Dearly Beloved

To Autumn,
Thanks for
reading!

ALSO BY
Rachael Rawlings

Dearly Departed
Dearly Remembered
The Parrot Told Me

Dearly Beloved

Rachael Rawlings

Hydra
Publications

Printed in the United States of America

ISBN: 1942212194
ISBN-13: 978-1-942212-19-5

Hydra Publications
1310 Meadowridge Trail
Goshen, KY 40026

www.hydrapublications.com

DEDICATION

I would like to dedicate this book to my best friend, Angela State Higdon. We grew up in Crestwood, Kentucky together, and our friendship has lasted through marriages, babies, teenagers, and all the rest!

Love you, girl!

Chapter 1

I woke in the dark. It wasn't the friendly dark of the city dotted with orange tinted lights hung over city streets. It was the cool dark of the country when even the fat moon, hung like a giant Christmas ornament, seems unwelcoming. Ahh, and it felt so real. I could feel the grass beneath my bare feet, the sweep of my nightgown against my thighs as I walked slowly between the trees. I could even smell the wet earth scent of the air after a rain.

The flutter of a bird in one of the trees sheltering the path made an explosive burst of sound. I jumped, wondering then why this wouldn't wake me up. These were really the clearest dreams that I had ever experienced, and in their clarity, I felt trapped.

I stopped walking for a moment and looked around. The trees were growing thinner, and the snake of blacktop that lead in front of me was familiar. Of course it was. Just the heat of the pavement beneath my bare feet, heat left from the autumn sunlight, made my stomach roll. This was the road. This was the place. Although I had visited it only two other times, both times without the knowledge or approval of my parents, I knew the very spot where my brother's blood had stained the pavement. Where his life had been snuffed out like a too bright flame. Here.

I fell to my knees, barely aware now of the sounds. It was a dying place, a place so steeped in sorrow that it took my breath away. I wasn't crying. It was too painful for that. I held my hand over my chest, trying to breathe.

The searing white of headlights appeared suddenly around a curve. The sweep of illumination caught me in the face, and my eyes closed. Perhaps I would be hit. Perhaps I too would die here one the road. Like Daniel.

But no, because this was a dream, and you didn't die in dreams, I continued to feel the ache of reality around me. The light remained, but dimmed, and I heard the vehicle stop. I climbed to my feet, the pale gown dropping around my ankles. The engine cut off abruptly, and the door swung open with an audible click, the lights on the interior coming on, revealing the figure of a single man, big and bulky in a jacket and knit cap.

I backed away from the road, fearful despite knowing that I was dreaming. It wasn't real, and yet it felt so very dangerous.

"Hey. Wait a minute." The voice was deep, the twang of Kentucky flavoring his words.

I slipped further back into the trees, away from the light. My sleeping heart was pounding, my sleeping breath coming in fits, wheezing from my lungs.

"No, don't go. Look, I just want to help." I saw him reach in a pocket, his face in darkness. Before I could bolt, I saw that he held a phone, the screen illuminated. "We can call someone. Your family? They can come get you. It's too cold to be out here. And it's too dark. I might not have seen you, and you could get hit on this road." He was moving slowly and speaking in what I could only assume was a reassuring tone.

I was panting now. I shook my head, feeling my long hair catch on branches as though the trees were reaching out to snatch at the strands. I didn't make a sound, just glanced back, moving away, away from the light, away from the faceless man.

"Wait. You can use the phone. I'll throw it to you. I won't even get any closer." His words had sped up. He stepped forward, the phone's lit screen still visible as he pulled his hand back. But was he throwing it, or doing something else?

Wake up, wake up, I was begging my mind. My heart was so loud now that I could barely hear his word. Wake up, please wake up, breath panting, backing into the dark. Wake up, wake up, wake up, Savannah, wake up!

I sat up with a jolt in my bed. My chest hurt, my hand clenched in a tight fist over my heart. I was alone. Thank God, I was alone. And home. I deliberately slowed my breathing, frightened that I might just scare myself into a breakdown. I kicked the covers off, looking at the pure white of my gown. Just a dream, no dirt on my feet, or grass stains on my nightgown. I frowned. My knees felt a little sore and when I pulled up the hem to look at them, they looked red in the dim light. Psychosomatic pain in my knees from kneeling at the roadside? Great, just what I needed.

"Forget it," I said aloud, relieved to hear my voice. I slid out of bed and tiptoed into the bathroom. In the mirror, the girl staring out at me looked like a ghost from the best horror film. My skin looked gray, and in the wavering light, my hair looked white instead of blond. It fell in tangles down my shoulders. I swept it up in a ponytail and pushed it back, away from my face. Dark circles were under my eyes and my lips looked chalky. Red eyes, shiny with unshed tears stared back at me. I grabbed a washcloth and ran it under water until it was hot. I held it to my face for as long as I could tolerate it and then pulled it away. My formerly pale complexion was now blotchy pink. Maybe better, I wasn't sure. I put the cloth back on the side of the sink and turned out the light. I would have gone downstairs to huddle in the kitchen, maybe drink a glass of water, or better yet, something hot. But I wouldn't now. If my parents found me up, there would be questions. And with the questions would be another visit to the psychologist whose job it was to rid me of these dreams, this grief, this guilt.

I returned to my bed and slid under the covers, sitting up against the headboard my knees pulled to my chest. I wouldn't have to be up early in the morning. I could sleep in late, and my mom wouldn't say a word. Then when I was up, I would eat whatever breakfast I could choke down and then sit at the table with my mom to do my schoolwork. I had always thought that I would hate being homeschooled, but when you were trying to run from the world, it suddenly seemed like a wonderful idea.

I put my head back and closed my eyes. It certainly wasn't the worst nightmare I had had, but usually the clear ones were all similar. I was by myself. I was in the woods. I was often there, at the roadside, looking both ways across the pavement searching for something, someone who would never come. Usually those dreams were so brief.

The last time I had encountered anyone in one of my realistic dreams was months ago. In that one I had been in the center of a graveyard, surrounded by a storm and talking to, well, to be truthful, I had been screaming at my brother's new girlfriend, Thea. In that dream, like this one, I had felt so present in the environment. I could feel the wind huffing at my back, could feel the sting of the sticks and leaves lifted from the earth in the tidal wave of air all around me. And the cemetery, in the cool blue light of the night, had looked so crystal clear to me. Even Thea's pale face, her curls whipped around her head in a crazy dance, was as detailed as a film played in high definition. However, I couldn't recall how it ended. Not really. I wished that I could. I knew that I had dreamed of seeing my lost brother, of Daniel, feeling the stiff fabric of his jacket and looking into the depths of his eyes. I knew he had spoken to me, but I could remember little else.

I gave up on trying to sleep and flipped the blankets back, standing and wandering over to my desk. I unplugged the cell phone and took it back to bed with me. Briefly I thought of the man in my dream, offering me his phone, asking me to call someone. And that was weird. Who would have thought that the scary dream guy would be offering his phone for an emergency contact? Crazy.

I frowned and switched on the phone. In the artificial light of the screen I opened a note taking app and began writing out my dream. I wanted to catch it before it was lost. I wanted to catch it before I was lost, or rather had lost my mind entirely.

I was late up the next day, but took extra care as I readied to go downstairs. My mother would be watching me with eagle eyes, just waiting to see that tiny crack in my composure. I frowned and added a little more blush to my cheeks. After I brushed my hair out I let it fall naturally down my back. With a final glance to make sure nothing was out of order, I jogged downstairs. My breakfast was laid out on the table with a note from my mother explaining that she had run to the grocery. I sighed. That was a relief. I had always been close with my parents, but the closeness was wearing thin. Before the accident my mother had been involved in her work, as well as a member of several charity groups and a Bunco club. Post-accident, all of our lives had changed. My mom had tried to go back to work, but when I started falling apart, she had left the job she loved to stay home with me and take over my education in the hopes that I would be able to return to school later in the year and graduate with my class. My father had begun to work longer hours, and my brother Thomas, the surviving brother, had left for college.

Without the twins, the house felt incredibly empty. I had gone from being the younger sister to two active guys with a large social circle and tons of friends, to an only child of overstressed parents.

The dreams had started just after the accident. The dreams at first were just minutes of time, so real, and so memorable. It had taken only one such episode to realize that my mind was visiting the place where my brother had died. At the time, Thomas had been in the hospital in a coma, and I had made it day by day, covering my fear and my grief just to be strong for my parents. I wouldn't tell them of my own agony. I powered on, trying to help bolster them as we set about the horrible process of burying one twin while the other lay unresponsive in the hospital. Now I could barely remember those days, and I honestly hoped it would stay that way. I didn't want those scenes to play back in my mind ever again.

And then the miracle happened. My brother Thomas woke from his coma. Life resumed but in a very different way. There was the coming home party, the visits to the therapists and doctors for my brother, and the odd relationship that developed between him and a girl that he had met just before the accident. As they grew closer and he grew stronger, I felt myself gradually caving in. I couldn't think. I couldn't concentrate. I wanted to sleep all the time, but when the dreams came, I became afraid of where they would take me, and I started to reject sleep. With that came the loss of appetite, the weight loss, and eventually, my parents took me to the doctor, fearing that I might need hospitalization to get my mood under control.

We stopped before my issues had become that extreme, but I knew that if my parents felt it was necessary, I would be back to seeing those doctors again. And sometimes I wondered if it wouldn't have been for the best. If a hospitalization with the isolation and constant therapy wouldn't have been good for me after all. But then it had all changed last fall. That was when I had the dream with my brother's girlfriend in the cemetery, that horrible, wonderful dream where I raged at the world, but ended up seeing Daniel.

Now I went to therapy weekly, did my homework, and tried to act like I was getting better. And in some ways I was. But the dreams, well the dreams weren't letting me move on.

When my mom got home, groceries in hand, I had eaten what I could of my breakfast and finished some of the work she had left out. I had research to do, a paper to finish, and an empty weekend looming.

"How is it going so far?" my mom asked nodding her head in the direction of my computer and the articles I had pulled up.

"Fine," I said keeping my voice light and unconcerned.

"Good. Well if you have any questions, I'll be doing the laundry. I need to get most of it done before tomorrow."

"Tomorrow?" I was only mildly interested.

"Thomas is coming in for the weekend." She turned and looked at me frowning slightly. “Don’t you remember?”

“Oh, sure,” I lied, my eyes back to the screen. Thomas hadn’t been home for three weeks, immersed as he was in his studies. And I knew that he had gone home with Thea to her small town in Kentucky. I tried not to feel vaguely jealous of that. Thomas needed Thea. He needed his new life with his new friends, miles away from his family and the grave of his twin brother. It was helping him put the tragedy behind him.

“He’ll be in on Friday, and I’m sure he’ll have all of his laundry with him.” She tried to sound irritated, but I knew she was pleased. She missed him; she missed them both, both of her sons.

“He’s staying til Sunday?”

“That’s what he said,” my mom responded, turning back into the laundry room.

I sighed softly. Thomas coming home should have been a good thing, but he was excessively sensitive sometimes. Of the twins, Thomas had always been the one who was most in tune with how everyone in the house was feeling, what they were thinking. Daniel had been the whirling dervish, bringing fun and trouble in equal doses when he came.

I looked back down at the keyboard and started to work. I wanted to get the paper well under way just in case I would get caught up in some plans for the weekend.

Thomas looked as he usually did, pale blond hair slightly too long, goldish eyes just a little too observant. When my parents announced that they wanted to take us out to eat, I wasn’t surprised. They were trying to be festive and to force me from my room as much as possible. Having Thomas here was an excuse to celebrate and to take me along for the ride. Thomas asked if I would ride with him, an unexpected question, and for the life of me, I couldn't think of an excuse not to. My parents took our riding separately in stride, making me instantly suspicious. It was a set up. I could smell it from a mile away. Apparently my attempts at deceiving my parents hadn't been as successful as I had thought. So they called in Thomas, my gentle sensitive brother who could pry a confession from a saint.

Thomas was ready for me. The radio was on an oldies station that I used to favor in my younger days, and the car was already running.

"What's the deal?" I asked, climbing in and buckling my seatbelt.

"Deal?" Thomas asked innocently.

"You know what I mean," I replied, turning in the seat and watching his profile as he backed out of the driveway. He glanced my way but didn't comment. "Thomas, I know mom and dad have put you up to this. They wanted you to talk to me, and they've called you home."

"So what do you think they're worried about?" he asked, turning the question back on me.

I frowned at his profile, unconsciously crossing my arms over my chest. "I think they're overreacting. I've been going to the therapist, I'm taking my meds, I'm not staying out late or going to parties," my voice drifted off at that.

"And maybe that's exactly what they are worried about. Maybe you haven't been out with friends, but do you even talk to friends?"

I didn't want to respond. I had friends, of course, and some good friends. But they were busy. As seniors in mostly college prep classes, as I had been, they were immersed in work, studying for exams, writing papers, visiting college campuses, and getting ready for the future. It didn't even include the dances, senior outings, part time jobs, clubs, and all the other extracurricular things that got in the way of keeping track of friends who were no longer there with them, namely me. And I didn't blame them. They were living the life that I had had.

"Van, they just want to make sure that they're not missing anything. You can be so good at covering up, sometimes we don't find out what's really going on until it's gotten out of hand."

He was talking about after our brother died. I had held up, supported our parents, and visited Thomas at the hospital while he was in a coma. I had gone to school, managed good grades, and helped arrange to bury my other brother. By the time Thomas had recovered enough to come home, I had used up every little bit of energy I had. The result had been fantastically bad.

"Thomas, what do you want me to say? Am I still upset, yes, and so are you. Do I miss him? Yes. We all do. I'm getting my work done and following all the advice that I've gotten from the therapist. Maybe it will take me a little longer!" My voice rose and I stopped, biting my lip and looking out the window.

"Okay, fair enough," Thomas said. We were pulling into the parking lot of the restaurant. "I know you're doing your best, I just don't want you to stop talking to us."

"It isn't really a choice, is it?" I asked, my voice brittle.

"No." He had turned into a parking space and put the car in park. "But Van, if anything happens to you, or with you, anything that seems unusual or something you don't understand, you come to me."

"What?"

He turned in his seat and looked at me, his eyes intent. "Look, I just want you to know that you can come to me, even if you feel like mom and dad won't understand. If you think something odd is going on, you tell me immediately."

"Thomas," I started, but my parents' car pulled up beside us and my father climbed out, smiling at me through the window. The topic of conversation, whatever the heck it had been, was closed for the time being.

And his strangeness didn't end there. When I asked him later where Thea was, he immediately told me that she was at school and staying there for the weekend.

"She isn't going home?"

"No," he said, almost as though he weren't paying attention to what he was saying. "She won't go home without me."

"Why?"

"Oh," he recovered himself, seeming to hear what he had said. "I meant that we were going back to her family's house next weekend. She had things she needed to do this weekend."

But that wasn't what he had sounded like when he first spoke. It sounded like she wasn't going to go home unless he accompanied here there. To protect her? From what? Her parents were nice people, if a little odd. The fact that her house was right next to a graveyard and her father had been the funeral director for the town, while seeming spooky to me, was normal for her. Thea, if anything, had always seemed wonderfully stable and even tempered. Considering her romance with my brother, who was going through a whole lot right now, was so successful. Well that proved to me that she was a good influence on him. Didn't it? There was nothing about those circumstances that would make me think that she needed to have my brother there for support.

So if it wasn't her home life, could it have something to do with the funeral I had attended in the spring? I had driven by myself down to Thea's hometown, just outside of Louisville, Kentucky, to attend a rather bizarre ceremony. A young boy's remains were found in a well on the cemetery property, later identified as a child who had gone missing decades before. When the boy had first disappeared, it had rocked the little rural community, but that had been a long time ago. But in a small town, even after all of that time, the discovery of the body had caused quite a stir. The town prided itself on its long memory, and the boy had lived in a house just across the street from the same cemetery that his body was found. That seemed to me to be even weirder. I had been in the house where he had lived and knew the people that lived there. My brother's best friend, Drew, was dating a girl that had moved there with her sister. And there was another sad story. The two girls lived there alone because they had lost their parents to an accident.

My brother's words came back to me, and I worried about Thea, but with my current mental state, I wasn't pointing any fingers. Perhaps the whole situation had affected her more than I realized. Maybe she felt like she needed Thomas to be there with her. Or it could just be new love. I made a face at that, and Thomas looked at me oddly.

"What?" he asked.

"Nothing," I said quickly and swung the car door open. "We'd better get going. Mom and dad are already inside." I gestured to their car parked across the lot and he nodded. I had avoided any more conversation for now, but I knew the subject of my mental health was far from dropped.

Chapter 2

My gown that night was the palest of pink, just a long tee shirt that reached almost to my knees. The material was soft, but didn't protect my skin well from the changing weather of my sleeping imagination. And that was where I was once again, in the chill of my dream state.

So real. How could a dream be so incredibly real? The fallen leaves, brown and damp, stuck to the sole of my bare foot, and I had to shake it off. The grass was slick, the pavement smelled of rain. I could hear the far off whistle of a train and the scurry and rustle of nighttime creatures. It was depressing how familiar the road was becoming to me. I knew just where the pothole dipped the road to the side, just where the white stripe had been repainted, and the hollow where the trees had been before the impact of my brother's car had caused his, and the trees', demise.

I walked to the edge of the road and balanced on the lip feeling the pavement against my toes. The barest of wind rushed in the leaves and a shower of light night rain dampened my hair. I licked my lips and stood very still. If I spoke, I didn't want my voice to be heard. Bad enough to talk in your dreams, but what if my parents caught me talking in my sleep?

"Daniel, are you here?"

My voice sounded so real in the silence, and I felt foolish for uttering the words.

A car came oh so slowly down the road, and caught me in its headlights. This was new. I had seen cars before in dreams, but none had stopped and no one reacted, usually the drivers' stoic faces had been soft blurs behind the glass. But this driver did. The vehicle slowed and pulled off the road, its wheels dipping into the grass on the shoulder. It was a truck, high seated with a powerful sounding motor that probably would have gotten stuck in the mud on the side of the road without the four-wheel drive I suspected it had.

I stood very still as though I could blend in with the darkness. The door of the truck opened slowly as a figure stepped out. No hat, just shaggy brown hair falling over a broad forehead, a rough blue jean jacket and pale pants. He stood next to the car door, and light seeped from the truck's interior illuminating him.

It was the man I had seen before; I was sure of it. The same broad shoulders, the same stance, the same truck. He stood in the light for a moment, and I was sure it was for a reason. He wanted me to see him. Whether it was to reassure me, or to make me fear him more, I couldn't tell. He moved away from the door but left it open, the light still glowing in the cab. He moved slowly, and I saw the dim light of his cell phone as he pulled it out of his pocket. Funny how those things were so important to us. In this dark scene, the artificial glow seemed to anchor him to reality.

"Hey," he said softly, his voice almost a low growl. "Don't go. I'm just checking on you."

I stood very still. It was the strangest sensation in my life, to be in a dream that seemed like reality. As he got closer, I could see the folds and seams of his jacket, hear the rustling of his movements, smell the acrid scent of exhaust from the truck behind him. I squinted and could read the icons on the screen of his phone.

"I have my phone if you want to call anyone, if you're lost or something." He had stopped moving. "I drive by here on my way from work. I've seen you a few times. Do you remember when I stopped last time?"

I stared at him dumbly, my mouth unable to work. He plainly was speaking to me; he could see me. I frowned as he took another step forward, and in turn took a step back from the road. It wasn't right. This was my dream, and I should be able to tell him where he could go, and when he should stand still.

"Sorry," he said quickly, and stopped moving. The moon was almost round, a three-quarter's globe that shed light in patches. It touched his face, and I could see him more clearly. His face wasn't traditionally handsome, and no one would ever call him pretty, but he was attractive in a rough way. He needed a shave and a haircut. His clothes were rumpled, a tee shirt under the jean jacket and khaki work pants. "Can you hear me?"

I was staring at him, stupidly, I'm sure. But again, it was my dream, and if I didn't want to talk, I figured that I didn't have to.

"Okay, so this is either one of two things," he now looked like he was talking to himself. "Either I see you, and you're here, but you won't talk, so maybe you're crazy because you're obviously not dressed." His eyes were on my face, squinting slightly. "Or you're a ghost, and I don't really see you. I'm just overtired, and I've made you up, or I'm just going nuts myself." He rubbed a hand over his face, looking suddenly very weary.

"A ghost?" I gasped.

His head jerked up, and he dropped his phone to the ground. Now he took a step back, more of a stumble in work boots.

I realized then that he had taken my comment as an affirmation, telling him that I was a ghost. Strange that the man in my dream suddenly looked afraid of me. He had dropped in a squat, one hand skimming the wet grass trying to find his phone without taking his eyes off me. I moved a step closer to him, looking at him more carefully. But no, he seemed real, very human, very disturbed. I put my hand out, I was going to speak, I was going to ask him what the dream was about, and why was he dreaming of me?

And then I was gone.

The dog woke me. My parents had reluctantly adopted a full grown Pit-bull mix named Daisy from a shelter just two months before. They had tired of watching me wilt away and decided that I needed a new responsibility. The decision to get a dog was spur of the moment when they led me to the shelter that day. It was supposed to be a surprise. And it was for all of us. I had looked dully at the puppies furiously tumbling and rolling around in the bins, ignored the sleek cats meowing at the cages, and sat on a bench in the front room. A young girl had barged in with a mutt on a leash, a sturdy shorthaired black dog with a smile stretching wide revealing a mouthful of teeth. The dog had entered the door, pulled backwards with some hidden agenda, and ducked out of the loop of her collar before the girl even knew what was happening. But instead of fleeing into the sunshine and freedom of outdoors, she had walked sedately to my side, plopped on the floor, and leaned her full body weight against my leg. I had to have her. From the moment we had brought her home, Daisy had settled into my room, and on cool nights, in my bed, more of a baby than any dog I had ever known.

Her enormous nose pressing against my neck woke me from my vivid dream, and it was a moment before I regained my senses and pushed her face away.

"Daisy, no," I mumbled. I pushed her harder, and she moved her heavy body to the end of the bed and dropped to cover my feet. I sighed and looked at the clock. It was nearly 5 in the morning, much too early to be awake. I frowned at the dog. The dream was so clear, so fresh in my mind. I reached out and unplugged my phone from the charger that I had relocated to the little table next to my bed. Without sitting up, I rolled to my side and pulled up the notes application on the phone. I put in the date and began writing as I had for the last several nights following the dreams. I described everything in as much detail as I could, from the feel of the grass on my feet to the smells of the woods and the pavement. And I added my visitor, the man that I had apparently dreamed up. It still seemed so funny to me that I had plainly scared him in my dream. I was sure there was some way to interpret that dream, to interpret all of them. I knew my tired brain was still dealing with the accident, with Thomas and Daniel. Whatever this new man was supposed to represent, well, it was beyond my understanding. With a second sigh, I closed out the app and lay back down. Tomorrow I would think about it. But tonight, well, at least I wasn't the one who had been afraid.

In the morning, I woke to a new resolve. I was going on a little trip to visit the place where my brother had lost his life. At this point I had little choice but to try. I needed to know why I kept going back there in my dreams. I could think of no other way to figure it out; figure myself out. I waited until my parents were gone. It felt wrong, sneaking out of the house like that, but I felt like it was something that I had to do. As I drove, I tried to count the trip as a success. I was driving! I hadn't driven but a few blocks in the last several months. The only long drive I had taken since my brother's death was for the funeral in Kentucky, the funeral for the poor missing boy that Thomas and Thea had helped find. Now I was experiencing a certain exhilaration in feeling the wheels turn beneath me, spinning out the miles, the space, the heady sense of freedom. The feeling remained even after I had stopped for a quick lunch. As I sat in my car, eating a chicken sandwich with unusual appetite, I realized that I was feeling better than I had in weeks, months even. I finished my meal and dropped the trash in the can before I left the lot pulling out on the mostly abandoned road to finish my trip.

It didn't take me long to find the accident site. My dreams had made me uncannily familiar with the area. I parked my late model sedan on the side of the street. Unconsciously, I realized that I had parked just where the man in my dreams had parked his truck. I unlatched my seat belt and turned off the engine. Finally I was here again, but while I knew where I wanted to be, I wasn't sure what I had planned to do once I got there. Did I walk into the woods? Did I just need to stand there in the shelter of the trees, my feet planted where my brother had left this life? The sun made a dappled pattern on the ground as I slowly walked off the side of the road. It was a gorgeous day, the leaves a golden/orange canopy hanging over me, a few brave flowers still flourishing in the grass. It was only a few yards to get to the crash site. The car, with its three occupants, my twin brothers and their best friend Drew, had slid off the road, leaving black rubber tracks that had gradually faded in time. The car had then turned sharply and slammed into a stand of trees, thrusting the left front quarter into the lap of the driver. Daniel had died at the scene. Drew had been found wandering in the woods, unaware of where he was or what had happened. Thomas was riding in the passenger seat. He was rushed to the hospital where he would stay for months, recovering from various injuries. The worst was a head injury that induced a coma, robbing him of his own twin's funeral and mourning with his family.

I sat on a stump rising from the ground, unsure if this was the remainder of the tree that had been in the accident. I hadn't visited the site with the car in place, nor had I seen the car after the accident. I hadn't wanted to, and I stood by that decision. To see the destruction would do me no good, I was sure.

But one thing I was learning was the accuracy of my dream. The leaves, the trees, the weeds growing wild in that raw patch of earth, all matched the memory of my dream. I hadn't been to the accident site in months. It was amazing that with the change, my mind could have predicted and then constructed the site so accurately with the changing of time and the seasons.

"Creepy," I said softly. The whole thing made shivers run down my limbs. I closed my eyes and tried to concentrate on the moment, the feel of the warm sun, the breeze blowing softly through the trees, the scent of earth and wood. Gradually I felt my heart cease the insistent pounding that had accompanied a very real panic. It was just a place, a piece of earth, a setting. There were no ghosts, no spirits, no unhealthy feelings.

I stood in the sun and felt a pang that I hadn't thought to bring something to leave here. Daniel wasn't much for flowers. He wouldn't have appreciated a bouquet. An honorary beer might have been suitable if I hadn't been driving. And under age.

I walked back to the side of the road and looked down its length where it disappeared around a leafy bend. It was a lonely site. But I was ready to leave now. I hadn't learned anything life altering, but I didn't feel worse for my trip either.

I wasn't sure why I felt compelled to check, but before I slid back in the driver's seat, I walked around to the back, my eyes on the ground. Was I looking for proof that my dreams were something more than what they were? Was I looking for proof that the man in my dreams had actually visited? But of course there were tire tracks. The ruts were deep, made when the ground was muddier, but it was a reasonable assumption to think that others might need to park here. Not that many cars might come by, but anyone related to the accident, Drew, Thomas, my parents, might have done the same as I had. The road was narrow, tree lined, it would be hard to find somewhere better to pull off. But in the back of my mind, I felt like the tracks might mean something. I shook my head at my folly. Stupid to be seeing something in the ordinary like that.

When I left the accident site, I had no real plan as to where I was going. It was literally in the middle of nowhere, and while I knew where the guys had been going when the accident occurred, I had no motivation to go any further. I wasn't ready to go home, but I knew I didn't have much time before my mother would be back from getting her hair done and running errands. I drove aimlessly for a while, finally emerging on a larger road that followed the railroad tracks. I entered what must have been a little commercial area and saw signs for the interstate. I stopped at a gas station to get a snack and took the next turn, unaware of which direction I was going but leaving the interstate signs behind. I passed a few little shops and buildings, turning again down a heavily treed street with large older homes on generous lots. A strange clatter pulled me from my thoughts, and I looked to the dash in alarm. My car made a second odd clunk and lights started flashing, engine warning, symbols, red and yellow, mocking my ignorance about cars and their mysteries. With a tug at the wheel that seemed to be becoming less responsive as the engine struggled, I pulled the car off to the side of the road. I wasn't in the center of any town anymore, but rather in the outskirts. I looked at the road stretching ahead of me in dismay. I tried the ignition once more and was rewarded with a cough and sigh from the engine. Well, damn.

Stranded. Stranded on the back roads of who knew where, my poor sense of direction and worse memory failing me completely. I pulled my cell phone from my purse and checked the bars. Good, I had a signal. But if I called someone, where would I tell them to meet me? I didn't know where I was. And my parents would go ballistic if they knew where I had been. And where was I? A field dotted with big shaggy beasts stretched off to my left, to the right, an empty field slightly overgrown and bordered by brush. I looked down at my phone again and an idea hit me. If I used the maps function on the phone I could find myself. Then I could call someone and tell them how to find me.

I flipped on the GPS and pulled up the map. After a moment, it registered my location, and a detailed map appeared. I suddenly knew where I was. My wanderings had brought me to the place that my brother most liked to visit. Crestwood was that small town in Kentucky where his girlfriend Thea lived, and the original destination of the boys on the day of the accident.

Relieved that I knew that much, I sat back against the seat. Now I had to decide who to call. The only people I knew in Crestwood were Thea, who was at school with my brother in Lexington, and Drew. If I called Drew, word would immediately get back to Thomas, and if he were worried enough, back to my parents. On the other hand, Thea was out of the question. She was a couple hours away at school. And that left, who?

Drew was dating a girl who had recently moved into town. They had met over the summer and had been inseparable since. Tori lived in one of the houses across the road from Thea's house, and the cemetery, and I had even been at her house, the house where the little lost boy had once lived. Tori might be the perfect person to call. I knew that she lived with her sister, and while I wasn't sure exactly what had happened to her parents, I knew they had passed away in a car accident as well.

I turned on the screen again and pulled up the phone list. My brother had put a bunch of numbers in my contacts before he had headed up to school with the admonition that I was to call one of them if anything ever came up. I wasn't sure if he had meant this particular situation, but I needed someone now.

Tori answered after the third ring much to my relief. I explained that my car had broken down and I was stranded. I gave her the information from the map on my phone and was relieved when she said she would be coming soon, no questions asked.

"Um, can you not say anything to Drew just yet?" I asked.

"Sure. Why?"

"I just don't want him going back to Thomas and worrying him. You know how they can be."

She agreed to my request, and I sighed in relief. It was a temporary fix, and I knew that. So I would go hour at a time, minute at a time, and I would manage events as they arrived. At least now I wouldn't be stuck out here alone.

Tori arrived in a massive old sedan, a privately owned tow truck following her. They both pulled off, and Tori introduced me to the other driver.

"He works over at Bart's Repairs," she explained. "He'll check out your car and see if he can get it going. If not, he can tow it to the garage, and we can decide what to do from there."

I stepped out of the way and waited in silence as the mechanic popped the hood. After a few minutes, he asked me to try to start the car, but the old engine refused to cooperate.

"We'll take it in and look at it," he said slowly, his voice warm and southern. "I think I have an idea of what's wrong. Should be an easy fix."

I nodded. Anything. I would do anything to get the car fixed and get home. But now it seemed that I wasn't going to be able to make it home without my mother knowing that I had cut out on her.

I climbed into the passenger side of Tori's car just after the tow truck hoisted my car like a massive metal fish. I watched as it hauled away my car, and reluctantly took out my phone.

"I've gotta text my mom," I told Tori, and then reddened, thinking that Tori no longer had a mom that she had to keep up with.

"Yeah, I have to keep my sister informed," she said lightly. "I might be twenty, but she still thinks of me as a kid sometimes."

I smiled, grateful that she wasn't asking questions, but aware that they would come.

We went to the diner. It was a cozy spot located in the middle of the little city, flanked on either side by shops and little boutiques. The building looked like it had once been just another office space, but the renovation had changed it into something that resembled a home more than anything else. A variety of antiques and mismatched pieces added to the down home feel. I had never been to Tori's work, but it felt comfortable to me. From Thomas and Thea, I had heard about its legendary desserts. Thomas had told me that Tori had been hired to deliver for the catering side of the business as the business grew. We settled at one of the tables, and Tori disappeared into the kitchen to get us something to eat while we waited on the car. I tried to look surreptitiously around the room. I noticed a small knot of kids gathered around the traditional counter in the front, desserts laid out in a lighted case. The diner served a wide variety of items, but most of the people at the tables were having coffee and pastries at this time of day. Small tables with mismatched chairs filled the center of the room. A few booths had been added to one side. The sugar, napkins, cream, and utensils were artfully laid out on an antique kitchen cabinet. There weren't that many people there, but it was too early for dinner, too late for lunch. I supposed my timing was pretty good since I hadn't caught Tori when they had a rush.

"I got you a little bit of everything," Tori explained, setting a plate in front of me.

My phone pinged, and I checked the message. It was from my mother, and she was plainly not satisfied with my explanation that I had gone out and the car had stopped on me. I typed in a quick return message trying to sound as close to the truth as possible. I told her I was having dessert with Tori, Thea's friend, and the car was being looked at. I left it to her to assume the reason I was here to begin with was to meet Tori. If she thought it was strange that I was meeting with a girl that I barely knew, she didn't let on. My brother had led her on a bit of a tangent while he was splitting his time between home and here, and I guessed she had assumed it would be better if she didn't ask.

"Is your mom alright?" Tori asked. Her hair that was once dyed multiple tones of blond and chocolate was now a silky brown and pulled into a loose ponytail. A lock of it fell into her eyes. Casually dressed in worn jeans and a tee shirt with the diner's emblem emblazoned on the front, she was wearing their uniform of sorts.

"She's fine. Just wondering where I was." I bit my lip and played with the straw from my glass. What to talk about?

"Drew said you were home schooled?" Tori broke the silence after a moment. She sounded curious. "Are you on a break?"

"I finished my work for the day," I told her, slowly picking up my fork and taking a small bite from the piece of cherry pie on my plate.

"That's good," she said, clearly waiting for another explanation. When I didn't respond, she continued, "I'm heading back to take some classes in the spring. Drew and I both are," she said.

"About Drew," I said slowly. "I really would rather you not mentioning this to him."

"This?" she asked. "You mean you coming here?"

"Yeah, any of this." I took a sip of the milk she had put before me. It was ice cold and obviously whole milk, tasting almost like cream.

"Why?"

She was honest, I had to give her that. "Drew will talk to Thomas, and Thomas will worry. I've been trying not to make Thomas worry. My parents already have me under a microscope."

She looked confused.

"I was just out for a drive, trying to relax. They'll never believe that. Then they'll try to figure out why I might want to go out alone, and it will just make them more concerned."

"Drew said you had some trouble concentrating. I hope you don't mind him talking about you. He looks after you like a little sister." She flinched then, and I thought it was sadly amusing. She had lost her parents; I had lost my brother. Neither of us knew how to handle the other.

"I've gotten much better, and I know exactly what Drew thinks of me." I blinked and glanced out the window at the parking lot and the elementary school just beyond and across the road. "Sorry, that sounded wrong. Drew is great, and I know he and Thomas are just trying to keep an eye on me. But I'm fine and I'm trying to be more independent. It's just hard when everyone is watching all the time. Like I'm going to self-destruct."

"Savannah," Tori started, but I cut her off.

"It's alright, but if you would just skip telling him." I hated to sound so pleading, but there it was.

She nodded, as her eyes narrowed. "Look, I know you don't owe anyone an explanation, but I think it might help you. Why don't you just tell me where you were off to, and I swear, as a fabulous dessert deliverer, that I won't tell Drew."

I was playing with a bit of cookie on my plate and took a quick bite, letting the chocolate melt in my mouth and giving me a moment to think. Tori was a wild card in the little group. Thea grew up in the small town. Despite her upbringing, was still a small town girl at heart. She was as all American innocent as they came, but Tori, well, she had an edge. And she had lived through tragedy and come out, perhaps a little more brittle than before, but strong.

"Okay, deal," I said abruptly. "I came out this way to go to the accident site. I haven't been there for a really long time, and I just got the urge. You know?"

The sad thing was, she did know. Her parents had died in a car accident, and I trusted that the incident might make her have a little more insight than most people would have.

"Did it help?"

I took another drink and thought for a moment. Had it helped? Had seeing the place where Daniel died made any impression on me? "No, not really," I admitted.

She nodded. "I've only been by where my parents had their accident a few times, but it never made me feel any better. I eventually decided that if I didn't need to go that way, I wouldn't. I don't know if it was a good idea or not." She stopped, her eyes gazing down at the tabletop.

"I'm sorry." I said it automatically, but I meant it.

"Me too," she agreed, and looked up to give me a small half smile.

The silence wasn't awkward, just a little sad. Here we were, two people who had lost so much, and neither of us had found the key to happiness. Or even the road to move on. We were just living one day at a time, waiting for the pain to go away.

Chapter 3

We stayed there for almost an hour until my phone vibrated in my pocket, and I learned that my car was done. We talked of the weather, of the desserts that Tori helped make in the tidy kitchen in the back, and the deliveries she made around town. I knew that she was filling the silence, trying to be kind. She talked fondly of her sister who was trying not to parent her and was successful most of the time. She talked about the move to the little town and how she had struggled to fit in.

"I don't know what I would have done if I hadn't gotten this job," she admitted. "I spend most of my time here, and I've met so many people." Her voice dropped to a more conspiratorial tone. "I was used to more of the big city. Here, everyone knows everyone else. They know their families, where they live, what job they have, even their pets. When I got Monty, my dog, most of my neighbors knew before I had even told anyone at the diner." She sighed. "But it's been really good for us, too. I guess you heard about the fire?"

I nodded. I had heard about the tragedy even through the fog of my own misery. Shortly after the girls had settled into their house, there had been a fire in the front room. Luckily it had been contained to the one area, but the damage had still been extensive.

"Once we started working on the house, people came out of the woodwork offering help." She smiled at the memory. "We had paint donated from the hardware store, flooring from the lumber sales, cleaning supplies from the dollar store. We had people from two different churches offer to come assist in doing repairs. The local women's club helped with the cleaning. By the time they were done, the house looked better than it ever had before."

I watched as her face lit up as she told the story. I knew the kindness of others. When my brother had died, we had had plenty of people offering help, to make food, the help around the house, to offer to drive me places. But time had reduced the offers until we had to stand on our own. I just hadn't been as successful getting over it.

"The area is nice around here," she said thoughtfully. "If you were going to have your car break down, it wasn't a bad place for it to happen."

I smiled at her. She seemed content that I didn't speak up, and I thought she understood. She was definitely from a different social circle than I was. I was the studious type, trying to remain under the radar. I wasn't a scholar exactly, but I instinctively was motivated to be the best at anything I tried, so I limited what I did to things that I knew I was good at. I suspected in school, Tori would have been with the alternative crowd, all loud music and raves. She would have an active social life, unlike me. But something had changed with her. In fact, her whole life had been turned upside down. For our differences, I felt a communion with her that I had seldom felt with anyone, at least not since the accident. Despite the slightly edgy way she had about her, with the black nail polish and the multiple earrings, she was easy to get along with, easy to talk to. She spoke of Drew just a bit, but the subject felt awkward. The Drew that I had known was the Drew of before. The more carefree teenager who hung out with my brothers and went boating with them when the sun was hot. He was the guy full of laughter and jokes, part of a trio that wrecked their own kind of havoc. But the trio was gone, and the pieces that remained were just trying to stand independent of the past. And the old Drew was a part of that past. So we avoided the hard topics and danced about the conversation. However, I knew it would come. I would have to face the present, with all of its pain and changes. So it was a little bit of a relief when Tori took me to pick up my car and then gave me directions towards the interstate as she headed back to work.

I sat in my car, letting the air-conditioning run as I watched her drive away. I wasn't sure if Tori would keep my secret. She had no reason to, beyond my request, and several reasons to tell. If Thomas indicated any worry about me, she might feel that she had to say something. But it didn't concern me as much as it should. Tori had been through a lot in her young life, and I think that might make her a little more sympathetic to my problems. It certainly had been nice to talk to someone who could understand me. Besides, worrying wouldn't help the situation, and I had bigger fish to fry.

As I drove away from the garage, my mind was racing. My drive back to Cincinnati would only take an hour, and I had already contacted my mom to buy some time. I drove slowly towards the outlined road on the directions Tori had given me, enjoying the view of the small town. I was feeling a bit of heady freedom and stopped one final time to get a large sweet tea from the gas station before hitting the interstate. The car's engine was chugging along, apparently none the worse for the breakdown. Fixing it had almost emptied my bank account, and I hated the idea that I might have to ask my parents for money. I shut down the engine and hurried inside.

The clerk called me "honey," and that made me smile again. I was in a rare good mood, but I knew that it wouldn't last. For one, I would soon have to face my parents about my little adventure.

I sighed. I should get a job; I should go back to school; I should get on with my life. It was like an incantation running through my brain. I stood by the side of my car and leaned back against the door, giant Styrofoam cup in hand. My life had nowhere to go but up. Seriously.

And then I saw him. There was a man standing just across the street. Behind him was a little fruit market, rows upon rows of rich hued flowers, mums I thought, framing him. He was carrying a crate full of some produce, dressed as I had seen him before in the worn jean jacket and casual pants. He stopped next to his truck, and I caught my breath, recognition striking again. I knew him. I recognized him. How could that be? The same man, the same truck, all from my dream? I stared at him for a long moment. There was no doubt about it. I had seen the man in my dream. The man who had asked if I was a ghost. The man who had been at my brothers' accident site. I watched with disbelief as he swung the door open and put the crate on the backseat, turning to slam the door. His gaze went across the road toward me. Then he stopped. I could tell the moment it registered with him, the stiffening that came with the shock. He recognized me. We stood for a long minute, frozen in our respective poses. He was staring at me, face hard, lips slightly parted as though mumbling something under his breath. The wind caught at his hair and ruffled to shaggy locks.

I could feel the wind tugging my long hair, a few golden strands drifting across my face. I heard the traffic crossing, the slam of doors, the babble of voices, of words. A short stream of cars blocked my view for a moment, and when I looked back across, I saw that he had moved. He was striding toward the road, the light wind blowing his hair back from his determined face. It was the first time I had seen him in the daylight. In reality, I corrected myself. But this couldn't be. I couldn't just meet him like this. I felt like I was standing at the edge of a rooftop, feeling the wind lift me, pull me toward the edge. And if I reached the edge, if I jumped into the nightmare, I didn't think I'd ever get back out.

I suddenly yanked my car door open and scrambled into the driver's seat. My fingers were cold and stiff, and I couldn't get the seatbelt locked, so I gave up, shoved the key in the ignition and turned it. The engine started with a muted roar and I threw the car in reverse, narrowly missing another car pulling into an adjoining space. I straightened the car and jammed the gear into drive. Eyes drawn to the street, I could see the man crossing the lanes recklessly, horns blaring as he blocked small town traffic.

I didn't hesitate. I didn't think. I felt like I was running from the devil himself, and I couldn't be stopped. I pulled away from the building and headed for the opposite side of the parking lot, pulling out onto the street in front of a minivan, hearing their horn wail in protest. But I got away. I was heading blindly down the street, only aware that I didn't want to meet that man in the real world. I didn't see the passing cars, the passing buildings. I drove over the speed limit, fighting tremors that shook my hands.

When I saw the interstate sign, I felt like crying. I had unintentionally come the right way. At the turn, I paused to pull my seat belt on and take a quick breath.

"Calm," I whispered to myself. "Calm down."

My heart didn't stop pounding until I was several miles past the exit on I-71. I narrowed my eyes on the road and kept driving. Just make it home; that was all I needed. I just needed to make it home. Somehow this confusion would all go away.

When I went to bed that night, I was almost sick with worry. I didn't want to have the dream, but I was tired from my day, scratch that, I was exhausted. I needed rest, especially if I were to face my parents in the morning with a convincing look of health and well-being. I took two allergy pills, hoping their sleepy side affect would let me rest soundly enough not to dream. Just after my brother's death, I had been given sleeping pills, and for those two weeks, I had slept deeply and dreamlessly. But the mornings had been unbearable, heavy headed and muddled, I had decided that I could not live that way and had stopped taking the pills. I still had them, and decided that if the dreams did not go away, I might have to resort to taking them again.

Terrified that I would dream of him again, I calmly sat on my bed and tried to reason why I had seen the man from my dreams in real life. It was obvious now. At some time while visiting Crestwood with my brother, I had seen the man. I hadn't consciously noticed him, but somewhere in my tangled neurons, I had stored away his picture. And probably the picture of his truck. Yes, definitely the picture of his truck, because I had seen it just as clearly. And then, without knowing it, I had stitched him into my dream. There was no reason I had chosen this particular person. I could only assume that on some level, my brain had chosen to keep him sharply in memory. Maybe he had been at the funeral? Maybe he had been standing there at the graveside when the little boy had been buried, and only now, I was remembering him? Or had I seen him at my brother's funeral? That would have been a mighty coincidence that he had known my brother but lived in Crestwood. No, I must have seen him in Crestwood. And now I dreamed of him. Strange, yes, but possible. Better than the alternative. That he existed only in my dreams, but somehow I had managed to conjure him up in real life.

Hopefully, between the medication and my sheer exhaustion, I would sleep soundly and dreamlessly. It was a little prayer that I tossed up before I finally slipped off to sleep.

I had no control of my dreams. When I looked around, I was exactly in the place that I had been during the day, the side of the road, the middle of nowhere, the place that my brother had lost his life.

And damn it, it was raining.

I had worn pajamas to bed, which I seldom did. It was almost like I was dressing for my meeting. They had tiny black dogs on them, a teasing gift from my dad after we had adopted Daisy. And sure enough, here in my dream, I still wore the same outfit. The blue background of the fabric looked black in the darkness, and I had a brief flash of concern. What if someone drove around the corner and hit me because they couldn't see me? I shook my head forcefully, angrily. What was I thinking? Getting hit by a car in a dream? But then that was ridiculous. Crazy. Insane?

I shifted uncomfortably. The wet leaves beneath my feet were cold, the air was cold, and the rain dripping in great plops from the trees above was even colder. I wrapped by arms around my middle and shivered. This was ridiculous. I needed to wake up and get out of this dream.

But I didn't. I stood still and shivered, feeling the wet drops of rain roll from my hair and down my forehead, dripping off my nose. I could taste the rain on my tongue; feel each wet drop hit my shoulders.

When the truck pulled off the road, I stood there, letting the headlights wash over me. I watched as the door swung open and the figure stepped out. He had changed the jean jacket for a windbreaker, probably for the rain. He was wearing blue jeans and heavy boots, dark in color. I almost laughed at myself. In my dream, he had dressed for the weather. I had not known it was going to rain, but the man in my dream did. He left the door open and the headlights on as he walked toward me.

"I saw you today," he said, his tone accusing. "I saw you at the gas station. You had me thinking I was talking to a ghost, the way you disappeared like that. But I saw you drive off, so you, lady, are no ghost."

"I never said I was." My voice sounded flat to my ears, but I was talking over the rain. It was beginning to soak into my hair and trickle down my scalp, and I shivered again.

"What the hell are you doing standing out in the rain?"

"I don't know," I replied honestly.

This answer didn't seem to make him happy, and he shifted from foot to foot, impatient. "Look, this is stupid. Come sit in the truck with me, and we can talk. I promise I won't take you anywhere unless you want to go."

It was the most realistic dream of all, but still a dream, so I nodded. He seemed surprised, and glanced at me as I followed him to the truck. He opened the passenger door and held it while I slid inside. It was warm; he had been running the heat, and the interior light remained on. He went to the other side and got behind the wheel, making no move to touch the keys in the ignition.

"Oh my God, are you wearing pajamas?" The light had illuminated the cartoon dogs in all their glory, and I pulled the cold damp fabric away from my skin. My feet were freezing, but I hadn't thought to wear slippers to bed. Which again was ridiculous when you had to plan what to wear to bed just in case you went dream walking.

"It's the middle of the night," I said and turned to look at him. "Why aren't you wearing bedclothes?"

He stared at me like I was crazy. This close I could see the reddish brown stubble on his cheeks and the laugh lines by his eyes. He had rather nice eyes, deep chocolate brown with long lashes that girls pay to get.

"I was at work. I have classes on some mornings to finish up my degree. In the busy season, the only time I can help with the bookkeeping is at night. So I work nights. That's why I drive through here almost every night." He was talking slowly like I was a child. He leaned forward as though to touch me, and I backed away. "That's my story, so why are you here?"

So now I had a choice. Did I tell him that this was all my dream? That he wasn't here, and neither was I? Did I tell him that although I too had seen him during the day, he wasn't real but a figment of my sleeping brain? It seemed almost rude. So I did nothing and ignored his question. "What were you doing in town today?"

He looked startled. "I was buying vegetables. I like my produce from local growers so I go shopping there about once a week to stock up." He was still staring at me. "What about you?"

"I was getting tea," I said honestly.

"Do you live around here?"

"No," I said, and looked toward the windshield where the rain was trickling down like tears.

"So why are you getting tea here? And walking on the road side at night?"

"I was visiting a friend," I answered sticking to half-truths. I felt a foolish flash of freedom, the freedom that came with knowing that none of this could be true. None would be remembered. "No," I amended. "I came to see this place. My brother died here. Right here." I gestured out the window to the road. "I wanted to see what it looked like now."

That shut him up. He finally looked away from me. He frowned out the front window, his face lit only by the glow of the dash lights. I felt an odd wave, like a pressure on my chest and looked at him.

"I've gotta go," I said quickly, knowing for certain that that was exactly what was going to happen.

"What?"

"I've gotta go. Leave. Me." My fingers found the handle on the flat panel of the door, and I popped the door open, wind pushing raindrops in heavy spatters across my face.

"Hey, wait," he was trying to throw open his door, but I was sliding out of the truck before he could manage to get around the front hood to me. My bare feet hit the side of the road with a squishing of mud, and I stepped away into the grass.

"Hey," he called again, coming around the front of the truck.

"Just a minute!"

The pressure on my chest was a warm push, and I could feel a strange shudder run through me. I turned toward him and I waved.

"Hey!" he called out again, but before the sound had finished ringing in my head…

I woke up. Oh, and I was cold. I knew now what it meant when people said chilled to the bone because it seemed like even my bones were shivering, clacking together like loose boards. And Daisy, her big body warm and solid, was lying across my chest. She was crying ever so softly, a delicate whine, but stopped when she felt me stir. She pushed her nose under my hand where it lay on the bed. I was waking up with an uncomfortable tingle. But I was dry, my hair, my feet, my pajamas with the goofy dogs, all were dry to the touch. I shoved Daisy aside, but gently, and she curled up next to me, moving her heavy head to my thigh. I sat up in bed and checked myself over. It had been so real, almost painfully so. I pushed a strand of pale hair from my face and felt the cool skin of my cheek against my palm. And I was still so cold. I pulled up a heavy blanket from the foot of my bed and tucked it around my shoulders. With the added heat, the shivers let up slightly. I breathed a few long breaths. It had felt real, that was for sure, but it hadn't been bad. For the first time, I hadn't been frightened. Confused, maybe, but not afraid. I had faced what I considered to be one of my demons and found it to be just a guy. Had I made him up in my mind? Well, obviously no. Maybe I had seen him when I had been down to visit Thea in the past, and my mind had just reconstructed him in my dream. Even if he hadn't been real in my dream, he was in my mind. The good thing, I supposed, was that my mind had made him a regular person, nothing to be feared.

I slid back down in my bed and pulled the covers more closely, leaning into the warmth of the big dog at my side. I would battle that dream later, but it no longer seemed quite so threatening.

I went for a successful week without dreaming, and the cool of October gradually transitioned into the cold of November. Halloween came and went with eager kids storming our doors demanding candy, but I honestly enjoyed the whole thing. I stayed home with my mom, and we watched old movies, none of which was scary, and drank hot chocolate. In our tidy suburban home, the worst scares we were likely to have would be from the neighborhood teenagers with zombie costumes. But even that was a comfortable routine.

I had honestly thought that the worst might be over. Seeing and talking to the man in my dreams, while flat out crazy, might have been the experience I needed to exorcize the demons. I couldn't have been more wrong.

When the doorbell rang, I stayed upstairs checking my emails and updating social sites. I had a vague idea that if I continued to try to remain in touch with my friends, even if indirectly, they would welcome me back once I was able to return to school.

The doorbell chimed again and I rolled off my bed, setting my laptop on the desk next to the window. Apparently my mom either wasn't home, or she wasn't going to get the door. I thought briefly about letting it go, but then decided that it could be something important. A flash of a dark evening, the grim faced police officer at the door informing us that there had been an accident, slipped through my mind. I would never hear the ring of the doorbell without the sting of alarm racing down my spine.

I jogged down the steps to the first floor landing quickly, pausing to peer at my face in the mirror at the base of the stairs opposite the coat closet. I wore no makeup, but my face looked fine. Pale, yes, but my skin tended to be that shade when I avoided the sun. I had braided my hair into a long plait that fell down my back, but a few strands had pulled loose. My jeans had seen better days, but they were comfortable, and I wore only socks on my feet. I had thrown on an oversized sweatshirt, so I was well covered. I wiped my hands quickly on the seat of my pants and smoothed my shirt with nervous energy.

One last glance in the mirror, and I pulled the heavy wooden door open and looked through the glass of the security door. The morning sun had burned off the fog that had muffled our house, and visibility was perfect. Even if it had been foggy, I still would have recognized the truck in the driveway and the man standing at the side of the porch looking toward the front lawn. I stood very still. This absolutely could not be. He could not be here. But he was. There was no doubt that I was awake and alert, firmly rooted in reality.

He seemed to notice the movement and turned back toward the house. His eyes met mine through the glass and some emotion crossed his face. Relief maybe? He took a step forward until his face was close to the glass.

"Yes," I said, making my voice even with effort. "Can I help you?" I didn't open the glass, but I knew he could hear my voice. I knew

I sounded like a clerk at a grocery store, automatic and falsely cheerful, but the words just slipped out.

"I found you," he replied. "I need to talk to you. I looked you up. I thought that this had to be the place." He sounded astounded, surprised at his success.

"I don't know what you're talking about." I started to back up into the foyer away from the door, away from him. I wanted to close the wooden door, but something made me want to keep him in my eyesight for as long as possible. I had an eerie feeling that if I blinked, he might just disappear.

"Wait!" His voice was loud and commanding.

I looked behind him onto the street. There was no joggers or passing dog walkers to hear him, whether good or bad. I stood still, frozen in place.

"I know you," he said, now his voice was lower and hard to hear through the glass. "Like I said, I looked you up on the internet. I knew that I had to find you. You said your brother had died there, and I found the article on the web."

"You looked me up?" It slipped from my mouth without intention.

"Yes," he looked around briefly, almost like he was worried someone might be overhearing our conversation. "I don't know what is going on with you, but I want to find out. That disappearing act you keep pulling is too crazy. It was making me crazy. So I started looking into your story, and it all just got stranger and stranger. Especially after seeing your brother's story in the paper. That was pretty easy to find. It was on the web and had all of that facts from the accident. I just matched the name with the address and found your Facebook page."

I opened my mouth to talk, but couldn't think of anything to say. He had looked me up because I told him about my brother. In a dream. I had met and spoke to him in a dream. There was no way he could recall the conversation. He wasn't real. Or I wasn't real. I felt almost sick, and wanted to sit down. I backed away from the door and sank to the bottom of the staircase. My legs would no longer hold me, and my head felt like it might float right off my shoulders. It was either sit down or fall down.

He opened the glass door and stepped in uninvited, but I could barely lift my head. "Savannah? Savannah, right? Look, I'm sorry. I didn't mean to freak you out. I'm not some stalker, I promise." He stood above me. I kept my head down, seriously worried that I might throw up on his work boots.

"What do you mean I said my brother had died?" My voice was faint and I was breathing heavily. I glanced up at him, seeing his soft brown eyes with those ridiculous lashes.

"When we met. That night in my truck. You were wearing your pajamas and walking in the woods. You do remember, I can see it on your face."

"I remember," I said, my head down, my hands over my face, breathing heavy. My skin had gone very cold and faintly clammy. Not good.

"You got out of the truck and, like, disappeared. It was like one second you were there, and the next you were gone. It seriously messed with my mind. It was dark and wet, and I was sure that you had fallen and hurt yourself. I looked for you for a long time on the side of the road, yelled for you, but you never came back." He squatted down in front of me, his face level with mine. I didn't look at him but concentrated on my breathing, swallowing the rising bile in my throat.

He turned and closed the wooden front door behind him, shutting out the morning sunshine. Slowly he lowered himself to the step, sitting one beneath me, so that the top of his head was level with my nose. This close I could see the dark chocolate striations in the color of his eyes, the hint of red in his unruly hair, and smell the scent of outdoors and soap on his skin. So real.

"I don't understand any of this," I said softly.

"Look. I'm sorry," he said slowly. "I really am. I didn't come to upset you. I just wanted to make sure you made it home safe. And to be honest, it was more than that. I wanted to figure out just where the hell you went that night. You know, the first couple times I saw you, I really thought you were some kind of ghost. And I don't usually believe in that type of thing." He was shaking his head and his voice sounded strained. "But I couldn't think of any other possible explanation. Where you went. How you left."

I looked at him again, his earnest expression. "I came home," I said faintly, truthfully. "And you don't have to worry, I'll be fine; I am fine." I lied. It wasn't fair to him to make him think his presence had completely rocked my world, even if it had. I concentrated on breathing, feeling my heartbeat, unconsciously practicing the calming techniques that the therapist had given me.

The sound of a car pulling into the driveway had me jerking my head up. Oh no, not now! I climbed to my feet. I stood on unsteady legs for a moment, backing away from him when he would have taken my arm to steady me. I stepped forward and around him tentatively and peered out the window to the side of the door. Then I let out a little gasp. It was my mother. And how in the world was I going to explain this guy in the foyer? If he told my other that he had seen me in the middle of the night at the side of the road, in my pajamas no less, I was in trouble. She was sure to call my dad first, the doctor next, and maybe a preacher to top it off. This was not going to go well.

"It's my mom," I said, and turned back to him. "I can't go into this right now, but I can't let her find you here."

He stood, confusion crossing his face.

"Look, I'll let you out the back. I'm going to say that a neighbor is borrowing our driveway. You can come back in a while to get your truck." I started rushing down the hallway with him at my heels. "I'll call you when you can come get it."

"Now hold on," he protested, but I turned back towards him.

"I can't do this now. I have to get you out. Then we can talk. I'll call your cell, and you can come get your truck. We can make plans about where to meet. And I'll try to explain; I'll try to explain everything." I was talking fast, then faster, my breath coming in hiccups.

We stopped in the kitchen, and I swung the back door open. He stopped at the doorway and pulled out his wallet. From it he extracted a business card and handed it to me. I glanced at the front, Travis Clark, professional landscaping and design. His cell phone followed along with an address somewhere in Kentucky, not far from Louisville, I assumed.

"You call me, and I'll come back. Then you and I will meet. You have to promise that, or I'll just come back again, and this time talk to someone. It's obvious that you're covering up something, and you're in trouble. I'm not going to stand by and do nothing. You call me." His face was grave and a little strained, urgent.

"I'll call. I promise. Now you have to go."

He stepped out on the back deck as the front door opened, and I heard my mother come in.

"Savannah, someone has their truck in our drive!" she called, and I heard the front door slam. When I looked back, he was gone.

Chapter 4

My mother took my explanation in stride. She had something on her mind, and I could tell that she had merely registered my excuse, not totally absorbed it. It wouldn't last. My mother was quite observant and the last year had made her more so. I needed to take care of my visitor.

I went back to my room and sat at my desk. First I looked up the website from the card. It was legit as far as I could tell. The website didn't have a picture of the man, Travis, I corrected myself, but it did give a brief background of the company. So what he was saying had been true. He worked as a landscaper just north of Crestwood. After consulting Google Maps, I saw that the shortest route that he could use to get from work to the Crestwood area would be just past my brothers' accident site. Of course, he didn't say that he lived in town, but I assumed he was living close by. I leaned back and looked at the computer screen. So my mystery man was real. A flesh and blood guy who just happened to be driving by and saw me. But saw me how? And saw me doing what? I hadn't been there on those nights. I knew I hadn't. I had been in bed, cuddled up with Daisy, having dreams. I sighed out a huff of air.

I knew I couldn't put him off. As soon as I heard my mother retreat to her upstairs bedroom to read, I closed my door and called his cell phone. He answered immediately, as though he had been waiting for my call, which I supposed he was.

"You can come and get your truck now," I told him, keeping my voice low.

"I still want to talk to you," he said firmly.

"I know, but I can't talk now. Just come and get your truck, and we'll arrange something later like I said."

"That's not good enough. I don't want to take some promise that you'll get back with me on your time."

"Look, I'm sorry that this isn't working for you," I said, my voice rising with irritation.

"It's not that, and you know it," he interrupted. "I want to see you today. I'm not in town for long. Remember? I had to drive pretty far out of my way to find you. I want to see you today."

"I didn't ask to be found!" I exclaimed, and immediately regretted my tone of voice. I dropped my voice to a whisper, "Okay, fine. I'll see you today. But not here. Not anywhere around here."

"Okay, fine, I'll let you choose," he responded, apparently satisfied that I wasn't getting out of the meeting.

We agreed to meet him at a coffee shop just off the interstate at 4:30, and I gave him the address. It would be early enough that my parents wouldn't worry, so I agreed to the time.

"Are you coming to get your truck now?" I asked.

"Yes, now," he said, sounding slightly aggravated. "I'll get it, and I won't come near your house."

"Fine," I snapped. I was angry, frustrated and scared.

"Then I'll see you at 4:30." The phone clicked off into silence, and I looked at the blank screen. What had I just agreed to?

I paced my room until I heard the rumble of the motor on his truck. I stood off the side of the window and watched him pull away, staying out of sight, but keeping my eye on him. The fact that he had found me, that he had walked right out of my dreams and showed up on my front porch, boggled my mind. And I had a big decision to make, and no way to coherently figure out what I was going to do. If I were honest and told him exactly what had happened, he would think I was crazy. If I told him that I did remember him, that I had deliberately appeared to him, then misled him, run from him, he would think I was a different kind of crazy.

Time seemed to speed by too fast. I ate an uncomfortable lunch with my mother while I tried not to look her in the eye. I was terrified that she would read me. I kept the conversation light, and when my mom started talking about a recipe she wanted to make for dinner, I let my mind drift.

Later, as I shut down my computer, preparing to leave the house at four o'clock, I honestly had no better idea of what I was going to do.

When I was ready to head out the door, I stopped at the foot of the stairs and took a few minutes to consider myself in the mirror. A little makeup had made me look a little less grave ready, slender jeans and a simple tee shirt with no logo. My boots were worn and comfortable. My hair hung in a long curtain down my shoulders, and I gathered it up into a loose pony tail. I chose simple hoops for my ears. I wanted to look normal. I wanted to look forgettable. It was a poor idea at best, but if he would just forget me, forget that he had ever participated in my madness, then I could forget as well. I grabbed my purse from my bed and shoved my phone in my pocket. I slipped out the door quietly not wanting to alarm my mother. Better to explain later than to be caught in a conversation before I could even leave the house.

The coffee shop was one the generic buildings at the end of a little strip mall. The coffee was good, not great, and I bought a cup and took a seat. I was early. That was the norm for me; I hated to be late to anything. Today it seemed important that I have some control over the situation. I chose a corner of the shop away from customers and staff. I didn't know what I was going to say, but I was pretty sure I didn't want anyone to hear it.

He came in at precisely 4:30, cool air washing in with him. He came directly to the little table I had claimed and dropped into a seat.

"You came," he said as a greeting.

"You made me," I replied, but I kept my voice light.

"I did," he acknowledged. "I just wasn't sure if you were really going to make it." He looked at me, eyes slightly narrowed. "I would have come after you, you know. I am serious about trying to make sure you won't be doing anything that reckless in the future."

"Yeah, I kind of figured that out." Now my tone was dry.

"So do you want to tell me why you are wandering in the woods at night in your night clothes?"

"One question for you," I said thoughtfully, "why do you care? You don't know me, or you barely know me. It's not like I'm your responsibility or anything."

That stopped him. I wasn't sure that he had ever thought over his motivation. "I guess it just seems like the right thing to do, or, I don't know, it seems wrong just to let you keep doing what you're doing. It's like seeing someone who is trying to hurt themselves. No matter who they are, or whether or not you know them, you still know that you should step in."

"I'm not hurting myself," I said stiffly.

"I didn't say that you were, deliberately. But the fact is, you're playing a dangerous game. What if it hadn't been me that stopped by when you're out there on the road? Or what if someone didn't see you and hit you? I just want to know the truth, whatever it is."

I looked at him, then glanced around, trying to determine if anyone was interested in our conversation. They weren't. The only other occupants were two women drinking coffee out of mugs and knitting, and a single man at a computer typing madly.

"If I tell you the truth, you have to not say anything."

"To?"

"To anyone."

He sat back and frowned. "You realize before this morning, I didn't even know your name. I'm not sure who you think I'm going to run to."

"I just want you to promise."

"Sure." He leaned back forward. "Tell me everything."

So I did. I had been keeping my secret for so long, it was an almost cathartic experience to say it out loud. And to give him credit, he was silent through most of my story. I began with my brother's death, and I quickly moved on to the beginning of the dreams. When I got to the part about seeing his truck, he looked like he wanted to interrupt, but didn't. When I described what he had said, what he had done during the meetings, he acknowledged with a nod. I hadn't been dreaming, he seemed to say with the gesture. When I told him of waking in my bed after our discussion in the truck, how I was dry and clean, no mud on my feet, no rain in my hair, he finally spoke up.

"What?" He stared at me wordlessly for a minute. "You've got to be kidding me! How can that be?" he asked, his face showing his mixed emotions clearly, primarily, disbelief.

"It can't," I said bitterly. "See my problem? It can't have happened. We can't have met in the woods; I was never out of my bed."

"And you're being perfectly serious about this?"

I glared at him, not responding to that stupid statement.

"Did anyone see you sleeping?"

"Really," I asked astonished. "You think that I drove in my sleep, an hour away in the dark, in the middle of the night? Then I met you, carried on a conversation, left you, ran out into the night to some hidden place where I left my car, and all the while, sleeping. Oh, and when I got back home, I must have showered in my sleep, dried my pajamas, put them back on, and gone back to bed."

He looked out the window thoughtfully. "So your explanation

would be what?"

"I don't have one," I snapped, my voice rising enough that the knitters paused their conversation and looked in our direction. I dropped my tone and leaned forward over the little table, wrapping my hands around the cup. "That would be my problem."

He was silent for a long moment as I sat frozen in my seat. There were no words that could describe my situation. There was no way that I could be lying in my bed sleeping while at the same time wandering in the woods. It couldn't be. But the fact that it was impossible didn't seem to be changing the fact that it had happened.

"So what are the chances that this is all a big joke?"

I looked at him, unsure if I should be pissed or amused. I settled for amused and just smiled. "Okay, so now you've heard my story, what's yours?"

He was frowning looking at the tabletop. H didn't appear to hear me. Or maybe he just didn't want to. I wouldn't have blamed him if he had just gotten up and left. He didn't know me, hadn't asked for this, had no idea who I was or what my life had been. It was pretty surprising that he had come to find me at all. Had he thought to find some crazy girl, lost in grief? If he had, I was pretty determined to disappoint him.

He shook his head and looked up at me. "I don't have a story, not really. I just happened to see you. I thought you were in trouble, so I stopped." He ran a tired hand over his face.

The bell at the door jingled a greeting, alerting the staff to another patron coming in, looking for warmth and caffeine. I looked up automatically and froze. Bethany Griffith, cheerleader, sweet and talkative, and no way to avoid her attention.

"Savannah!" she squealed in greeting.

"Hey, Bethany," I said faintly.

I watched her blue eyes flicker between my face and Travis's, appraising.

"This is Travis Clark. He's...."

"A new friend," Travis interrupted. "Nice to meet one of Savannah's friends."

"Yeah," Bethany agreed. "Great to meet you too. I've known Savannah for, like, ever." Her smile was genuine, and I couldn't help but smile back. I had run away from all these people, and felt a flash of guilt. Perhaps I could have given them a chance.

"So what's up with you?" I asked her.

She grabbed a chair from an adjoining table and pulled it close.

"Well, not too much, but you know how school is." She leaned forward and whispered, "you did hear about Mr. Sanders..."

I listened, bemused, as she eagerly filled me in on the latest gossip from school. Her subjects flitted from faculty to students, from who had broken up with whom, and what team was dominating in their sport. I glanced surreptitiously at Travis, and he gave me a slight smile.

When my cell phone buzzed in my pocket a few minutes later, I excused myself and answered the call just outside the glass doors. It was my mother, predictably. I reassured her that I was fine and told her I would be home soon. It was a good time to leave. I could slip away with Bethany's presence as a distraction.

"I've gotta head out," I said as I reached the table.

"Oh?" Bethany sounded disappointed.

I smiled as Travis stood as well.

"You don't have to go," I said backing away from the table.

"I really should," Travis replied. He stood, suddenly seeming taller and larger. "I'll walk you to your car."

I nodded. There was no way to get away without this conversation. And how would it end? If the guy was smart, he would give me his best wishes and send me on my way. There was no way that he could still think I was normal. Sane.

I told Bethany goodbye, but couldn't promise when I would see her at school again. With everything that was happening to me now, it didn't look like I was ready to join the real world. I was obviously losing what little stability I had. But someday, well, someday I would be better, ready to carry on in my normal life, and it was nice to know that it was waiting for me.

I stopped by my car, the keys resting in my hand. I still felt it, the little surge of nerves, of uncertainty before I climbed behind the wheel.

"So," Travis started, his eyes on my face.

"So I'll be fine. And thanks for not saying anything to Bethany."

"I wasn't going to say anything to your friend. I never thought about it. But I don't know about the being fine part."

I shoved the key in the lock and pulled open the car door.

"Wait," he said, reaching his hand out.

"I appreciate you trying to help," my voice sounded odd in my ears.

"Are you just going to run away?" he asked incredulously.

"I don't really have a choice," I responded. "I'm not running, I'm just moving on."

It sounded stupid, once the words were out of my mouth, but I hadn't anything further to say.

"So you won't let me help you."

"I don't know what you can do." I responded.

He dropped his hand. "Will you talk to someone about this?"

"You mean a shrink?" I asked, my voice harsh.

"Hell, I don't know. Just someone you trust."

I almost asked, who? Who did he recommend me to talk to? Who would understand? But I bit my tongue. If I acted like I didn't know what to do next, I felt sure that he would feel obliged to interfere. And I knew I didn't want that just now.

"I'll find someone," I said finally. "I'll talk to someone."

I had no intention of telling anyone about my dream walking problems. But the pressure was getting so great, the pressure that made me feel as if my backbone was wired together with steel, that I couldn't bend, couldn't even sit to get my breath. It was making me miserable.

I shouldn't have been surprised when Thomas called on my cell phone. I had asked Tori to keep quiet, but I had also felt sure that she wouldn't want to hide anything big from Drew. And Drew would naturally feel that he needed to talk to Thomas. And so the circle led back to me.

"What's up?" I asked, as though it was completely commonplace for my brother to be calling me. He had called me only a handful of times since he had left for college in September. Since the accident and his recovery, he had suddenly seemed so much busier than before, and worst, wildly distracted.

"That's what I was going to ask you," he replied, his voice calm and easy.

"Nothing is going on here," I said, voice still casual.

"Okay, fine. A group of us were going to get dinner and go out to the movies this weekend. Thea suggested I ask you to come."

Thea had asked. It made me wonder. Was she asking because she wanted to keep in touch with her boyfriend's sister, or had she talked to Tori? Had Tori told her about my visit? I stood still, phone to my ear, my eyes focused outside. I could go. I liked Thea, and I had known Drew forever. Tori was fun too, in her quirky way. She understood me. And I had to admit that being with Thomas was somehow very comforting for me. He wasn't Daniel, I knew that, but he was a connection to Daniel, somehow closer than even our parents seemed to be. He was still my big brother, the one who had taken up for me when I was in the second grade and another kid had called me names. The one who teased me about my crush on one of his friends in middle school, the one who had embraced me from his hospital bed, comforting even when he was in pain.

"So Thea wants me to come?"

Thomas snorted on the other end of the line. "Well yeah, like I would want my younger sister hanging around," he said, a light chuckle in his voice.

"That's what I thought," I said back, my voice haughty. I wanted to joke with him, to recover the carefree relationship we had once shared. But it was forced, and we both knew it.

"Just come for a couple days; just stay the weekend. You can stay with Thea for the night. I'll even come up and get you."

I opened my mouth to protest, but stopped. So someone had told him about my reluctance to drive. I hadn't wanted to burden him with my problems, so I had explicitly asked my parents to not say anything to him. But apparently that hadn't happened. Despite my disappointment, I knew he understood. He didn't drive much himself. The memory of the accident, while erased from his mind, had lingered in his subconscious. The fact that he was offering to drive told me how much he wanted to see me, and once again, I wondered why.

"Sure," I said slowly. "I'll come. But you don't have to drive me. I'll call you when I leave, and I'll drive directly to Thea's."

"Good, great," he said, but he sounded surprised. He thought I wouldn't come. I could tell it in his voice. But I needed to prove something to him, and to myself. I needed to get out of the house, get out of my brain.

After we had hung up, I curled up on my bed and leaned back against the headboard. I had one other concern that I had to face, no matter how much I might want to deny it. If I were going to spend the night out, what would happen if I had one of my dreams? Or would I dream at all? Perhaps just being away from my home might cure me of something. Dream walking, crazy talking, whatever was happening to me.

And directly related to that, I was worried about Travis. I didn't think he'd come by my home again, there was no reason for him to, but I couldn't leave without knowing that he wouldn't tell my parents about my problems. Our problem, I corrected in my mind. If he was on the crazy train, I was definitely the conductor. I needed to make sure he wouldn't be bringing any of his concerns and dropping them at my parents' feet. I pulled my phone from my pocket and switched it on. His number was in my recent call history, but I hadn't added it to my list of contacts. Doing so would make him a regular in my life, and I wasn't ready for that addition.

I decided on a text. But how to word it? Dear fellow crazy person, don't stop by my house and freak my parents out? Leave me alone for a few days? You are not allowed near my family? Keep my secret?

I settled for a brief message, 'Travis, I will be out of town for the weekend. If you need to contact me, please use this phone number'. I signed it Savannah and reread the words. It was brief and to the point. It wasn't rude. Sure, it was an invitation for him to call me. But that would be better than him calling my parents. And at this point, with my scary habits running off the charts, I couldn't blame him for wanting to track me down. I had thought he was in my dreams. He had thought I was a ghost. Which of us at this point was the most unhinged?

I sent the message and laid back on my bed. I would need to clear the trip with my parents, but since I was visiting my brother, that wouldn't be a problem. Then I would need to pack a bag. It didn't need much, but I hadn't stayed away from home for a while.

My phone chimed, letting me know I had gotten a message. I checked it, expecting a response from Travis. I was right. He wrote only 'ok', no further communication, but at least I knew that he had gotten it. I got back to my feet and jogged quickly down the stairs.

Chapter 5

I didn't know what I had expected, meeting my brother and his friends, but it wasn't just a night out with buddies. I had been sure there was some sneaky ulterior motive behind the invitation, so when we actually did load up in Thea's old wood paneled station wagon, I was pretty surprised. We went outside of the little town of Crestwood to a nearby shopping center off Westport Road to buy our movie tickets. The line was fairly long, and the smell of popcorn as we waited brought back cheerful memories. As I watched Thomas laughing at something Drew had said, and punching him playfully with a grin, I felt myself relax. Thea had dragged Tori to the front of the theater where there were lines of knockout roses slowly losing their blooms preparing for the winter. I saw that they were gathering up some of the faded petals and watched with interest. I was well aware of Thea's artistic ability. In fact, I was the only one from our family who had gone to see her show while Thomas was still in the hospital. It was true that I had gone because some of the story that she had told my parents, that she had met Thomas on the trip that we had taken together to her hometown, was totally false. I had known that because I had been on some of those trips. But at the time, beyond telling her that I knew the story wasn't accurate, I wasn't about to say anything negative to her. I had been so grateful for what she had done for Thomas. We had all felt that it was her presence that had brought him out of his coma. I also had an inner feeling for Thea that was undefinable. There was something so trustworthy about her, so calming. But perhaps I wasn't completely honest with myself. There was a time that I had mistrusted her, and her hometown, and the whole circumstance of the meeting. But that was a long time ago, and now I could see how good she was for Thomas. How much she was helping him through this. And I could see how much he cared for her.

"Van, you coming?" Thomas' voice interrupted my thoughts, and I saw that he held the tickets and that Thea and Tori had joined us. Only I was standing frozen on the pavement, lost in thought.

"Sure," I said, and forced a smile.

The movie was awful, supposed to be funny and failing, but the guys liked it, and it was nice to see Thomas and Drew laughing again. We drove back out to Crestwood for our dinner, and by that time I was starving. The restaurant had the best pizza in town, a locally based place that served thick crust pizzas and salads piled high with real bacon as well as an array of veggies. It was good, but the company was better. I had missed this.

I tried not to check my phone, but I was worried. I didn't think that Travis would show up at my house unannounced, but I didn't know the guy. And there was something else. He had seen me in my dreams. He was the only proof that I had that I was actually walking in my sleep, and definitely not in the traditional way. I still had a nagging concern that if I never saw him again, if he disappeared, that I would be proven insane. It was almost a blessing that I had seen Bethany at the coffee shop. Otherwise, I would have had no witnesses to the meeting.

After dinner and a stop at Dairy Queen for ice cream, we drove the short trek back to Thea's house. It was funny how the tiny city blended so seamlessly with the very old and historic buildings around it. Built long before electricity and plumbing were a must, Thea's stone home was a testament to past beauty and practicality. Her house was situated at the front of the lot, the porch opening onto a few steps that led down to a cracked sidewalk flanked by mums in rich fall hues. The stones were a warm golden color, and light seeped from between sheer curtains at the windows, fringed with lace.

Thea's parents greeted us as we came in, her mother at the kitchen table apparently grading student's work that she had brought home with her from the local high school. She had a gigantic mug of coffee at her elbow and a plate of cookies in the middle of the table that smelled freshly baked, making me regret eating ice cream earlier. As I watched her sort through her papers, I remembered my art classes, how fabulously unsuccessful I had been and had to smile to myself. The A I had gotten in that class was for good bookwork alone.

Thea's father had an antique clock taken apart on their kitchen table and was painstakingly cleaning each piece with an old handkerchief. I knew that he had taken early retirement. He now spent his free time gardening, doing odd jobs in the neighborhood, and crafting furniture in his wood working shop that he sold for a tidy profit in local stores. His former job, though, had taken its toll on him. He had been a funeral director and manager of the local funeral home for years, and the effort that it had taken to comfort the grieving and deal with the passing souls showed on his features. I couldn't imagine ever wanting that job, but knew from what Thea had said that it was a position that had been handed down from father to son.

Thea was a mix of her father's calm nature and her mother's artistic style. Thomas had proudly shown us pictures of some of her more recent work, and I knew that she had made a name for herself through her unusual flower arrangements created from dried blossoms, forever frozen. When I had been at the art show while Thomas was recovering in the hospital, I had seen her most prized piece, the sculpture of the figure in flowers that was stunning and disturbing in turn. I knew that she continued to do her art, although much of it remained on campus in Lexington where she and Thomas were in their second year of classes.

I could hear the flurry of activity out the back door and peered outside. Tori had stopped by her home to check on her sister and bring out her massive dog, Monty, on a leash. He was prancing in the back yard with Thea's genial beagle, the pair of them making an amusing odd couple as they played. We went out back as well, settling on benches in the gazebo, nestled in the twilight. Tori's home was across the street and down a few houses, just at the curve of the road. The yellow paint, a soft buttery color, glowed gently under the streetlights. I felt a little wave of emotion when I saw how pretty the house looked. I couldn't believe that someone had set a fire in the front room of the old home. They could have successfully burned the whole thing down, if Tori hadn't woken and rushed downstairs with her sister. The damage had been significant, despite their quick responses, but the community had stepped in to help with repairs. When it was all completed, the exterior siding had been repaired and painted. The window that had been broken was replaced. The scarred and singed wood floors had been sanded and refinished. A platoon of ladies from the local Women's Club had descended to help air and sponge away the lingering scent of smoke. It was as though the town had banded together to erase the damage that someone else had inflicted on the two girls.

In all, it seemed like a great place to live, except for one thing that made me want to glance over my shoulder at the most unexpected times, and dread when the lights would be extinguished.

Just next door to Thea's historic house, and directly across the street from Tori's, was a grand old cemetery. Floydsburg Cemetery had been around for a good long time with graves dating back from the 1800's, and plots still open for more recent inhabitants. And it was beautiful. It really was, with its rolling hills, carefully planted and tended flowers, mature trees stretching out over picturesque stones, and the Chapel itself. Thea had lived here and grown up with it right next door, her bedroom window overlooking the graves. For her it was home, and as normal as any neighbors would be. For me, well, I just couldn't feel that way. All those souls, all those bodies spread out over the land.

I shivered and pulled my sweatshirt tighter around my shoulders. The dogs had finally grown tired and curled up together on the wooden floor. Thea sat on one bench, knees drawn up to her chest, Thomas sitting next to her, close, but not too close. Opposite was Tori, bending down to pat Monty's head as he stretched out taking up most of the floor, and Drew with his too long legs and unruly dark hair sat next to her. I looked at Drew for a moment and sighed. Drew had been almost a brother to me for many years. He had met my brothers when they were all in elementary school and had remained friends with them both. He had been in the accident that had killed Daniel and injured Thomas, and he walked away without a scratch. His bouts with confusion and memory loss were concerning. He didn't remember anything from the accident, and I knew that it preyed upon his mind. The fact that he had walked away while his closest friends had been so damaged did not seem fair. The tragedy had marked his life almost as strongly as it had marked mine. But I was happy for him in finding Tori. Her spontaneous personality had pulled him out of the depression that he had been sliding into, and I could see more spirit in his dark eyes now.

The conversation was light, about school and weather, the upcoming holidays and plans for the future. I found myself drifting while the words spilled around me, not listening, but secure in the presence of so many other people. I must have drifted off to sleep because the next thing I knew, Thomas was tugging on my long braid.

"Time to go to bed," he said, smiling at me. "I think we've bored you into a stupor."

I shook my head sleepily. "I just haven't gotten much rest lately," I said, my mind muddled.

"Then come on. You can sleep in tomorrow." I stood with him, following the group into the house. Drew and Tori left with a wave, and I followed Thea upstairs. They had a tiny second bedroom that Thea's mother had used to create her various art projects. It held a daybed with an old soft quilt. Thea's beagle, Baxter, chose to stay with me. He was curled up on the floor next to the bed side, a sleepy sentry, and I patted his head before rolling over, nestling in the warmth.

I slept without dreaming.

The next morning I woke early and stretched, admiring the view out the window. I could see the street out front, the old homes lined up like ornaments decorated in their autumn finery, the leaves bright splotches of crimson, gold, and orange. The sun was out, but the temperature wasn't likely to rise over 50 degrees.

I slid into a pair of jeans and threw a sweatshirt over my tee shirt to ward off the chill. Older homes were charming, but this one was drafty as well. Baxter, Thea's hound, lumbered to his feet and followed me out the door, galloping down the steps with surprising agility and waiting at the front door to be let out.

I told him to wait and wandered into the kitchen. Thea was alone in the lemony yellow light, a laptop computer open in front of her and a coffee cup in one hand. When I entered she smiled a welcome.

"Thomas has gone out with Drew. Tori went in to work, but we will meet her later." Thea stood and switched on the coffee pot. "Do you want something for breakfast?"

"Coffee is fine," I responded, noting that she had some flavored creamer on the counter.

"Toast?" she offered, and unwrapped a loaf of bread from its foil cocoon. "Tori brought it from the diner. Bythe is the best baker in town."

"If you insist," I replied grinning. Baxter was dancing more insistently at my feet. "Do you want me to let him out?" I asked, gesturing to the anxious dog.

"Yeah, that'd be fine." She took out a long bread knife and began sawing at the loaf. As the bread heated in the toaster oven, she pulled out butter and honey harvested locally. The radio was on in some room, and a tinkle of melody sounded in the quiet.

The coffee maker sputtered to a stop and I helped myself to the coffee and creamer. It was hot and sweet and delicious. "I slept really well last night," I said on a sigh as I eased down at the table.

She brought a plate of buttered bread and put it on the table between us, adding napkins and the honey and some jam. "Good. Thomas said he didn't think that you had been sleeping well."

"Is it that obvious?" I asked wryly.

"Not to everyone, but to him, yeah. He worries about you."

"I know," I said frowning, "and I don't want him too. I'm doing fine, aside from the sleeping thing."

"Bad dreams?" Thea said casually.

I felt my cheeks heat. "Why do you say that?"

She shrugged, her warm brown curls falling into her eyes when she looked down. She swiped the locks away with the back of her hand and got up to pour herself another cup of coffee. "I just remember you talking about the dream you had had when you came and visited me."

I could feel my face get redder. I could easily recall that time shortly after my brother had come out of his coma, when he and Thea had just begun dating, that I had had a vivid dream where I came to the cemetery. My mind unwillingly went back to the dream where I had just appeared like a ghost among the graves. I ranted like a mad woman, crying out in total despair, blaming the accident and my brother's death on her, on myself, on anything just to make the pain go away. I could recall standing in that dark place, screaming wildly, the wind whipping the trees, my hair, my clothes into a frenzy until the world seemed ready to explode with my grief.

And then he had come to me. As I was out in the cemetery, screaming my fury on the innocent Thea, Daniel had come to me. And I could still vaguely feel his arms as he had held me, and called me pet names from our childhood. Sometimes I thought that in my dream he had told me that I wasn't to blame for what had happened to him, but sometimes I thought that that was just wishful thinking. In my recollections, I imagined that I knew he wasn't completely gone from me. I knew somewhere, perhaps not in this world, he was there waiting for me, for us.

After the dream, I had woke in my bed, confused and frightened, but not nearly so grief stricken. But guilty, hell yes, I felt guilty. For as much as it had been my dream, and therefore happening only in my head, I felt that I owed Thea a big apology for the way that I had blamed her.

To the confusion of my family, at my insistence, I had come to see Thea after that and told her the truth. I told her that I had dreamed about her, and that I had not been fair or rational in my feelings toward her. Thea had accepted the apology and the story with surprising calm and acceptance, as though getting apologies for someone's dream thoughts was common for her.

Now I felt a fission of fear. What if? What if I had actually appeared to Thea, as I had to Travis? I looked at her with caution. She was calmly eating toast, her eyes drifting toward the window over the sink that looked out into the sun dappled lawn. In the bright light of morning, it all seemed ridiculous. But it had seemed that crazy when I had opened the door and let Travis in my house, feeling his heat and his solid presence. Knowing that I had spoken to him before, but never while I was awake.

I drank in the silence but my mind was racing. Should I? I felt so alone in my crazy feelings, and Thea fairly exuded calm and serenity. I took a deep breath and put my elbows on the table, my fingers wrapped around the warm mug.

"That dream was very real." I said softly. "And I've had some other's that have felt like that."

Thea stopped chewing and her eyes rested on my face, sharp now. "You've dreamed like that again?" She asked.

"Yeah, I've had lots of dreams like that, or at least a dozen," I estimated. "And it's hard to get over them in the morning. I just feel so tired." Her expression was making me feel antsy, like I had said too much. I began to regret my honesty. This confession could do nothing to help. "Thea, don't tell Thomas about this. He'll just get more worried, and he'll get my parents upset."

"I won't tell him anything you don't want him to know," Thea said solemnly, "but I think you would be better off if you were honest with him."

"Honest," I said, wrapping my hands more tightly around the mug. "How honest do you think I should be?" I spoke like I couldn't bite the words back. "These dreams, Thea, they are so real, they're almost more real than the mornings that come after. I see places, people, and remember them like I had seen them just an hour before." I leaned forward. "Have you ever had a dream where you met a stranger, and later met them in real life and remembered them? You can remember your conversation? My dreams are that real!" My words had sped up and I closed my lips tightly to prevent anything else from spilling out.

"Are you sure they are dreams?" Thea's voice was soft.

"Oh, my God, what else could they be?" I cried. I could feel my eyes welling with tears, and wiped at them with the palm of my hands. "I can't be going crazy, Thea! I can't do that to my parents, or to Thomas. I know he's doing much better, but I also know how much he has been hurt. And my parents, my God, my parents have had to deal with too much already!"

"Savannah, Thomas is doing fine, and there's nothing he would like better than to help you," Thea said, her voice low and urgent.

"There is no way to help," I burst out. "Thea, these are not ordinary dreams! I see to the place where Daniel died, I walk there in my dreams, and I can see and smell and feel everything so clearly. But I'm not really there. I'm just dreaming it. I even went out there a few days ago during the day to check it out to see if it looked the way it had in my dreams. And it did. It was exactly the same, down to the tire marks on the side of the road!" I took a deep breath. "And there's this guy that I saw there. He pulled off the side of the road in my dream, Thea. He pulled over and talked to me like I was a real person. He said he saw me walking and wanted to help. He said that I was standing out there in my pajamas on the side of the road in the trees. He offered to let me use his phone." I laughed a little hysterically, and I swiped at my cheeks again, barely aware of the tears sliding down. "All in my dreams! This was all in my dreams, I thought. But then I saw him while I was awake. I saw him in town, around here, and later at my house. He came to my home and found me because he said I told him my brother had died at that place. He figured out who I was! I told him in my dream, but to him it wasn't a dream."

I stopped talking, my breath coming in gasps, expecting Thea to say something, but she certainly didn't respond as I thought she would.

"Savannah, your brother needs to talk to you, to tell you the truth. They aren't dreams, what you're having, and he and I both know that. He's been holding some things back from you because he was afraid that you couldn't handle knowing. But now I think that it's clear that you can't handle not knowing." She reached out and covered my clenched hand with her own. "You have not been dreaming; it has been real. And it's not just you; it's your brother too. You are not crazy. You're bilocating."

I took a long, hot shower, waiting for my brother to return. Thea was cleaning up our breakfast mess, and she had called my brother, demanding that he get back as soon as he could.

I was trying to clear my head, but with little success. Thea had promised answers, and I was just waiting for them.

After I finished bathing, I pulled back on my warm clothes and sat in the little guest room, combing my long hair absently while looking out the window. This place was certainly different than what I was accustomed to. My neighborhood was filled with carbon copy houses, set one next to another, well-manicured lawns blending together in a carpet of green, now turning pale and sickly in the cold. Here, each house was as individual as the family living within, all of them older than the oldest inhabitants, their glass eyes having looked at decades of history and change. Had they seen the likes of me before? Had they seen someone who could be sleeping in her bed at one moment, and walking in the woods another? I impatiently tugged my hair back in a loose ponytail and pulled on a pair of thick white socks, my brother's, which I had taken the night before because I had forgotten to bring my own. I went to the top of the stairs and took a deep breath, holding the railing for dear life.

Downstairs I could hear the rumble of voices from the living room. It was more than just my brother and Thea, I felt sure. Drew's dark tones could be heard, although he was saying far less than Thea.

"You should have said something long before this," Thea was saying, hands outstretched and trembling slightly in a gesture of aggravation.

"Well, I get that now," my brother responded, and then caught my movements and looked toward me. "Van," he said softly.

It struck me again as I watched the light blend into his pale hair and paint his face with warmth how very like me he was. Our coloring was the same, the same fine bones, the same stubborn chin. But as much as I saw myself in Thomas' face, I saw his twin, my crazy, spirited Daniel so much more. The photos that showed the three of us growing up could have been snapshots of triplets if I had been closer to their age. But I knew that it was a little club that I would never join. The twins were a matching set, a troublesome duo, the two halves that made something of a whole. Standing outside and looking in I had been jealous, I could admit that now, but more than that, I had been a little hurt, alone. Now, looking at Thomas, I saw more of myself in him. He was alone now.

"You should have said something," I said softly, frowning. "Thomas, what has happened to us? What have we done?" I felt bruised and tender and prickly all at the same time. "And now I want to hear the whole story. All of it!"

"Sit down. I'm not going to talk to you if you're going to just loom over me," he responded, his tone so even and reasonable.

I dropped on the chair across from where he and Thea were seated on the couch. I immediately tucked my feet under me, drawing into myself unconsciously.

"I'll start, but Tori's on her way. She's involved in this too, and I want you to hear her side of the story." Thomas' voice remained infuriatingly calm.

"Tori too?" I felt a little betrayed, like there was a secret that everyone had known but me. "Fine," I said shortly, biting back any other words.

Thomas heaved a sigh and looked at me closely. "This all started with Daniel and one of his ideas," he said, his face tight at the mention of his twin's name. "He was after something when we came here the first time; he just never bothered to tell any of us what it was." He leaned forward. "I'm talking about the first time we came out here. We were all together, going from site to site, all those cemeteries and churches."

I nodded. The first time I had come to the little Kentucky town, we hadn't known anyone. Daniel, full of mischief as usual, had driven, Thomas next to him, Drew and I in the backseat trying not to be concerned. But it was summer and scorching hot, the leaves heavy and green, making the cemetery 10 degrees cooler with the shade. As a group we had climbed out of the car, and I could distinctly remember complaining because I was hungry, and Daniel had promised us lunch, as though lunch would be our biggest concern.

We had wandered the cemetery, Daniel going off on his own, attempting to unsuccessfully get into the closed Chapel. I eventually had settled on a bench placed directly next to an old well which was covered and unused. I think I had texted some of my friends, complaining about the heat, and fussing because my brother had persuaded me to come here and now I was bored out of my mind.

"Daniel was looking for something," Thomas said as he looked around the room at our faces, "he just never bothered to tell us, any of us, what he was looking for."

"I knew that," I said dismissively. "But he was always coming up with some kind of quest." Daniel had been the one looking for treasure maps at the beach when we were children, the one venturing into caves as young adults, fearless and curious. As teenagers, we had traveled extensively on day trips, going from one small town monument or tourist attraction to another. After a while, the trips had started to blend together in a slide show of the unusual and banal, Daniel's hunches and foolish ideas.

"Well, this time, it was real," Thomas said, his voice hoarse and strange. He reached into his pocket and pulled out a black pouch made of fabric. "This was what he was looking for, but never found."

He spilled out the content onto the table in front of us, a necklace. It was a heavy old piece, too big to be worn just as an ornament. It reminded me of the crosses I had seen hanging from rosaries that the nuns carried when I used to volunteer at St. Gabriel's soup kitchen. The chain was a heavy gold, and the cross was stamped with patterns.

"Where did that come from?" I asked.

"We found it here," Drew said, but he looked anything but happy. "We were trying to trace Daniel's steps, and it led back here."

The front door swung open and Tori walked in, her jeans still dusted with flour from the baking she had been doing. "Okay, where's the fire?" she asked, as she strolled in and stopped immediately upon seeing the necklace on the table. "Oh," she said, and slid into a seat on the other side of Drew.

"We are trying to explain," Thea started slowly, "well, everything."

"That's a big job," Tori responded.

I leaned forward to look at the cross as Tori dropped into a seat. I put out a tentative finger to touch the thing, and pulled back quickly.

"Where did you find it?" My voice was choked with some emotion I couldn't name.

"Remember the boy in the well? He had it with him." Thea picked up the cross and cupped it in her hand. I watched as I thought back to the sad little funeral I had attended months before.

"Tell me," I insisted.

Thomas leaned forward and took the cross from Thea's hand. "This was taken from a grave site off the coast of Spain. The man who was buried with it was a reformed pirate named Juan Madino. Trust me, it took some work to find out all this information, but we figure that Daniel must have been way ahead of us in this." He pushed his pale hair away from his face with one hand, still holding the cross with the other. "The pirate had been literally saved by a religious Sister that he knew. He was being threatened by another pirate back in eighteen hundreds when Sister Francisca appeared between the two men and stopped the fight. She just appeared out of nowhere, and I imagine scared the hell out of the two men. Madino was a changed man after that, needless to say. But the stranger thing was that while Sister Francisca was supposedly seen by the pirates and all of the other men on the dock that day, she was also seen in the convent by the rest of the sisters that lived there."

"That's where we got the term bilocation." Thea looked at me, her face earnest. "We looked it up in some of the religious books that my parish priest had. Bilocation is something well documented in the Church's history. Several saints were said to have bilocated. It essentially means that while you are one place doing one thing, you can also be somewhere else, truly there, not just some kind of spirit, but with a body and mind."

My mouth opened to protest, but my voice held in my throat. There were no words. This couldn't be real.

"Let me finish before you ask any questions," Thomas said gravely. "Sister Francisca gave the converted pirate the cross as a gift, and when he died, it was buried with him. In the 1800's, his tomb was plundered, and although some of his belongings eventually turned up, the cross was never found." He paused for a moment. "Fast forward a little. In Tori's house across the way there was a family who had built the house and lived there with a son and daughter. At some time, the wife's father, an old scholar, moved into the house as well. He was known for extensive traveling and had a collection of things that he had found from all over the world. But he was a strange old man, a recluse. He became even stranger as he lived there, coming out of his rooms only occasionally, barring himself in and demanding that his food be served to him in his rooms. It sounded like he was just getting paranoid, or maybe suffering from some mental problems like dementia. Now we're not so sure."

I found my gaze traveling to the window. I could see Tori's house set off the road, across the way and a few houses down. Under its shelter of trees, the shade staining the ground, it looked a little haunted.

"And one day, the boy disappeared."

"You don't think his grandfather…" I closed my mouth before I could utter the words.

"We don't think so," Thomas said firmly. "The stories were that the grandfather went out searching for the boy. They said people would see him in the middle of the night, searching, walking the streets. And then one day, the grandfather didn't answer his door when they came to give him his meal. He was dead, there in his room, sitting at his desk."

"And you found the boy's body in the well with the cross?" I felt confused about how all of the facts would link up.

"We think, and this is only our speculation, but we think that on his travels, the grandfather found the cross and brought it home with him. We also think that he realized that something was going on with his new treasure after he moved into the home with his daughter. Remember, before moving in with her, he was a teacher, a traveler, a lecturer. When he moved out here, he locked himself in his room, cut himself off from the public, generally, he became like a different person. And people said they would see him walking at night, but the family insisted that he hadn't been out of his room. We think he was bilocating, moving around in his second body while still staying in his room at home."

"And the boy?" I sounded impatient because I was. This wasn't some bedtime story with a happy ending, this was my sanity at stake.

"We think the boy found the cross and took it with him. We think that he accidently ended up in the well. And no one in the family had any idea what happened to him. But the grandfather knew one thing. Both the cross and his grandson was gone."

"And his 'bilocating'?" I asked, using my fingers to add quotations in the air.

"That continued, we guess. So the old man knew that the cross couldn't be far away. Not like it had been taken back to another country or something." Thomas dropped the necklace on the table in front of him.

"So we figured that Daniel had followed the trail as far as the cross ending up here with the old man." Drew put in, seeing my frown. "He knew what he was looking for, and he knew where it was, but no specifics. So he wanted to hunt around in this area. And he brought us all along. You, me, Thomas, Daniel. We think now that everyone on that first trip out here was affected by the cross."

"What?" I rubbed a hand over my forehead. "Affected?"

"We think that Daniel might have been aware of something changing after our first visit. He was so hot to get back here. He was going crazy with his research. Remember how he had let his grades slip and mom and dad were so pissed?" Thomas sat back slowly. "I wonder now if it was happening to him. The bilocation. Guess we'll never know for sure."

I looked at him, noticing how his face seemed paler, tighter. "But why us? And why now? That cross had been in the well with the little boy for years. What made us different?"

"That's a really good question, and one that we haven't figured out the answer to," my brother replied.

"So Daniel got you and Drew to come back here, not telling you the truth, that he was looking for the cross, but getting you to come just for the fun of it?"

Drew nodded. "I remember him calling and asking if I wanted to ride out here with him. He was so excited about something, and you know, it was hard to ever get him to settle when he had something on his mind."

I could remember the day with painful clarity, but put it out of my head. Daniel hadn't asked me to go on the trip, and I hadn't wanted to go. The last memory of my brother that I had from that morning was his flash of a smile and wave as he pulled out of the driveway.

"And the trip? The ride down? Are you remembering anything else from it?"

Both of the guys shook their heads.

"I didn't remember anything about the trip, and I was pretty messed up after the accident," Drew confessed. "I didn't know what had happened, or why. So I spent time going back and forth from home and here, trying to get some answers. I just couldn't see you all," Drew's voice was heavy with pain as he looked toward me, seeing, I knew, my brothers and I as a tight little family of pain.

"I was in the hospital," Thomas said slowly. "But that's where my story gets really bizarre. I was unconscious in that bed, in no shape to do anything, but Van, here's the weird part, I did do something."

Chapter 6

"I've lived here all my life," Thea said, taking up her part of the story. "I've seen people wandering the cemetery, classes visiting to take rubbings of the stones, wedding parties in the chapel, you name it, people do it." She frowned a little. "I've run off my fair share of people behaving badly. I've got a bat, and I'm not afraid to use it!" She smiled a little, and I thought of what she must have looked like when she was younger, wild curly hair and flannel pajamas, running out in the cemetery at night. "But when I saw Thomas walking in the cemetery, I knew there was something different about him." She took a deep breath. "I finally got up enough guts to go talk to him. But he was so, I don't know, insubstantial." She pressed her hands together. "He didn't seem to be real. He didn't want to tell me anything about himself, even his name. He seemed to just appear out of nowhere, and just like that," she snapped her fingers, "he would be gone. There was a time that I wasn't sure if I wasn't seeing things, seeing people that weren't there."

"I don't think I knew my name," my brother added. "It's hard to describe how it felt. It was very dream like. I don't know if I even thought about what was happening to me. I was just living in the moment." He stopped and looked thoughtful. "I remember walking in the cemetery. I knew there was something I was looking for. I knew that I had a reason to be there. But beyond that, I was just existing. I couldn't remember the accident, or my life before the accident, you, or Daniel." He looked apologetic, as though he could have controlled what he could remember. "But I think my situation was different because of the head injury, all of my injuries. I was just being, outside of myself, and not really remembering who or what I was." He sighed. "When Thea came out to meet me, it was the first time that I started to feel awake."

"He was so close to being a ghost, I didn't trust myself, or my feelings." Thea's eyes had gotten damp and she sniffed lightly.

I shivered at her term. If he had been a ghost, if I had lost both of my brothers, it was too much to think about. My mind refused to go there, that terrifying possibility. I found myself thinking about the first time I had met Thea at the hospital, and the visit I had taken while she was presenting at the art awards. "So your story about knowing each other from before the accident?" I asked.

"Completely made up," she admitted honestly. She blinked rapidly, composing herself. Of course, I had known her story was made up. I had been on the first trip. "But how else could I explain to my parents why I cared about this guy, this person I had never actually met who was in a coma in a different city? At first I just wanted to see him. I needed to figure out how crazy I was. I mean, in some way, I knew I had met Thomas, we had talked, we had even walked together. But when I found out about the accident, that Thomas was in a coma and Daniel," she didn't finish, just stopped and bit her lip, looking a little teary eyed again. "When we first met, Thomas just seemed like, well, he seemed confused, and alone, and lonely. Then I found out that he had lied about his name, that he didn't appear to want to admit to who he was, and that's when I started getting totally freaked out. And he pulled his disappearing act more than once, and I was back to thinking I was crazy. When I found the newspaper account of the accident, I thought I had lost my mind. But for the first time, I knew that he had been real. I just didn't know who I was seeing, Thomas or Daniel. I decided then that I had to go and see him, whoever he was."

"And you came to the hospital," I breathed, recalling the earth shattering hours after my brother had miraculously woken. He was speaking and coherent, not at all like other head injured patients who emerged in stages. The doctors had been baffled. He had defied most known cases of brain injury, emerging from his coma completely and all at once. "You came to visit, and he woke up."

"I remembered Thea perfectly," Thomas stated, still sounding surprised himself. "Better than my life before the accident really. It was as if I had been awake with her the whole time, not in the hospital bed at all. I could only vaguely remember the visitors that came to the hospital, and that was foggy even after I was fully alert. But Thea was different. I knew who she was, where she lived, and all of our conversations." He paused. "I didn't recall anything about the accident, but I knew the things that I had experienced while I was in a coma. But only while I was with her." He shook his head as though to clear it. "I can't explain it, Van. It's like I was living another life while I was in the coma, and when I woke up, I retained all of it."

"And now?" I was almost afraid to ask.

"I haven't had any of those types of experiences since I came to." Thomas leaned back, clasping his hands before him, his usual calm and serene self.

I stared at him and felt a deep compulsion to just scream. How could this be? I felt a little sick, and more than a little alone. Waking from his coma had cured Thomas. Obviously that cure wasn't an option for me.

"But I have," Drew interjected.

"What have you done?" I said, breaking out of my frustration.

"I have had those experience, just like you, Savannah." Drew looked at me steadily. "And we're going to figure this out."

If my brother's story had been strange, Drew's story had pushed the whole thing into the bizarre range. While Thomas had been bilocating without any control, at the mercy of whatever was causing it to happen, Drew had plainly gone far beyond that. Drew was controlling what he was doing. He could go into his room, lock the door, and with complete deliberation, go to sleep and awaken in another place of his choosing.

"It hasn't been perfect," he admitted. "I've only tried to go to places that I know pretty well. And I don't do it often. I'm just not sure how safe it is."

I sat in utter awe and a little fear. "So you try to do it?"

"I didn't at first," he explained. "I had come here to look into some of the places that Daniel had taken us. I found myself drawn to stay here, so it seemed easier to just find a place to stay and live here for a while." He dropped his head and rubbed his eyes slowly. "I didn't know what I was looking for, but I felt like I just had to do something. There had to be a reason that we were all going through this." When he looked up, his eyes were full of painful memories. "Daniel was gone, Thomas was in a coma, and I was walking around like I hadn't a problem in the world. I was just so damn guilty. So I decided that I would come here and take up Daniel's quest. I wanted to find out what he was here for, and to be honest, I wanted to know more about the crash."

Thomas looked at him quickly, surprised.

"Man, I don't remember much about the accident. I really don't. But I just couldn't figure out how it had gone so wrong. All the cops on the scene said we were going the speed limit, there were no other cars involved. I just couldn't figure out what would make Daniel go off the road like that."

"I thought that the police said it looked like Thomas was avoiding something. A cat or dog." I looked between the two guys.

"That's what they said," Thomas said thoughtfully. "But I don't remember." He ran a tired hand through his hair, and I knew that discussing the accident was upsetting him. "I've tried so hard to think of the moment, or even the hours before the wreck, but they're just gone."

"Yeah," Drew said softly, "but for me they shouldn't be gone. I should be able to remember something."

"Drew," I reasoned gently, "they found you walking in the woods. You didn't even know where you were. Just because they didn't put you in the hospital doesn't mean that you didn't hit your head. You may have been hurt yourself and didn't know it."

"I know," he said harshly, "but I still feel like there is something important that I should be remembering. It's just slightly out of my reach."

I felt sad listening to Drew's story. After the accident, I had barely seen him. He seemed to have melted into oblivion, and I had to admit, it had made me angry. He hadn't so much as visited Thomas in the hospital. No, that was wrong. He had come, but only occasionally and only briefly. And at the funeral, he had been a shadow in the background. Now I could hear what he was feeling, and it hurt me to see his pain.

"None of this had been easy," I whispered.

"I'm so sorry Savannah," he murmured. "I knew you were going through hell, but I just couldn't be there."

I nodded, silent. Thomas reached out and took my hand. "Things are going to be different now," he said firmly. "But we need to hear about what you've been doing."

It took the rest of the afternoon for me to describe my dreams. I had to repeat them in detail, and more than once. It had taken me a few minutes before I realized the extent of my problem.

"Thomas, I have one real question, and I want the real answer. I dreamed I came to the cemetery. I dreamed that I stood out there and then, well," I turned to face Thea where she was curled comfortably on the couch, "I was screaming at you." I glanced to Thomas, but immediately read the truth in his face. "It wasn't a dream, was it?"

The room stilled and Thomas leaned over to take my hands again. This time, I jerked back, the realization striking me like a dash of cold water.

"Oh, my God! You knew! You all knew! You knew that it wasn't a dream when I came here. You knew I was bilocating!" I was breathing hard, the feeling of betrayal sharp and bitter.

"Van, wait," Thomas said quickly.

"Wait!" I stood, my feet tingling as the circulation flooded my system. "Are you serious? All this time, I thought I was going crazy, and you knew! You knew that I wasn't!" My voice had risen in pitch and loudness.

"Van," Thomas' voice was deep, trying to be soothing.

"No!" I fairly screamed at him. I had the horrible sensation that the walls were closing in on me. My world was shrinking into a pinprick of heat, of betrayal. I turned and stormed out the front door, disappointed when the hinge caught, and I couldn't hear the bang. I walked down the steps, hesitating on the front sidewalk. I had nowhere that I wanted to go. Nowhere that I needed to be. I stalked down the sidewalk running parallel to the road and turned into the front gate of the cemetery. The ground felt spongy at my feet, but I wasn't paying attention to anything. My mind was full of memories. I could almost see myself that horrible night that I had come, no appeared, at the cemetery and screamed insanely at the world, at Thea. In truth, a truth that was still hard to believe, I had actually bilocated to the cemetery, gone completely crazy, and then, well, that was the question. I slowly walked to the place that I vaguely remembered in my dream. But it wasn't a dream. I stood under the trees and pictured in my mind what it had been like. Standing there, feeling an unnatural wind whip around me, feeling the push of the air, the pressure of the atmosphere sinking in like that threat of a heavy rain. In my memories, I could picture Thea's pale face, here curls dancing madly around her head. And then. I sighed and slowly sank down on one of the graves. I had seen Daniel. Or at least, I felt like I had seen Daniel. That part of the dream, while not completely clear, still seemed as real as the rest.

"It was real," Thea's voice was soft and I realized she had been standing silently for a few minutes, giving me time. I looked up into her soft eyes and read the sympathy and the pain.

"What was real?" I saw that she was alone. "Thea, what was real?"

"You were here," she said gently. "I found you out here."

"The wind was blowing. Crazy."

"Yes," she agreed. "The wind was wild, and you were so upset. You were crying. You didn't really know what you were saying. When I saw you, I called Thomas."

"Called him," I repeated numbly.

"I called him on his cell phone and told him that I was with you. He went into your room at home and said that you were lying in bed. You were taking a nap. You didn't wake up. That was when we knew that it was happening to you too."

"He saw me," I breathed.

"At the same time that I saw you," she agreed, nodding. "But Savannah, he never meant for you to get hurt. He realized what was happening, just like I did, but he didn't know what to do."

"He didn't say," I left the words hanging. He hadn't said anything. He hadn't so much as hinted that I had done something that was physically impossible.

"You were having such a hard time with Daniel's death," she told me honestly. "He didn't want to tell you anything until he knew that you could handle it. Or until you were ready."

"It wasn't his decision," I said, my voice low and bitter.

"Maybe not, but think back. Do you remember what you were like then? You were pale and so thin. You looked like a hard wind would blow you away. He was just trying to protect you."

I sighed and pushed my hair back. "Protect me," I mumbled softly.

"You know that's true. That's how all the guys are. Trying to protect us."

I looked at her perched in the shadow of the trees. The cemetery seemed to frame her with color, and I thought back to when I had seen her that night. "You know what else I saw in my dream," I said, looking at her closely to read her expression.

"What?"

"Daniel. I remember seeing Daniel." I waited but she didn't reply. The indecision was plainly written on her face. "He came here. I swear I remember him coming here. He talked to me," I felt hot tears blur my vision, but I could see her clearly enough. "You saw him too," I said, choking on the words. "I can tell by the way you're looking at me. You saw Daniel."

And she had. For her, it was as hard to explain as it was for me to hear. She did see my other brother come to me. She had seen him clearly, well enough to know without a doubt that it wasn't Thomas. And she hadn't told anyone about that experience. At least, not until recently and that was when she and Tori had been talking about Tori's parents.

"She felt like she heard her father call to her the night of the fire. She feels sure that she heard him and he woke her up. She got her sister out because of the warning, and they ended up being fine." Thea knitted her fingers before her and looked thoughtfully back to the house. "I've never believed in the vengeful spirits that are supposed to haunt people and places. But this, well, I believe in this. I think that you and I saw Daniel because you needed him, and Tori's father came to her because he was needed."

I was still crying, but this time it wasn't just the sadness, it was some relief. I had hoped for some resolution, and although this was nothing like I had ever anticipated, it was an answer. And in the memory of Daniel, I finally felt like I knew that Daniel still existed. He lived on.

"Thomas?" It was a choked question, but she understood.

"I haven't said anything." She looked down at her clenched hands for a moment. "I didn't know what to say. Or how to say it."

"He doesn't know."

"No." She looked at me, her face somber. "There's been just so much happening, I didn't know…" but she stopped then because we could hear the squeal of the gate as the rest of the group entered the cemetery.

As night fell with velvety darkness, I was once again tucked into the little bed in Thea's house. I would be going back home in the morning. Home. Everything would be the same in our tidy house, but my life had taken an abrupt turn into the twilight zone. I had thought that telling my story to my brother would be the grand culmination of a horrible hallucination.

Of course, now I knew that it hadn't been the end of anything. It had been the beginning.

The story was over. I had described my dreams, my experiences. And it brought me to full circle. What was I to do now? On one hand, the reality that I had started to realize with Travis had come true. I really had met him all those nights. I had walked the road and seen the accident scene. I had been there.

"What am I going to do about Travis?" I asked no one in particular.

The dog rolled over and yawned, his long pink tongue like a wet ribbon.

"You're not much help," I told him, and he gazed up at me with warm brown eyes. "Ok, fine." He got up and leaped with surprising agility into the bed. We curled up together and the night was soft and dreamless.

At breakfast, Thea and Thomas seemed to be watching me with concern. Not obvious, but certainly palpable. I had lived under the watchful eyes of our parents long enough to detect the subtle signs of worry.

"So what are we doing now?" I asked over the rim of my mug. The hot chocolate was rich and filling, and I was drinking it slow.

Thea was looking at me with sympathy. "We have a lot to figure out just now," she said. "Let's just take one step at a time."

"And my next step?" I asked softly.

"You're right where we are," Thomas replied softly. "We have to figure out everything we can about the cross. Then we have to find out what causes this phenomenona. Then we have to figure out how to turn it off." He looked over at Thea for a moment before turning his eyes back to me. "But there is something else that you need to be aware of. Especially now that we know you are bilocating again."

"That's one way to say it," I said.

"We're not the only ones who can do this," Thomas said, his face grave. "There's someone else who can not only do this, but who's trying to find the cross too."

Drew and Tori returned to the house as we finished packing up our things. Thea and Thomas were heading back to college, and I was heading home. The thought of leaving now, returning to my real life, my real world, with the scary possibility that I might take a trip at night, was terrifying. But I had to go. I couldn't hide out at Thea's house. I couldn't follow my brother up to school. So I was going home. But not before I heard the rest of the story.

"I became aware of him almost as soon as we moved into the

house," Tori began.

'Him' was the other person who could bilocate. The mystery man who was after the cross and the secret to our ability.

"He's been ahead of us this whole time," Tori said flatly. "Before I got here, before we moved here, I'm almost sure that he had broken into my house. He came here while Mrs. Lucy was living in the house. She said she thought someone had been through her things. I think now, well, I think for sure that he was here before. He was looking for something."

"He who?" I asked.

"That's our problem," Thea said frowning.

"We don't know who it is," Tori agreed.

"All we know is that Daniel wasn't the only one looking for the cross. And we're almost sure that whoever was breaking into Tori's house could do what we can do." Drew sighed and leaned back slowly.

"He can bilocate?"

"I think he can," Tori broke in. "It's the only thing that makes any sense, and I know it doesn't make much sense at all."

"What do you mean?"

"After we had been living in the house for just a few weeks, I was getting the feeling that someone had been in the house. It was little things. Shoes moved, keys misplaced, furniture shifted, just little things. And sometimes I would wake up and be sure that I could hear someone moving inside the house. But I didn't believe it myself, and when I tried to tell my sister, she just thought I was getting dramatic." Her eyes flickered out the window. Through the trees and across the pavement, her home could barely be seen. It was cast in shadow, an old home with a very long history. "I heard him there, in the house. So I went looking for him. It was stupid, I know, but sometimes I get a little carried away."

"Sometimes?" Drew's eyebrows seemed to creep toward his hairline.

"So anyway, one night when I followed him, he spoke to me. He wanted me to give up. He called me little girl." Tori sounded angry now. "He was creeping around in my house, looking for something."

"And now we think that we know what he was looking for." Thomas looked out the window as well. "He was looking for the cross."

"We think that he was ahead of Daniel. We figure that he's been at this for quite some time. Ms. Lucy hadn't been living in the house for a while before we moved in. And we know that he was trying to get in her house while she was still here. She said as much.

"So after she moved out, why didn't he just come in and tear the place apart?" My mind was flying through possibilities.

"That we don't know. He may have gone through the place, several times over. When we got here, the house was empty and in pretty bad shape. He could have spent days going through it."

"But he didn't find what he was looking for," I pointed out.

"Apparently not. And we really don't know why he returned after that. We don't know what triggered him back to the search, assuming that he had ever given up."

"But you think that he knew about this long before Daniel had come upon it?"

"Had to," Tori agreed. "He was coming here when Ms. Lucy lived here, but we don't know where else he has been looking. He could have been creeping around some of the other houses, the cemetery, the chapel, Thea's house!"

Thea's nose wrinkled in disgust. "You really think he might have been breaking in here looking for the cross?"

"He could have," Tori agreed. "We don't really know what he was doing for all of that time. What we do know is that we stumbled on the cross ourselves. As it was, in that well with that poor little boy's body, it might never have been found it I hadn't dropped my bracelet down there."

I nodded. I had heard about Drew climbing down the well and finding the poor little boy's bones. I shivered. So very sad.

"So somehow, this person found out about the story and came here looking for the cross. Then Daniel found the same story, or something similar. The two of them must have been on parallel paths the whole time."

"Or Daniel talked to this guy."

No one spoke after my words slipped out. I watched as Thomas' face whitened.

"That could be. I never really thought about it, but it makes sense. Daniel and this guy might have actually met, discussed this. They might have shared ideas. But Daniel would have had no idea what kind of person this guy was. He would never have dealt with someone who was breaking into houses."

"But you know this guy isn't just breaking in." I looked thoughtfully over to Tori. "How do you know he can bilocate?" I asked. "That he didn't just find another entrance?"

"He got into my house without ever opening any doors or leaving any trail. I've searched that old place. I knew every single door and window. I had no idea what he was doing, but Drew knew."

Drew was actually smiling. "I had figured out how to control it, just a little, by then. And I suspected from what Tori had told me, that I knew who was breaking in. I knew it had to be someone like me, someone who could do things. And then I saw him."

"You what?"

"I saw him. Sort of. I saw him appear just outside of Tori's house one night. One minute he was there, the next minute, he was gone. Just gone. So I knew that he could do what I did. And I recognized him. I think he's been tailing me too. I had seen someone watching me when I was working or when I went into town. It was frustrating me, and scaring me a little. And after I saw him here, I knew that he had to be the one that was getting into Tori's house. I didn't know her well at that time either, but it pissed me off to think that this guy was just coming in whenever he wanted to." His smile was more of a grimace. "So I bilocated myself so that I could catch him in the act. I went into her house too. But I didn't catch him. And unfortunately, she caught me."

Tori punched him lightly in the arm. "You scared the crap out of me!" she exclaimed.

"Yeah, well, I didn't mean to," he replied lamely.

"And now?" I interrupted. "You've had the cross," I looked pointedly at my brother and he nodded his assent. "And the guy has given up?"

"I've had the cross with me, on me, at all times," Thomas said, "but I can't say I think he's given up. I think he's just biding his time. He's been at this a long time."

"I hate to ask a dumb question, but have any of you said anything to the authorities?" My eyes scanned the young faces around me.

"I couldn't even get my sister to listen to me," Tori answered. "She thought that I was exaggerating."

"I wasn't going to say anything to our parents," Thomas agreed softly.

"We just haven't had any real proof of anything," Thea said slowly. "We have the cross, but that doesn't prove anything. And we're afraid to volunteer information about us."

"No way I'm going to tell some scientist about what I can do," Drew burst out. "I don't want to be locked away in some lab while they dissect my brain!"

I felt a chill and rubbed my arms absently, suddenly realizing that I was in the same position. If what they had said was correct, I could be in two places at once. That would be a good reason to either lock me up, or make me some great science experiment.

"Okay," I agreed. "I can see where that might be a," I hesitated, "a mistake."

"So we're going to just continue as we are?" Thea was looking from one of us to the other anxiously.

"We can't do anything about the other guy until he tries something." Thomas shrugged. "I will hold onto the cross. As long as we stay around a lot of other people, we can assume that he won't tangle with us."

"Thomas, how do we know that the cross isn't affecting other people? How do you know that by taking it to another location, it's not, like, bleeding its abilities to all kinds of people?"

"We've thought of that," Thea said softly. "And we don't really have any assurance that it couldn't affect anyone else. But it doesn't work on just anyone. I've lived here all my life, and I've never had any kind of experience. And I haven't heard of anyone else saying that they have had problems."

Thomas nodded. "We think that it was just the little group that came down in the first visit. We are the only ones who came away with the ability, you, me, Daniel, and Drew."

"And whoever 'he' is," I added.

"And yes, the guy who is after the cross, and we are assuming the original old man living in the house, the grandfather who brought the cross here to begin with."

Thea spoke up, her brow furrowed in thought. "You know, there is one thing that I had forgotten about." She looked at Thomas and Drew. "When did you say that you came here the first time?"

Drew answered her as we all looked at her.

"You know, there was an earthquake here around that time," she said, almost to herself. "With everything that happened, I forgot about it. It was a small tremor, barely noticeable, but it was on the news. It caused car alarms to go off, and some pictures fell of walls, but no real damage."

"An earthquake?" Drew looked like he was trying to process the information but was unsuccessfully putting the pieces together.

"You're looking for an 'event'," I said, making quotation gestures. "What made the cross switch on the power? What changed?"

"The cross had been with the little boy for decades. Suddenly, it's making people change in bizarre ways." Thomas leaned forward.

"And the change is restricted to just a select few people, and they aren't even locals."

Drew seemed to catch some of the enthusiasm. "If we were here in the cemetary, and the guy whoever he is, had followed us..."

"And the earthquake caused the cross to shift or jostle, then maybe it was triggered in some way." Thomas finished the outlandish thought. But it didn't feel that outlandish to me. Something had happened to change me, to change us all. And if it wasn't a blessing sent from heaven, as it had been with the Saint, then what had it been?

"Why them, why us?" I burst out.

"We just don't know." Thomas reached out and caught my shoulder. "But we're working on this now, Van. We're going to figure it out."

Chapter 7

So I went back home. My head felt so full of thoughts and conjectures, facts and assumptions that I thought it might just float off my shoulders. I had come to Kentucky with a fear, with a huge unknown that I felt like I had to handle on my own. When I left, I felt very different. This wasn't something that I was tackling alone. I had people to help.

It was hard to pretend to my mom. It has always been difficult to hide things from her. Now, with just us in the house, I felt like she was on constant watch. As I prepared for dinner on Wednesday night, I rolled around my arguments in my head for a final preparation of my point. We had made a decision, there in Thea's comfortable kitchen. I needed to get a handle on my new ability, and sooner rather than later. So we decided that the best way for me to work on this was to be with someone who knew a little about controlling it. There was only one person that I knew and trusted with something so monumental. There was only one person I knew that could bilocate.

Drew took the whole thing on with easy grace. He had known me forever, and we were comfortable in our roles. He would work with me to practice how to control my talent. I would bunk with Tori in the guestroom of her house so I could stay close. And Tori could be our lookout in case something were to happen while we were 'away'.

"So next week I think I'm going back to Crestwood to hang out with Drew and Tori," I said casually as I set plates on the table. Three each, three plates, three cups, three knives, forks, and spoons, the little family laid out in tidy places.

"Tori?" My mom turned from the stove and looked at me.

"Yeah, Thea has a friend that lives across the street. That's Tori.

She and Drew are dating." I finished placing the last piece of silverware and grabbed a handful of napkins. "Tori is the one whose parents died last year. She and her sister moved to Crestwood, so her sister could get a job at the bank. They bought an old house across the street from Thea's."

Mom nodded. She had heard much of this from Thomas on one of his visits home, but I had a reason for reminding her.

"Tori and her sister have been in the house for about a year and haven't gotten everything fixed up. Tori's sister is so busy working, and Tori works at the diner most days. Tori wants to start college soon too." I tucked the last napkin under the plate. "So she really wanted to get some things done in the house before she heads back for classes in January. She said she still had boxes to unpack, and she wanted to paint some of the rooms upstairs." I paused and scooted a glass slightly closer to the plate. "You know, they were the ones that had the fire in the front room."

My mother said nothing, but she was watching me now.

"So I told her that I could come down and help. I can do my school work while I'm there, and I thought it would be really nice to have their house looking fixed up in time for Christmas."

I had dropped the ultimate guilt word. In our house, Christmas was a big celebration. We had lots of family traditions that we followed faithfully. To suggest that I wanted to do something for someone to help them prepare for the holiday was a sneaky ace in the hole. I knew my mom well enough. She would be hard pressed to refuse me.

"I didn't know you were such good friends," my mom said slowly.

"Well, we haven't been. But I did go visit her just a few weeks ago," I reminded her. "When I was out there this last weekend, we all spent time together."

"You had a nice time with Thomas, didn't you?" mom asked, her voice strangely gentle.

"Sure," I said quickly, "and it was great seeing Thea and Tori, and Drew, of course. I'll probably see him a lot while I'm down there." I waited to see her response.

"Will Thomas be coming in?"

I had expected that question, and I had already asked him. "Yes, he'll be coming in on Friday, and he said that he would ride with me home for Saturday and stay for the Thanksgiving break." I felt a guilty twinge. Using Thomas' visit home to bait my mother into letting me go was low, but I needed to be with Drew to figure out what to do with myself. I didn't like the deception, but it seemed unavoidable.

"And you're driving?"

I nodded, relieved. She wasn't protesting, just checking with the plans. That meant that she would be okay if I left. I watched as she turned the heat down on the food and glanced back at the table. Next week there would only be two place settings. But I couldn't think that way. Eventually we would have all left home. My parents would be fine, they were strong, but I hated any pain that I would cause them. And I had a bad feeling that I might cause them more heartache soon.

With things settled at home, I headed up to my room to start planning. I needed to have all my school things in order. It was important to me that I didn't let my mom down. She had given up a lot to be my full time teacher, and I wanted my scores to reflect that.

I had four days to cover a whole lot of material. I doubted that I would spend much time on my studies once I was in Crestwood. I was trying to get as much done as I could before I left home. Then I could 'hand in' my assignments gradually over the week I was gone to show my mom that I was doing what I had promised.

I hesitated at my computer. I had work to do. I did. First I wanted to check something. I typed out the term 'bilocation' in the search bar and started to read. An hour later and pages and pages of responses read, I felt more confused than reassured. Bilocation was fairly well recorded. It was also closely linked to religion. The stories were mystical and miraculous. It didn't reflect my experience. I tried to find the story about St. Francisca. It took some digging into some historical documents, but I was able to at least read a summary of the story myself. It left me with more questions than answers

.

I was still feeling a mixture of excitement and dread when I finished packing my car for the week. My mom was inside, making sure that I didn't forget anything, medications specifically. I wasn't going far. It was just an hour and a half away, but my mom had the look of someone who preparing their child for a trip out of the country.

Daisy galloped out on the lawn and skidded to a stop at my feet. She would miss me, I knew. I wasn't even sure where she would sleep without me home. Normally she would be with me each night. I looked apologetically into her sweet face and bent to rub her ears. With a sigh, I straightened and finished tucking my purse in the car between the seats.

I put my computer bag in the front seat. The laptop was new, an unexpected gift from my parents. I think they were trying to prepare me for my return to school. I looked grimly at the bag lying on the seat next to me. I couldn't picture going to school just now. Not with everything up in the air the way it was.

"Okay, so I called your brother and he said that he'll see you next weekend," my mother told me. "I put some money in your purse in case you girls decide to go out." She stepped back and looked at my car critically. "Your dad filled up the tank and said that everything was running fine."

"I know," I said softly. "It's fine, Mom." I smiled. "If I need anything, I can just drive home. It's not like I'll be far away."

"Sure," she agreed, but her eyes kept scanning the car as though looking for anything amiss. "I put your medicine in your purse. It's in a baggie."

"I already packed some," I reassured her.

"Well, now you'll have extra if you need it."

I nodded. "I'll call you when I get there. And I'll call you to let you know how we're doing."

Mom smiled, but her lips trembled and I had the horrible premonition that she might cry on me. I leaned forward and gave her a quick hard hug and climbed into the driver's seat.

"You have your phone?" Mom asked quickly.

I held up the device and pulled the door closed. "I'll call," I mouthed through the glass, and started the car. She stepped back off the drive and stood for a moment in the driveway, the warm autumn sunlight giving her a halo of gold. I backed the car out and turned the wheel, maneuvering deftly around the mailbox and the trashcans at the side of the road. As I accelerated away, I could see my mother still standing in the driveway, a lonely figure bathed in light.

The drive was singularly uneventful. I made it to Tori's home just as the sun had dipped behind the overhanging limbs of the maple trees in front of her house. Her lawn, more moss than actual grass, suffered from the perpetual shade, but for now was a carpet of color, falling leaves painting a canvass of impressionistic dabs of gold and orange, brown and flame red.

Tori came out to meet me. Her enormous dog, Monty, was following at a gallop. He hit me with his paws at my shoulders, pushing me back against the closed door of my car before Tori could call him off.

He welcomed me with a huff of meaty breath and a very wet kiss.

"Monty, down! Down!" Tori yelled, marching through the leaves to get to us.

With one hand, I pushed Monty off me, and rewarded him with a vigorous ear rub once all four feet were firmly on the ground. "It's okay," I said, a laugh in my voice.

"We're working on the jumping up," Tori warned, "but so far it's not taking well."

"He's just excited," I said watching the big dog fairly dancing.

"He's always excited," Tori said darkly. "Come on, let's get you inside."

Tori's house was surprisingly cozy. The overall neglect had been replaced with artful repair work, cheap and creative. They had decorated with a mixture of old and new, some pieces from their parents' house, while others were obviously added later. As I stood in the living room, Tori's sister, Liz peeked around the door.

"I'm fixing dinner. I hope you haven't eaten. It's a new recipe!"

Tori tried to stifle a smile. "And you're trying it out on us tonight?"

"Yes, smartass," Liz said, making a face. "I used the crock pot so it should turn out okay." Liz turned back into the kitchen, stomping a little in fake frustration. She looked very different from Tori. Where Tori's hair was dark, Liz had light hair with a heart shaped face. Tori looked like an impish elf, where Liz had a classic beauty, long limbed and graceful. Their eyes were the same shape however, and their smile was similar when they laughed.

"I appreciate you letting me stay here," I said to Liz's back as she took the top off the pot and stirred the steaming contents.

"That's fine," Liz said. "We have plenty of room."

Tori gestured for me to follow and we clattered up the wooden staircase. The second floor was cut up into four small bedrooms, and a hallway, all with wooden floors scarred and scuffed from use.

"This is Liz's room," Tori explained pointing to the first bedroom. The door was cracked open, and I could see the neatly made bed with the floral bedding, the tidy dresser with perfume bottles and framed pictures, and the lacy curtains framing the window.

"This is Liz's office for now," Tori breezed by another closed door. "And here is our guest room." When she opened the door, I had to smile. The bed was just a mattress on a metal frame, but they had put a striped comforter on it with several plump pillows. A small table was next to it, painted a gleaming black, that had doubtlessly come from some second hand store and been repurposed for the room. The dresser that was pushed up to the open wall was a beautiful old piece made from cherry wood, gleaming in the lamplight. "The dresser was my parents'," Tori said, as way of explanation. "We couldn't bring everything here, but we took our favorites."

"It's very nice," I said, feeling a little choked up. The girls had lost so much. Their parents, their home. "The whole room is great!"

"You can just drop your stuff in here," Tori continued. "My room is the last one." She ducked out of the room and continued to the next door. I almost laughed out loud when I reached her doorway, but stifled the impulse. Tori's room was a mix of crazy patterns and decorations that traced her lifeline like a three dimensional diary. There were wide eyed stuffed animals, well-worn and loved, two Barbie's pinned in their original box shoved on the top shelf of a bookcase, stacks of picture books here, with worn chapter books propped next to them, and still more novels lined up to fill the rest of the shelf. She had posters taped to her walls, one with Kermit the Frog, one with some teen heartthrob that I had forgotten his name, and another movie poster from Harry Potter. Framed pictures were placed around the room, but only one showed her parents. It was on the little table next to her bed, and it was tilted toward the head of the bed as though she had grabbed it as she lay and turned it to study the frozen faces. The rest were still shots from the past of her and her sister, her giant dog, Monty, and one with her and Drew, a close up with just their smiling faces. Her bed was half made with a black and white patterned comforter over gray sheets. Her desk had an old computer set up with an equally old printer and stacks of papers covering the rest of the top. Mounds of clothes, shoes, and bedding dotted the floor.

"I didn't clean up today, so I guess I'll have to do it later," she said, shoving a pile of pillows over on her bed. She sat and huffed out a breath. "Liz thinks that you're here just to get a break from being home. And she was totally fine with it. She's just happy that I'm meeting some other people around here."

"You're sure she doesn't mind," I said hesitantly as I sat in the desk chair.

"Sure I'm sure," she responded. "And it will give her some time to go out on her own. I don't want her thinking that she has to babysit me, but she has a hard time letting that go."

I nodded. That I could understand. I felt like I had been living under a microscope for a very long time. “You work tomorrow?” I asked.

“I told Blythe that I would be in in the afternoon,” she replied. “Drew will be coming over and you and he can start your lessons, or whatever.”

I nodded again. Lessons. It was certainly a strange concept, but I couldn’t think of anything better to call it. What else would it be, learning to control how I bilocated? I tried to push the vision from me. It was all too strange. And thinking about it too much would doubtlessly freak me out.

“Then the day after tomorrow, you’re going with me on a delivery,” Tori continued.

“What, where?” I asked, surprised.

“They are having one of their monthly meetings where they play games and make plans for their activities for the next several weeks. They usually order pastries to have while they ‘discuss’,” she threw air quotes around the word discuss, and I laughed at her expression.

“What are the discussions about?” I asked.

“They gossip. It’s just their excuse for eating fattening things in the morning.” She shrugged and smiled. “But it will give you a chance to meet Mrs. Lucy.”

“Who?”

“Mrs. Lucy used to live in this house. She and her family have always lived around here. Her family built the house. The missing boy and the grandfather were her relatives. Distant, but still related. So she knows stories.” Tori leaned forward, her voice low. “She doesn’t know about Drew or what you can do, but she heard someone walking in this house while she still lived here, and she knew something weird was going on.” She glanced at the door quickly. “We found pictures and papers from her things that were moved out of the house and never looked at. The old man had letters and journals. We were able to piece together quite a bit from the information that she had.”

We heard a movement from below and then Liz’s voice over the hum and rattle of the furnace firing up. “Dinner,” Liz called, “and come get Monty out of the kitchen. He’s gotten something from the counter again!”

It was hard to fall asleep. Darkness had settled so completely here, with the window facing the woods behind the house. But dinner had gone well, and I had felt very comfortable helping them clear up the plates and wash dishes in the old stainless steel sink.

Monty had enjoyed dinner immensely, dropping his big fuzzy head in my lap as I ate and rolling his big brown eyes in my directions to plead for a scrap. I had resisted for most of the meal, but couldn't help but sneak him a bite or two as we were cleaning up. He was plenty tall enough to lay his head on the table without even lifting a foot from the floor, so I knew that he could easily take what he wanted. But he was practicing self-control, and had settled around me.

After dinner and cleanup, we had gone into the front living room to watch TV. They didn't have cable, so the selections were limited, but I wasn't paying any attention anyway. Tori had gotten out a deck of cards and we played a few hands of double solitaire before going upstairs. Because of the early mornings for both the girls, Liz because she had to be in Louisville by the bank's opening, and Tori because she was helping prepare for the breakfast rush with Blythe, we headed up at 10:00 o'clock. I read for some time, choosing a mystery book that I had read before and knew the resolution. It was comforting, the assurance that everything would be fine in their fictional world.

By 11, I decided that I too should try to get some rest. I didn't know exactly when Drew would be over, but I suspected that he would want to get going early. I had no idea how these lessons were supposed to go. How did one teach the control of out of body experiences? How did one know if they were doing it correctly? Would I just one day be able to automatically rise from my still body and go where I pleased? It was frightening as well as exhilarating.

But in truth, if I had known how the lessons were to proceed, I would not have been looking forward to them at all.

"You are not trying at all, Savannah," Drew said, his voice exasperated.

"I am!" I protested, but without enthusiasm.

"Right," he said darkly. "You've checked your phone three times in the last five minutes."

"I have not," I said, but I knew that he was right. I wasn't concentrating. It wasn't working. I wasn't learning anything.

"Van, you have to try a little harder."

"I am trying. Or I was," I argued. "Drew, you said yourself that you fell into controlling this. Well, I'm not falling. I can't get my mind empty enough!"

He ran his hand through his hair, "Okay, fine, let's stop for lunch."

I watched as he slowly unfolded himself from the couch. His long limbs seemed to go on and on, but he could move with surprising grace. He came to the chair and reached out a hand. I took it and let him pull me from the chair.

"Do you want to go out?" he asked.

"Yes!" I said with too much enthusiasm.

He frowned. "Fine," he said darkly.

"Tori said that she would be at the diner for the lunch rush. We can go over there and you all can introduce me to Blythe," I said, sounding like this was a great educational act on my part. "Tori told me she wanted me to meet some of the people from around town."

"Come on, then," he agreed. "I have to put up the mutt."

Monty had been watching our experiments with interest from his place on the floor. I didn't know much about poodle mix dogs, but he seemed to have an especially understanding look on his face, as though somewhere in his furry brain he was comprehending what we were doing and sympathized with our plight.

"Where will he stay?" I asked, feeling suddenly guilty for leaving behind our companion.

"He stays in the bathroom. Don't worry, he likes it in there. He lays on the floor when he's hot, on a towel when he's cool. I'll give him one of his bones to chew on." Drew patted his thigh and Monty's eyes rolled up to gaze at him. "Come on, pup," Drew beckoned. Monty looked unimpressed. "Monty," Drew said, his voice going a little deeper and sterner. Monty's eyes went to me and I stifled a smile. He could tell which of us was the push-over, and he wasn't above using his puppy cuteness to get what he wanted.

"Come on," I said gesturing, and Monty rose to his feet.

Once he was safely ensconced in the bathroom, I grabbed my purse and we headed for the door.

Technically, we could have walked to the Diner. It was almost that close. On a warm day with bright sun, it would have been tempting. But a drizzle of rain had started just before sunrise, and the ground was mushy and damp. Besides, the weather was just getting chillier.

At the diner, we left the car unlocked and parked out front. It was that kind of town. You didn't need to lock up where ever you went. Of course, Drew's old Ford wasn't exactly a sought after car, so I knew he felt confident that no one would mess with it anyway.

The diner smelled wonderful from our place just inside the door. We hesitated there before choosing a seat. Tori came out after a moment and waved enthusiastically.

"Hang on for a bit, and I'll take your order. Then I can take my break and eat with you." She hurried back behind the counter and tucked a lock of hair behind her ear, an ear pierced at least three times from what I could see, as she rummaged around for a pen and pad.

"What's good?" I asked Drew, watching as more people filed in and out.

"It's all pretty good," Drew responded. "I usually get the combination with the sandwich and soup, especially on cold days."

I chose grilled cheese and tomato soup, which Tori assured me was the gourmet version compared to what she made at home. As she went to get our food, I took a moment to examine the patrons. There were a variety of people. Young moms with toddlers in mismatched high chairs armed with crayons or goldfish crackers sat next to an older couple sharing a piece of dark chocolate cake and lingering over coffee. Two men in business suits eating sandwiches and deep in conversation were by the door, and another table held a group of young guys in painters pants splattered with a rainbow of shades were parked next to the window.

When Tori returned, she had her tray loaded with our choices, and she laid out the food and then sat down across from me and next to Drew.

"So?" she asked immediately, "How did it go?"

"It didn't," I assured her.

"Not yet," Drew corrected, and turned his dark gaze in my direction. "Van has to be more patient with herself and with me. This is all new territory for all of us."

"I'd like it to be a whole lot quicker," I said wryly.

"You sound like me," Tori said. "I hate waiting for anything. But if you figure it has taken Drew over a year to get where he is, it's unreasonable to think that in one day you're going to know what to do."

I nodded slowly. "Okay, yeah, you're right about that. I just feel like we don't have much time."

"And I understand that," Tori agreed. "But just because you don't get this figured out this week, doesn't mean that you won't have some control."

The door to the kitchen swung open and a middle-aged woman with red hair and a no- nonsense attitude swept into the dining room and started making rounds at the tables. She refilled drinks and took plates, but mostly talked to the different customers, seeming to know everyone's name on sight, as well as a topic of conversation for each.

"Blythe?" I muttered under my breath.

"That's her," Drew responded, and smiled.

When she approached the table where we were sitting, her eyes went first to the plates in front of us to make sure that we were eating. Next her sharp gaze flitted from face to face, and I had the distinct impression that she would miss very little.

"And you have to be Thomas' sister," she said by way of greeting. "There is that family resemblance."

"Hi," I replied, feeling suddenly shy.

"Your brother comes by with Thea almost every time they are in town. And he can really eat!" she exclaimed.

"Oh, yes," I agreed, relieved that she had provided a common topic. "He always stays thin, but he eats twice as much as I do. He and Daniel could polish off an entire pie between the two of them." As soon as the words were out, the name was out, I felt my breath catch, ready for the pain. But although the ache was there, it seemed lessened somehow.

"I imagine they were quite the twosome," she agreed, easing onto another topic. "And how are you liking staying with Tori and that crazy dog of hers?"

"Monty is great," I said, feeling a genuine smile. "I have a new dog at home. She's a pit-bull/lab mix. She's the sweetest thing. She sleeps with me every night."

"Dogs are good," she replied. "They keep you laughing." She looked at our almost empty plates. "Do you all need anything else? Dessert maybe?"

"Oh, I'm full," I said quickly. "But the soup was delicious."

"I'll send home some pastries with Tori when she heads out," Blythe assured us. "And you all come around again." She looked at Drew pointedly. "I know I'll see you again," she teased.

"That is for sure," he said smiling.

We watched as she moved away. "Blythe has college aged boys herself, so she has her eyes on all us around here. But she's a great person to know. She knows everyone in town, everything that goes on here, and most of the town's history."

I sat back and looked out the window briefly, studying the play of sun and shade in the lot. "And what does she know about all of this?" I asked softly.

"I don't know about any of the old mysteries," Tori said firmly, "but I've asked her to keep a look out for any new faces in town. If someone tries to comeback to finish what they started when they broke into our house, hopefully Blythe and some of her friends will know something about it."

Chapter 8

The next day, I helped Tori load up the pastries for the retirement home under Blythe's watchful gaze. We had a sample of almost everything, many of which I could attest to their quality. The goodies that Tori had brought home with her the night before had been absolutely delicious.

Once the boxes were loaded in Tori's giant sedan, we headed a few miles away where the new retirement community provided a comfortable home to many of the local senior citizens. The building was still fairly new, and set off the main road. The brick façade was impressive with pillars and artfully placed dried flowers and corn husk arrangements to celebrate the fall season.

When we approached the door with our arms full of boxes, the doors swung open and a staff member greeted Tori like a long lost friend.

"Did Blythe remember the muffin for me?" she asked excitedly. "She said she still had some cream cheese ones, and I missed out on them the last two deliveries."

"It's in the bag on top," Tori said grinning. "She said I needed to drop it off before the older folks start to pick over the selection. I don't know why we bother to put them out on trays. They're gone before we can even get them to the table."

The grateful woman snatched the bag off the top and opened the bag. "Ah, I'm not even going to wait. I'm eating this now!" She smiled like a little girl with her favorite candy.

"Tori!" An older lady with lovely curled white hair and a lavender sweater set came bustling over to help the girls. "So glad to see you here again! And you've brought a friend! Are you working with Blythe as well?"

"Mrs. Coffey, I knew you'd be out here to help!" Tori gestured me to follow with our load of boxes. "Savannah is just visiting and offered to come along for the ride."

"And how is your young man?" the older lady asked, ushering us into the dining area which was already beginning to fill up with hungry seniors.

"Drew is fine. Savannah is actually one of his longtime friends."

Mrs. Coffey's eyes seemed to see more than what I was comfortable with, but I forced a smile. "Drew was best friends with my brothers since grade school." I said.

The older lady's eyes softened, but she thankfully held her tongue. "Well Drew is a very nice young man," she said instead. "And Lucy has been hoping that you would come by soon."

I followed as Tori stopped at a large round table and began setting out the boxes, flipping the tops open. A small group of ladies filed out with trays, plates, napkins, and a cart laden with a silver carafe of coffee and a tall pitcher of iced water. Cream and sugar were quickly set out along with colorful napkins in fall colors of orange, yellow, brown, and gold.

"There's Lucy now," Mrs. Coffey said cheerfully, and I watched a spry woman with gray curls navigate through the dining room, a cane clearing her way and offering a minimum of support. It looked like the cane was mostly used as a subtle weapon, and I smiled unwillingly.

"Tori, honey, I'm so glad to see you!" Mrs. Lucy called, and took Tori's hand in a firm squeeze. "You are looking absolutely lovely. That shade of color on your hair is so becoming!"

I was surprised to see Tori blush a little, but it made me smile more. Tori had told me that Mrs. Lucy had lived in Tori's house before she had moved to the retirement home. She had also said that she had gone to the ladies for advice about the house and the history of the area. Now, seeing them together, I could tell that the feelings between Tori and the ladies were much stronger than that. It was a sweet friendship, and knowing what Tori had just gone through with the death of her parents, it was one that the younger woman had desperately needed.

"Mrs. Lucy, this is Savannah. You remember meeting Thomas? This is his sister."

"Of course," Mrs. Lucy said, her smile bringing laugh lines to her face. "Your brother is such a nice fellow."

"Yes, he is," I said, and realized that I meant it.

"And now you're here visiting with our Tori!" Mrs. Lucy

seemed delighted. "I'm so glad she is spending her time with some other young people. She can be so serious."

"She and her sister are letting me stay for the week," I volunteered. "We're going to decorate for the holidays."

"A giant tree," Mrs. Lucy said suddenly. "When I was a girl, we would put a giant tree in the front room and decorate it with glass balls and garland. I may have some of the ornaments down in storage still." She seemed to catch herself and said quickly, "If you girls wanted to use some of the old things. I'm sure you have some decorations from your family."

"No," Tori responded. "I mean, yes, we have some things from mom and dad, but I would love to use some of your family's things as well."

"It would be so nice to have decorations that were originally in the house," I agreed, picturing the lovely ornaments.

"Then you'll have to go down and look through those boxes again," Mrs. Lucy stated. "I know you went through them before to find some pictures and notes about the house and my family. But this will be more fun."

Tori nodded. "Sure. We'll have to come back after I'm off work, but I would like to find some of the things. Things that you're not using yourself."

Mrs. Lucy shook her head. "They will have a tree put up in some of the rooms here, but I'm not planning on using one in my little apartment. I will enjoy the ones that they have."

"If you're sure?" Tori said, a question in her voice.

"You can use whatever you find," Mrs. Lucy responded. "My family has already taken what they wanted from the house when I moved. I doubt those boys would be very sentimental about some old ornaments."

"Then we'll come out tomorrow evening," Tori said.

"And we'll enjoy seeing you again," Mrs. Lucy assured her.

We lingered over a muffin and coffee with the ladies for another hour, Tori's lunch break. When we returned to the diner, Drew was there to pick me up. I reluctantly left Tori and her friend Anna waiting on tables and climbed into the Jeep with Drew.

"Mrs. Lucy was very nice," I said, watching Drew's profile as he steered onto the main street.

"She's a great lady. Tori has really gotten attached to that group. It's good for her." He looked thoughtfully out the window. "In fact, the whole move has been good for her and her sister. They were able to start somewhere new, and they've gotten to know a lot of people in town. It's an advantage to living in a small area like this. Everyone looks out for everyone else."

"And you?" I asked. "Has living out here helped you too?"

He shrugged. "I'm getting along," he said. "I get paid enough to live." He paused for a moment. "That's not really true. Most of the people here have gone out of their way to be nice to me. They were like that before they even heard about the accident. I think it's that small town hospitality that you hear about. Besides, I've met some good people, met Tori and Thea, and now," he sighed, "I just want to get all the rest figured out."

"When it first happened," I said slowly, "I didn't see any end to it. With Daniel gone, I felt like my life had turned into a bad dream. And then just as I felt like I was starting to come out of it, like I could finally see a time when I would be able to live again, the dreams started. It's been a mess, and a tragedy, and I guess it's our job to live through it."

Drew looked at me with sympathy. "We will figure this out. Daniel left enough for us to start on, and we are learning more every day. This isn't going to be an instant cure, but I feel like it will get resolved."

I sighed. "And in the meantime, you're going to make me practice again, aren't you."

His response was a broad teasing grin, and I could tell he was glad that I was breaking the tension.

"Okay, so I have a question for you." I looked out the window again, watching as he pulled into Tori's house. "When I 'bilocate'," I made air quotes around the term and grimaced, "I always show up in the woods wearing my pajamas." I swung my door open as he threw the car into park. "Every time, no matter the weather, I am standing there in my nightclothes. While you, well, apparently you are wearing your normal clothes, like you're dressed for the weather."

"I go to bed fully dressed," Drew said, eyebrows raised. "Seemed like an obvious thing to do when I knew I could control it."

"So the first time you did it, accidentally, I mean, what were you wearing?"

"Sweats," he responded firmly. "But that's what I wore to bed, so that's what I had on when I was 'bilocating'," he made the same gesture and shut the car door behind him.

"Okay, that all makes sense," I said slowly, "but what about Thomas? When he showed up here at the cemetery, he wasn't wearing a hospital gown. And I know for sure that that's what he had on in the hospital."

Drew looked thoughtful. "I had thought about that, and I think I might have figured it out." We had gotten to the front porch, and Drew opened the front door that we had left unlocked since morning. Small town security or Monty, the place just seemed safer than at home. "The last thing that Thomas would remember wearing was the clothes he had on just before the accident. He didn't bilocate again after he came to in the hospital. So he was wearing what he last recalled wearing. And the same could be said for us. I was wearing sweats to bed, so when I bilocated, I was wearing sweats. You were wearing your PJs, so what you had on when you appeared in the woods were the same PJs. I think that you end up wearing the last thing you recall wearing before you bilocate."

I pondered his logic as I put my purse in my borrowed room. I could hear the clatter of the dog racing around the room and the creak of the door as Drew let Monty out to play in the backyard. I had so many questions still. I had so many ideas. And things weren't getting much clearer. In fact, the more I thought about the situation happening around us, the more tangled it seems to become.

I was licking the gooey chocolate from my fingers, looking like a child just after the infamous cookie jar incident, when the diner door swung open and he walked in. He. Travis. The guy that I had least expected to see, but in retrospect, should have known would come around. After all, he didn't work that far away from Crestwood.

He was dressed for the rainy weather, ball cap pulled down over dark hair that curled at his collar, jacket splattered with dark droplets, and jeans with his tennis shoes. No work boots so he wasn't going to work. A day off, I supposed.

He didn't see me. He strolled to the front counter and leaned on the scarred surface looking into the kitchen. Blythe came out, tray in hand, but stopped to greet him warmly.

"Travis, there you are! I haven't seen you for over a week! I was starting to worry that you'd found somewhere that served better coffee. "

"It's not your coffee that I'm after," he replied smiling comfortably. "I just want you for your peanut butter pie."

She didn't ask him for his order but put a mug in front of him and poured the coffee. Without putting the tray down, she grabbed a plate and deftly swung open the refrigerated cabinet and pulled out a pie stacked high with decadent whipped cream. The piece she cut him was generous, and her smile was wide and full of humor. “You get started with this and then let me know if there’s anything else you need,” Blythe said, handing him silverware and napkins.

Tori was back in the kitchen, but the diner was emptying out. We were planning on leaving as soon as she was done and heading over to the retirement home. Tori wanted to get the decorations from Mrs. Lucy, but more importantly, she felt like there might be more information that she and Drew had missed the first time they had gone through the old papers from the house.

Travis’s arrival had put a wrench in the plans. He hadn’t seen me, but he would. I couldn’t hide out here forever, and in truth, I didn’t want to. I felt guilty. When Thea had talked about how terrifying her encounters with my brother had been, it had reminded me painfully of the times that I had spoken to Travis and then left, blinking out like a figment of his imagination. I had been so obsessed with how I felt, how the dreams were affecting me, that I hadn’t thought about it from his point of view, even after I had met him at my house and in the coffee shop. Now I was looking at him through a new perspective. Here was this young man who had seen someone on the side of the road and had stopped. He had said he wanted to help me, and from what I knew of him now, I could believe that. In retrospect, it seemed even more amazing since he said he had seen me many times. I had to wonder how many times. When I had seen the flare of headlights in the distance and stood to the side of the road in my dream state, had he had actually seen me standing there ghostly, in the dark? He had said that he was forced to work nights to get paperwork done for the green house. Who knew how many times, exhausted and confused, he had passed me as I stood on the side of the road, thinking that I was a figment of his imagination. And then he had stopped to see how I was or to help me. And for him, things had gotten no better. I had first run from him and disappeared; then I had spoken to him and disappeared. In either event, I had lead him to believe there was something other worldly about me, just as my brother had unintentionally done when he had visited Thea in the cemetery.

And now he knew that I was real, and he knew the connection between the spot where he had seen me and my brothers’ accident. But what he didn't know, and what I couldn't explain, was how I was managing to appear and disappear.

I pushed out another sigh when I thought of our last conversation. I had told him what I knew. I had told him about the dreams, about waking up in the woods, and about waking again in my own bed with no memory of how I had traveled. And if what Thomas and Drew were saying was true, and I was bilocating, the truth of story was even stranger than any fiction that I could make up.

As I was still watching him, my mind churning through all of the new information that I was just now trying to digest, he turned and our eyes met. The look of recognition that crossed his face would have been humorous if there hadn't been just a flash of fear as well.

So it was true. Having me here, seeing me again, was scary to him. In fact, at this point it was even worse for him than it was for me since my experience was starting to make some crazy sense, but his experience was still like some crazy nightmare.

He didn't hesitate but quickly slid off his stool at the bar and crossed the floor, leaving his coffee cooling at his place. His brows were lowered over those dark eyes, and hair looked a little longer.

"Savannah?" It was a greeting and a question.

"Travis," I replied, keeping my voice and my gaze steady.

"I didn't expect to see you here," he said slowly, his eyes scanning the table in front of me where I had laid out a notebook and pen to take quick handwritten ideas as they came to me. Pushed farther from me was the empty plate with just the suggestion of icing, chocolate to be exact, that had graced the best piece of cake I had ever eaten.

"My friend works here," I said softly. "I've been here a couple of times."

"Your friend?" It was a question, as though placing me in his world would make me a little more real.

"Tori." As though the word had conjured her, Tori came out of the kitchen, her eyes bright with curiosity and caution.

"Van, I'll be done in about 15. Are you ready?" She was checking on me, and at the same time, assuring me that she was there and watching the exchange. From her expression, I could see that she wasn't familiar with Travis. He wasn't a regular in the traditional sense, but it was obvious that Blythe knew him, so he must have come around at some time.

"Sure," I responded, but Tori stayed there, her eyes skimming from Travis to me. "This is Travis. He and I met at the accident site," I said meaningfully.

"Oh!" She seemed at a loss for words. I had told her about our meeting, but at that time, my main goal was to figure out how best to control my travels, not to work on the relationships I had started during my out of body experiences.

Travis was looking between us both, clearly curious.

From behind us, Blythe called out an order and Tori turned. "I have to help with this one. If you are okay?"

"I'm fine," I reassured her. And I was. I had no idea what I was going to say to Travis, how I was going to explain anything, but I felt more sure of myself since I had started my lessons with Drew and knew that I wasn't the only one going through this supernatural adventure.

Tori hurried back behind the counter and I looked at Travis. "Sit down," I commanded, and dropped back in my seat. "I'm going to be leaving in just a minute."

Travis nodded and sat, his eyes still trained on my face like he was memorizing my features. "What are you doing here?"

"I have friends here, like I told you. I'm staying with them for a week and trying to get my life straight."

He hesitated a long minute before asking, "Are you still dreaming?"

I glanced around us. The lunch rush was gone, and the diner held only a few people finishing up desserts or drinks, most involved in their conversations. "I haven't had one of those dreams for some time," I said softly. "But I am getting help, and I have talked to someone."

"Good," he said, almost automatically. I could see by his face that he was still trying to figure me out. "And you're doing okay?"

"I'm fine." I hesitated and slowly reached out and put my hand lightly over his where it rested on the table. "And I'm sorry that I've upset you. I hadn't thought about any of this from your point of view, and now I realize that this hasn't been easy for you either." His hand was warm and a little rough under my fingers. "I know that you felt like you needed to help me, but I am getting some help now. And by the way, you're not crazy, and I'm not either."

He just stared at me, dark eyes confused. And that was how Tori found us. She strolled out, her apron gone and her purse over her arm.

"Van, we need to head out now if we're going to go through all of those boxes," she said abruptly. She looked businesslike, brisk, and a little protective.

I quickly pulled back my hand and leaned back. "Okay," I responded, getting to my feet.

"Savannah," Travis started. But he didn't say anything more.

"I'll probably see you around, Travis," I said lightly, and turned. We quickly left the building, the hot of the sun hitting the window and setting it ablaze. I didn't see Travis watching until we had backed out and the overhang of the roof had blocked the sun. He was standing at the window, framed by the glass, with an unreadable expression on his face.

Mrs. Lucy was waiting for us in the lobby of the retirement home. She had already picked up the key for the locked storage area where her belongings, once packed from her old house, had been stored in the lower level of the facility. Tori and Drew had already been down in the room looking for information before they had found the cross. The boxes of material from the old man's collection had given them just a glimpse into what his life had been like. I had seen only a few pieces of what they had found, but Tori assured me that there was more, much more, just waiting for us to explore.

"You take this key and bring up whatever you like," Mrs. Lucy told Tori, tucking the key into her hand. "I'm not using any of those things any longer, so you can take whatever you want."

"Would it be alright if we looked through the pictures as well?" Tori asked.

"Pictures? Well of course, you can go through any of it. If you happen to come across a little album with my initials on the front, could you bring it on up? I think I lost it in the move, and it has pictures from when the mister and I were first married."

"Sure," Tori said, happy, I was sure, to have a mission. If we could find the album for Mrs. Lucy, then we wouldn't feel like we were just looking through her things to unearth her family's dirty secrets.

"When you're finished you can stop by and tell me what you found." Mrs. Lucy was smiling, false teeth making a Cheshire grin on her wrinkled face.

"We will," Tori assured her. "And we won't be too long."

The basement was refreshing after dreading what I had thought would be a dirty and dark affair. The corridor was well lit, and the door opened easily. Although the space was small, Tori showed me how she and Drew had dragged boxes out into the hallway to go through the contents before returning them.

"The ones on this side we pretty much finished," she said pointing to a stack of boxes, their lids marked with a green checkmark. "We went through and sorted out the papers. Some of this was from when Mrs. Lucy lived there, but most was from before. Her ancestor liked to write and I think he kept everything he ever laid a pen to. There are receipts, journals, books, and tons of loose papers. We found those pictures in this box over here," she tugged a box away from the stack and pushed it out into the hallway. "I may have missed some things, so we need to go through this one again."

I nodded and helped her tug a few more boxes from deep within the room. "And these newer ones?" I asked, seeing some totes made of plastic.

"Those are Mrs. Lucy's things. But they might have her album or the Christmas decorations," she said nodding. "We can bring those out to look at quickly. Why don't you start on those while I go back through the older things?"

I pried the lid off the first of the totes and breathed in the old scent of roses and dust. Inside was a stack of forgotten clothes, some dresses folded with yellowed paper, a few hats that had been carefully tucked in with scarves and shoes, and a small stack of greeting cards. "There are probably some of her old clothes from when she was younger. I doubt she'll need any of these." I snapped the lid back on and found another tote. As I went through more of her things, Tori was cutting the tape on some of the older boxes, pulling out handfuls of paper and pictures, scraps and bits of detritus.

We continued that way for a time until I popped open a container with layers of tissue paper and small cardboard boxes. Slowly I pulled out a single wrapped bundle and unfurled the paper. A single silver glass globe was nestled there, the old finish slightly faded but still beautiful.

"I found one!" I said, raising the ornament into the light.

"Oh," Tori said, jolted away from what she was studying. She stood and came toward me, a stack of photos still in her hands. "That is beautiful. We'll have to use those!" She stood over me as I unwrapped several more, revealing multicolored treasures.

I rewrapped some of the ornaments and pulled the box to the side. "We can just take the whole tote with us." I went back to opening other containers while Tori headed back with her pictures. We worked in silence for some time. After a bit, I opened another box to find more wrapped pieces. Carefully, I pulled the newspapers loose. Inside was a wooden statue, small and roughly formed. It looked vaguely like the human form, but with exaggerated features. Next was a heavy metal piece that looked like a short staff. The handle was twisted into an ornate pattern.

"I think I found someone's collection," I said, holding up the third item. This one was a collection of coins, rough and well-aged, but unfamiliar. "There are all kinds of antique things here."

Tori stepped closer. "I would like to look through those things when we have more time," she said slowly. "I'll ask Mrs. Lucy if we can take a few of these boxes with us. Then we can go through them more slowly."

"I would bet some of these things are worth some money," I said, holding up the coins.

"Once we have it figured out, we can ask Mrs. Lucy what she wants to do with them. Maybe some of them should be in a museum. The cross definitely could have been."

"What are you going to do with it?" I asked.

Tori shrugged. "Once we figure out how to get rid of this mess, I guess we'll see about returning it to the pirate's grave. It wasn't causing any trouble there," she hesitated, "that we know of."

I agreed and stood up. I pushed the container next to the one with the ornaments and went to the next. We continued that way for another hour until we had combed through most of the items. Tori had gathered two cardboard boxes that she wanted to look more closely at, and I had the two totes that we had set aside. It took us four trips to get the things out to the car, and then we stopped to talk to Mrs. Lucy and Thelma for another half an hour, drinking hot apple cider and warming up. We explained about the things we had packed and what we thought might have been stored in the boxes.

"I thought most of his odd collection had gone to the historical society, but maybe some things were overlooked," Mrs. Lucy said.

"We'll make sure and return everything to you so you can decide what to do with it." Tori assured her.

"It's nothing that I need," she said smiling. "But it will be good to have some of it on display if they decide what to do. A nice family legacy."

Chapter 9

Back at Tori's house, the sun was setting like a round ball of flame over the treetops casting heavy shadows. Tori parked her huge car next to the house and flung open the back door. We had needed both the expansive trunk and the back seat to hold all of our boxes, but I was glad that we had brought them all. It was the first time that I was being allowed to help with the research, and I was anxious to get started.

Tori went in first to bring out Monty. He was still investigating the front yard when Drew pulled up in his Jeep, the sides spattered with mud.

"Where have you been?" Tori asked, looking over his muddy boots.

"I was out at the priests' house. Out by St. Benedict. They had some yard work to be done before the winter."

I watched him bend to greet Monty as the dog eagerly sniffed at his jeans, intrigued by all the new and delicious scents.

"Your timing was good. We have all these boxes to get in." Tori gestured to the car and we started unloading, carrying the containers up the stairs and into the only other room that wasn't being used.

The extra bedroom that Liz had been using as an office was mostly empty. There were a few empty boxes left over from their original move, and an old desk that appeared unused, making it apparent that they had made no attempt to make it a livable space.

"Just drop them in here," Tori said. "We'll take the decorations downstairs after Thanksgiving when we get a tree."

I glance around the room. It was painted a plain white, probably done while Mrs. Lucy still lived there. "Is this your office?" I asked.

"It was a bedroom," Tori said. "But I don't know how long it's been since anyone lived in here. It just wasn't my favorite room, so we haven't done anything with it." She shrugged. "We'll eventually use it for an office when we need to."

"Let's grab some dinner and then we can start going through this stuff," Tori said. "I think we have some frozen dinners downstairs if that's okay with you all."

"I'm starving," Drew stated. "I'll eat anything!"

After dinner, we went back up the stairs. Tori pulled a pole lamp from the downstairs living room to help illuminate the empty room. The window was unshaded by curtains, but the sun had made its last spectacular show in a colorful sunset as it sunk below the horizon, and the moon was providing no help.

"This tote is the one with all of the ornaments," Tori began, opening the lid of one box and setting it aside. "Mrs. Lucy said that we could use any of the decorations that we could find," she explained to Drew.

He nodded. "I'm not surprised. She's a nice lady."

Tori began pulling out the glass globes, pausing to admire each one, before rewrapping them carefully. At the bottom of the box, she pulled out a book and held it up triumphantly. "It's the photo album," she said smiling broadly.

I stood and went to bend down next to her to look at the pictures. There were in black and white, and there weren't many of them, but the ones we found were lovely. Lucy in her dress, an elaborate lace concoction with a long train and a crown holding up a heavy veil, smiled out of the frame with a mysterious look that few women could perfect. Mrs. Lucy hadn't been beautiful in the traditional sense, but she had certainly been striking and it was easy to see why she would have wanted to keep a copy of the photos.

"We'll take this out to her soon," Tori promised, putting the book gingerly to the side.

"This one has all of the collection things," I said, pulling the top off the second container. "Maybe we need a table or something to set these things on. I would hate if they got stepped on or broken."

"There's a card table in the basement," Tori volunteered.

"I'll grab it," Drew said.

"It's in the laundry room. The light should be on down there."

He nodded and ducked out of the room while Tori bent to open one of the older cardboard boxes. "I think that these are papers that the family collected, but they don't look like anyone has tried to organize them." She took out a handful and shuffled through. "This might take some time, but we still might find something else from the grandfather."

Drew came in with a folded table and set it up. While Tori sorted papers, he and I took out more pieces from the tote, unwrapping them, and placing them on the table.

"I don't know what most of this crap is," Drew said, wiping dusty hands on already dirty jeans.

"I guess it's just part of his collection. We'll have to look to see if he has any papers to identify them." I unwrapped a particularly ugly statue of some kind of animal, rough and made out of wood, and put it on the table. "What's this?" At the bottom of the tote was a wooden box. I carefully lifted it out and deposited it on the table with the rest of our finds. Tori stopped paging through papers and looked at it with interest.

"The lid won't open, but there's a key hole," I said, dropping the last of the wrapping back in the now empty box.

"I wonder where this one came from," Tori said.

"It could have been anyone in the family," I observed. "It was in a tote, so it might be Mrs. Lucy's or belong to one of her other family members."

"It was in with the collection, though, so it could have belonged to the old man," Tori responded.

I rummaged around in the bottom of the box looking for the key. "I don't see any keys. Did you come across any in the boxes?" I asked.

"No," Tori said frowning. "I don't remember seeing any keys while going through the storage room before either. Maybe Mrs. Lucy has the key."

"She might," I replied. "Or it might have been lost in the move."

"I'll stop by tomorrow to check when I bring her the photograph album."

The funny thing was we already had the key. Tori checked with Mrs. Lucy in the morning and the older woman explained that she didn't know anything about the box and hadn't any idea what had happened to the key. She was, however, delighted that we had found the pictures for her.

Drew and I spent the day alternately playing with Monty and practicing our bilocation techniques. I was hopeless. No matter how much I concentrated, relaxed, and tried to psych myself into another state of mind, I remained painfully vigilant and firmly set in reality.

Drew had to leave just after noon, so I spent the remainder of the afternoon reading through papers from Mrs. Lucy's things. My week was going fast with half of my days already spent, so I wanted to be of some help before I returned home. I had texted my mother daily, and called her twice. She was fine, she insisted, but the guilt twisted in my stomach. I would have liked to be honest with her, to tell her what problems that we had been thrown into, but to do that would be betraying the rest of our group. And Drew was right about one thing. If I approached my parents with the seemingly impossible story of bilocation and magical crosses, they would have me to a doctor's office before I could finish my story.

So I told her of painting and decorating that we hadn't done, but added in truths like visiting with Mrs. Lucy, since she actually had lived in the house before, and going to the diner to meet Blythe and try out all of the fattening goodies that she made.

When Tori came home, we returned to the upstairs room where I showed her the items that I had categorized and placed it little piles, the notes and letters, receipts and tickets. Then we puzzled over the box again. We studied its sides, messed with the lock, jiggled and shook it, and finally gave up. But our answer didn't come until we weren't even thinking about the mystery. At dinner, Liz was talking about the renovations that they had done after the fire when Tori gasped.

"The key!" she exclaimed.

I stared at her, waiting to see what revelation would follow.

"I think I have the key to the box." She stood quickly, almost knocking the chair over behind her and hurried up the stairs. I stayed at my place and Liz and I exchanged looks. Tori was back in just a moment.

"I found this in my closet in my room. It was hidden between the shelf and a piece of wood. Someone really didn't want it to be found."

"Really?" Liz was looking skeptical as Tori held the key out in her palm for us to see.

"I would have never found it, but something caught on the nail that was holding up the piece of wood, and I managed to pull it down."

"Let's try the box!" I said excitedly.

Liz looked at us frowning. "What box? What are you talking about?"

I realized that there was quite a bit that Tori had neglected to share with Liz. And I knew from her expression that she wanted to keep it that way.

"It was a box that was with Mrs. Lucy's Christmas things," Tori explained. "She didn't remember it, but we knew it had been here in the house. She told us it was okay if we opened it."

"And is that part of the junk upstairs in the spare room?" Apparently Liz had been upstairs and seen the mess we had made.

"Yeah," Tori agreed. "We saw some old stuff that Mrs. Lucy had in storage. She said that she had a relative that was a collector. We thought if we found some cool antiques, we could find out what it was worth for her."

"Just keep it in the spare room," Liz said standing and starting to clear the table. Tori and I exchanged glances and quickly got up to help. It was a near miss. Too many explanations would eventually get us into trouble, and we didn't need any more trouble.

It was late when we finally went upstairs. We had watched the television with Liz for some time and gone up later. We took the box from the spare room into Tori's room.

"It doesn't look that interesting," I said, holding it in my hands at eye level. It was wooden, but plain, with no ornamentation besides a decorative square carving in the center of the lid. The bottom had four small carved feet, similar in design to the square on the top, and the front had a single key hole framed by a square metal plate now tarnished to a gray black.

Tori brought out the key. "I only found this accidently when I was packing up some things after the fire. It was hidden in such a weird way that I kept it and took it with me. With all of the troubles after the fire, I forgot about it."

As I held the box, she angled the key and inserted it into the lock. It turned with little effort.

"It worked!" I said excitedly. I had half expected that it wouldn't.

"Good," Tori said with a gusty sigh. "Let's put this on the desk."

I handed her the box that she placed next to her old computer. I'm not sure what I had thought would be in the little box, but I felt my shoulders slump when I saw more papers, more receipts, more painstakingly written notes. Tori took the first sheet off the top and studied it.

"This looks like someone was taking notes, not very thorough, just an outline. It's describing statuary." She paused and skimmed the page. "Look at the sketch!" she said excitedly. "You know what this is, don't you? These are notes about that ugly statue of the dog thing!" She flipped the paper over and strolled over to the table. "Here. It looks just like it."

I slowly pulled out the next paper in the stack. It was a lined receipt, not from any computer, but handwritten and very old. "I think this is the receipt from when the statue was bought."

"Wait," Tori said, "if it has records of when this thing was added to the collection that the old man had, maybe he has records from the cross." She hurried back to the table and put the paper down. "We can go through these and sort them. They may already be in some order, so I don't want to mess it up. But we may be able to find something more about the cross."

I stood beside her as she carefully flipped and stacked the first couple of pages so that they would remain in the same order as they were arranged in the box. The next few sheets were more of the same, notes with sketches, some of the objects matched what was set up on the table, while others didn't look familiar at all. If he had once had all of the pieces in the collection, I wasn't sure what had happened to the other objects because they hadn't been stored with Mrs. Lucy's things.

"I haven't seen anything that looked like this," I said, holding up a black and white photograph of a mask, its features twisted in a savage grin.

"Some of the things were given to the historical society. Probably a big part of the collection was hauled there with his books and papers that he kept in his study. I don't know why these things weren't with them." Tori flipped another page. "Might be that these were in another room of the house and packed separately."

We were more than halfway through the box when Tori cried out in triumph. "I know this picture! I've seen a photocopy of it!" It was a drawing of a nun in full traditional habit standing between the menacing figures of two men, obviously dressed in sailing attire.

"Is that the pirate?" I asked.

"This is the picture we found in our research. This is Saint Francisca and the pirate Juan Madino." She pointed to the other figure. "This was the guy that was going to run Madino through with his sword. She saved his life by appearing between them. And at the same time, the sisters in the convent swore that she was with them praying."

"Bilocation," I breathed.

Tori pulled out a rolled canvas, secured with twine. She tugged at the string and it shredded between her fingers. "Oops." She gently unfurled the canvas, revealing a clumsy painting of a man, a pirate. "Madino," Tori said victoriously, "and check out the necklace." Laying against his chest, prominent against the white of his ruffled shirt, was the heavy gold shape of the cross inlaid with the blood red stones. "This is what we've been looking for. A way to connect the old man, his collection, to the cross and the nun."

Drew was over the following morning early enough to see Tori before she was scheduled to leave for work. Liz had gone into town early, so their only observer was Monty, and he was just happy to be included.

"I'm not sure where this actually gets us, besides reinforcing what we already thought, but it is interesting," Drew said, looking through the papers.

"One of the notes actually seems to be a letter from Saint Francisca. It confirms that she gave him the cross," Tori pointed out.

"I agree. It is good stuff. And I can see why it was locked up. This wasn't meant for everyone to know. This is the direct link between the cross and the old man and the bilocation. This shows that something can be traced from Saint Francisca, to the cross, to this place. But we still can't really tell who else is trying to get the cross." Drew ran his hand over his face, his dark beard showing scruffy under darkly ringed eyes.

"One thing at a time," Tori replied, carefully replacing papers into the box.

"I just wish I knew where Daniel had gotten his information," Drew murmured to himself. "It wasn't the same way we found it. He didn't ask anyone around here, and Mrs. Lucy didn't know him."

"There was a name on his documents," Tori said. "Maybe we should start there."

"Yeah, okay, but I think Thea has the papers." Drew looked toward me. "We had so many problems last year that we sent all the important things away: the cross, the research information. We kept some notes though." He looked at Tori. "I'll grab my notes and come back this evening with them. I can text Thomas to make sure we get the name."

"I have to head for work," Tori said regretfully.

"I'll be in for lunch," I volunteered quickly. I didn't have a lot of time left to stay in Crestwood, but I didn't want to spend all of it trying to meditate with Drew. I knew somewhere deep inside that I wasn't learning anything, despite how determined he was to teach me. Going to the diner would give me a break from the lesson.

"Okay, good," Tori responded. "I have a few deliveries earlier today, but I'll be back in time to have lunch with both of you."

"I got the hint," Drew said wryly. "I'll make sure to give Van a break so she can get something to eat."

Tori nodded her satisfaction. "We're getting somewhere. I can feel it."

"I certainly hope so," I said softly.

We got nowhere in our practice of bilocation. And I tried. I really did. But my mind seemed full of history, dates and pictures of antique jewelry and sacred symbols. And then there was the dread of heading home. While I had been there, tucked in the tiny guest room in Tori's house, my dreams had been completely normal, barely remembered, and leaving me comfortably tucked in the bed each morning.

Lunch was delicious, but I was pretty sure that there was nothing sold at the diner that I wouldn't like. Tori sat with us while we ate, noting when the Chief of Police came in with some of his fellow officers, and the dentist from across the street dropped by for take-out. She seemed to know most of the diners, and they spoke to her like she had lived there forever.

Drew dropped me off at Tori's house after lunch, and I ducked inside. The wind had kicked up a little, but the temperature was still in the 60's, tolerable for the season. Monty greeted me joyfully as soon as I opened the bathroom door.

"Okay, so what are we going to do?" I asked him. "Tori will be home for dinner, and Drew will come back later, but for now, it's just you and me."

His tongue lolled out of his grinning mouth. He looked behind him, and when he saw that I was still watching him, trotted to the door. He stood, nose almost to the crack around the door, and looked back at me.

"You want to go outside?"

He danced a little and grinned back at me.

"Okay, let me find your leash," I said, going over to the hooks by the door. It was there, along with a few jackets. I borrowed one of the light jackets and pulled the leash down. Monty dropped to a sit, waiting patiently for me to attach the hook of the leash. Once done, Monty led me to the door and pushed at the crack with is nose.

I opened the door and we slipped out, closing the door behind us.

The air was brisk and glorious. The leaves had mostly dropped to the ground, but the autumn sun was brilliant. I held the leash loosely, and let the dog lead me down the road until he paused. He wanted to cross the road. I realized that he was probably accustomed to going over to Thea's house. No traffic. The road was quiet, peaceful. I crossed with the dog and stopped at the entrance of the cemetery.

There was a truck pulled to the side of the lane, a rather mud spattered vehicle, a familiar sight. My mind registered whose it was, and why it looked familiar, before I actually saw him. Travis. He was standing at one of the graves in the center of the front of the yard, head down, thoughtful. His hands were tucked in the pockets of a navy blazer, and he wore khaki pants with brown dress shoes. This was not his usual fashion.

I stood for a moment, unwilling to interrupt his thoughts. Monty had no such hesitation. With a quick tug, the leash slipped from my grasp, and the dog went galloping toward Travis, quiet considering his size.

Travis looked up seconds before Monty leaped at him, massive paws landing in the middle of his navy blazer.

"Monty!" I gasped.

He gently pushed the dog down and commanded him, "sit." The voice was firm, and Monty responded promptly. I sheepishly leaned down and pet Monty's ears, feeling awkward and embarrassed.

"Hey," I said softly. A breeze caught up a whirlwind of browned leaves that danced just in side of the gate to the cemetery, the loose wind catching them on the perimeter.

"Hi." He stood studying me, his expression sober.

"Sorry about the dog. He's Tori's. I don't have the best control of him." I saw with dismay that there were now streaks of dirt on the jacket.

Travis followed my gaze and looked at the smears of dirt. He dusted them with his hands, but it did not help. He ignored the marks and looked toward me.

"What are you doing here?"

"I'm still staying with Tori. For a couple days, at least."

"The new girl at the diner?"

"Yes," I said nodding. "She is something of a friend of the family."

"So then you're going back home?"

"Sure," I replied. "But don't worry, I've told my family about what is going on with me." And it was partly true. I had told my brother, and he was family. Keeping my parents in the dark was a necessary evil that I wasn't giving up.

He looked skeptical, but that was okay. I didn't have to prove my truthfulness to him. As long as he didn't come looking for me at home, and stirring things up, it was fine with me.

He looked suddenly weary. "You know, I don't want to cause any trouble, and if you think you have this all under control, fine." He hesitated. "But just so you know, there are some other strange things that are happening around here. You aren't the only ghost in this neighborhood."

I stiffened. "What do you mean?"

"Just that. You're not the only person who is creeping around, vanishing with no explanation. And I may not be aware of much, but I know when things are getting too strange for me."

I held my breath, fear catching me. Who else was creeping around? What did he mean? I wanted to ask, but I wasn't sure what to say. If I drew out the conversation, there was a chance that he would want to hear my story. And I wasn't ready to go into that.

"I'll be leaving soon. And I'll be out of this area, so I'll be safe." I was saying it knowing it was a lie. I was leaving, but I wouldn't be staying away. Until we knew what was going on with our strange new ability, and could somehow get rid of it, I wasn't likely to just leave and never come back. Besides, there was something of this place that tugged at me. I wanted to be here.

He seemed to take my explanation in stride and bent to pet Monty. "So this is your friend's dog?" he asked, totally changing the subject.

"Yep, this is Monty," I replied, grateful for the change.

"What kind of dog is he?"

"Some poodle mix," I said, recalling Tori discussing his lineage.

"He's awfully big for a poodle," he responded, cupping a hand under Monty's chin and raising his head to look into his eyes.

"It's a big poodle," I said smiling. "She adopted him. But he's a good boy." I looked at the smudge of dirt on his jacket. "I'm sorry he got you dirty. You're all dressed up, too."

"I'm going to visit my Granny and take her to dinner. I promised her I'd look in on Grandpa while I was out here." He gestured to the grave in front of him.

I could read the name. Fredrick Bennet Hench. "So your family is from around here?"

"For a couple of generations," he agreed. "Granny lives over in

LaGrange now, but her family was here in Crestwood when she was younger. That's when some of this land was a farm. Really different from how it is now."

"I can imagine," I said looking around at the cemetery. It was a lovely old place. The stones of the chapel were worn to a mellow gray brown. The flower gardens surrounding the building were heaps of dark earth sprinkled with leaves, but I knew in the spring they would be mounded with colorful blooms. But the area felt so very old. All the houses, built in a row of differing facades, faced the cemetery as they had for a hundred years before. And Thea's house, the original home for the caretaker for the cemetery, was tucked to the side of the lawns, separated only by a thick stone wall that outlined the property. It was an area that time had forgotten, except to soften the edges.

Travis checked his watch and frowned. "I've got to get going."

"Sure," I said, tugging Monty's leash until he was back at my side.

"Then I'll see you around?"

I forced a smile. I would, I guessed. I would see him again. It was just a mystery as to where, when, or how.

Chapter 10

Drew was over after dinner, but if Liz thought there was anything strange about our retreating upstairs to the little room to look through our collection from Mrs. Lucy's house, she made no comment.

Drew put his papers on the table among the strange artifacts that we had found in the totes, and he rifled through the pages.

"Here's the name," he said, pointing to what was obviously a copy of a bookplate attached to the title page of some old manuscript.

"Edwin Morrison. You said he was a professor?" I was looking over the paper, my fingers hovering over the print.

"That's his name, but there was a note that Daniel wrote that has his phone number too," Drew responded. "I found it later in some of the papers we pulled off of the flash drive."

I felt an almost painful pang in my belly. The flash drive had been one of the funny gadgets that Daniel had used to keep organized. After the accident, neither the emergency workers nor the police had found his cell phone and the flash drive. Thomas had gone later with Drew, Tori, and Thea to the junkyard where the car had been deposited. Among the wreckage, they had found the flash drive, miraculously still in working order. They had taken all the documents that Daniel had painstakingly scanned onto the drive and printed them out. Copies had been spread among the group to ensure that the information would never be lost again. That, as well as the information that Thea and Tori had organized into a binder was now in front of us.

Drew pulled out a page and dropped it next to me. The familiar writing made me ache. But the copy was clear enough to read. "There he is. Maybe this is as good a place to start as any. If Daniel started with the guy, then maybe we can too. And he might know if anyone else was looking into the cross."

"I'll call," I said firmly.

"Why you?" Drew asked, his face looking set and stubborn.

"Daniel was my brother. I can say that we found some of his papers and were wondering what it was all about. I can say that we were just following up since his death." I licked my lips, feeling a tingle of nerves. "I'm the only one, besides Thomas, that it would make sense to call. We would automatically have had access to his things."

"She's right," Tori volunteered. "If you contact him, it's going to make him suspicious. He'll wonder why you want to know what was going on with all the research. It might make him want to go back and read the information himself. And the last thing we need is one more person meddling into this mess."

Drew nodded. "Fine. But I don't think we should call from your home phone."

I pulled out my cell phone. "I'll use this. I'll just ask him a few questions. I can read people fairly well, I think. I should be able to figure out if he knows anything about this." I dialed the number and waited patiently as the ring buzzed in my ear. I didn't expect anyone to answer. I had an idea in my mind of an elderly professor's office at the university, filled with bound books and stacks of research papers. At this hour, he would be at home, drinking wine from fine crystal and smoking his pipe.

"Hello?" The voice caught me completely off guard and I had to look back down at the paper to remember who I was speaking to. "Mr. Morrison?" I asked, my voice a little breathless.

"This is Professor Morrison, or Dr. Morrison if you prefer." The voice was smooth, slightly high pitched for a man. I felt like I had been corrected for some ghastly oversight.

"Oh, I'm sorry Dr. Morrison," I said hastily. "I'm sorry to bother you, but I think that you knew my brother, Daniel Meridan."

There was a silence on the other end of the line, a quiet that felt thick and wrong.

"Dr. Morrison?"

"I'm sorry," he responded slowly. "I'm trying to recall the name. Can you tell me what this was in regards to?"

"I think he wanted to borrow some materials from your library." I answered truthfully. "We found some papers with your name on them, and thought that he had come to you with some questions."

"We?" his voice was mild.

"My other brother and I," I said quickly.

"I'm afraid I don't understand."

"My brother Daniel," I said, through a throat that felt very tight. "He passed away in a car accident. We are just trying to follow up on some of his projects that he wasn't able to complete."

"Oh, I am very sorry." His voice was smooth, little inflection.

"Thank you," I responded. It was always difficult to respond to that. The 'I'm sorry' that meant so little, especially to this man who didn't even recognize my brother's name.

"I'm not sure how I can help you."

I felt sure he was going to hang up, so I blurted out, "Wait! We want, um, we wanted to see if you knew what Daniel was doing with the information you gave him. Do you remember?"

"Daniel," his voice pondered over the word. "I think I may recall your brother. Blond, was he? And a teenager?"

"Yes," I breathed, "that sounds like Daniel."

"And you say you have some papers from me?"

"We saw your name," I said quickly. "In the papers, Daniel had a copy of your bookplate. That's why we knew who you were."

"I had no idea any of those papers were still around," he said, almost to himself.

My heart was beating fast. "But," I said softly, hoping for some new information, my breath catching.

"Well, frankly, I don't actually know what your brother's plans were. He didn't say. He asked to take a look at some of my materials, and I allowed him, of course." He paused, "I wish I could help you. But I have no idea what your brother was really looking for. I had assumed it was for some paper he was completing for his degree."

I felt my heart sink. Daniel had remained true to his nature. He hadn't told this man what he was doing either. "Oh, well, thank you anyway," I said slowly, jolted out of my revere by Drew waving. He mouthed something and I realized what he was asking. "One last thing, Dr. Morrison," I said quickly.

"Yes?"

"Do you know if anyone else has asked to see the same material that Daniel was using? Anyone asking to see your library?"

He was silent again and I held my breath. "No, I don't believe so," he said at last. "And I do need to go now. Again, I am sorry for your loss."

The silence in my ear seemed to take up the whole world. Gone. He had hung up leaving us more in the dark than before. One of our leads was gone.

I couldn't sleep. I was hot, I was cold, my skin felt alive with prickles of anxiety. It wasn't like the other nights. Something was wrong. I restlessly swung my legs over the side of the bed and sat in the darkness. Monty had chosen not to sleep with me that night, and I missed his warm, reassuring presence. Actually, I missed Daisy too. And I missed home. And I missed my mom and my dad and the reassurance that each day would be something that I could handle, that the world was based in reality, and that there was no such thing as ghosts and the boogie man.

I climbed out of bed and straightened my shirt. I was wearing long pajama bottoms and a short sleeve shirt. I had thought a lot about my discussions with Drew, and had decided, for now at least, to dress carefully before I went to bed. My long hair was in a braid down my back but I could feel the wisps of escaped strands brushing my cheek. I impatiently smoothed my hair back and went to the door, opening it slowly and carefully.

The hallway was empty, the window casting a pale square against the wooden floor at the end of the hall. I walked carefully over the worn floor boards, not wanting to wake either of my hostesses. There was nothing wrong, nothing to alarm them about, and I didn't want to bother them if it wasn't necessary.

I crept down the stairs with no particular goal in mind. The house lay dark and quiet, stirrings of wind and old wood playing a symphony of night sounds. At the front door I stopped and peered through the window. Without knowing exactly why, I pulled open the door. The breeze that flowed in was cool and damp. I saw the pair of tennis shoes I had discarded earlier to the side of the door and slipped them on. I grabbed a jacket from the chair set next to the door, Tori's I thought, and stepped outside.

I didn't for a moment think that this was one of my dreams. I wasn't bilocating. I could remember waking up, and I was dressing to go out, but it held a similar feel of unreality. As I stepped across the porch and down the stairs, I felt a tingle of apprehension.

What was I doing? Why was I out here?

At the road, I paused and looked right and left down the empty pavement. When I crossed, my footsteps were the only sound. At the gate of the Floydsburg cemetery I hesitated, but it wasn't closed, so I walked in. The grounds were lit by a ghostly glow that came from the chapel itself. I hadn't passed this way since seeing Travis, but nothing had changed. The big old trees stretched bare limbs over the grounds making patterns of moonlight and darkness. I stayed on the paved and then gravel path. The graveyard itself wasn't frightening, it wasn't ghosts that scared me. It was…

The shape that moved among the graves was pale and wavering. It moved toward me and I forced myself to stay in place. As it drew closer, my breath caught. Daniel? Was it Daniel, come to visit me in this place where life and death were but a thin line?

"Savannah," the voice said, and then I knew. Not Daniel. Never Daniel, never again, but this was his twin, his other half, my other brother.

"Thomas?"

He stood before me. He had dressed better for the night in dark jeans and a long sleeved shirt. His skin was pale in the dim illumination, but there was something, just something not quite right about him.

"What are you doing out here?" he asked, hands catching my arm.

"I couldn't sleep. I felt like something strange was happening."

"There is something happening. He's back. You need to get inside and lock the door!"

"What about you!" I demanded.

"I'm not here anyway," he responded cryptically. It took me a moment to think. For his words to sink in.

"You're not," I said softly.

"I'm here, Van, but not all of me. Thea is watching me at school."

I had heard of it, I had learned and studied, I had done it, but I hadn't experienced seeing it, and that was enough to make me doubt my sanity.

"Why?" I asked, my voice faint.

"He's coming back. He must know that we have something, or he's found out something. But I know that he's back, and he's going to try to get to you."

"How? How do you know all of this?"

He ran a hand through his hair and blew out a breath. "I can't answer that. As crazy as it sounds, I thought that I heard a voice in my head. Or words in my head. And I knew that I had to come out to the cemetery to find you and to protect you."

"A voice in your head?" I was shivering now. There was no more wind than before, but the cold seemed to be seeping through the thin material of my clothes.

"It's difficult to explain." He looked behind me, not really seeing, but remembering. "You know how close Daniel and I were. How sometimes we would have the same idea at the same time?"

I nodded feeling that little pain.

"So it felt like that. Like I was hearing one of his ideas." His eyes returned to mine. "It doesn't really matter how I felt. The point is, this isn't a safe place for you anymore. You need to go in that house and warn Tori. You need to tell Drew. Then you need to go home."

"No!" I cut him off with my words. "I'm not running away like that. And you're assuming that he wouldn't follow me. If I leave, it won't be because I got scared away. Tori didn't run. Neither will I."

"Van, I know how you feel. And I'm not asking you to abandon everyone. I just want you safe until I can come home."

I looked at him, finding it hard to believe that I was just looking at a shade of him, something cast from the true him.

"I'll be careful. And I'll go back in the house, and I'll warn Tori. I'll talk to Drew. I'll even give you a call every hour on the hour. But I have one more day here to help figure out what is going on with us, and I'm not giving up a second of it."

"Van, you just don't understand," he began, but then stiffened visibly. His gaze went toward the house across the way where Tori slept in ignorance.

"What?"

"I thought, no, I see something. Someone moving. Come on!"

He started to jog across the uneven yard, dodging around the gravestones, with great loping strides. I followed, still fast but not nearly as fast, my braid slapping a rhythm against my back. We didn't pause at the street but ran across the slick shine of the blacktop. The door was still open and the porch was empty. If anyone had been hiding out front, they were gone now. Gone inside the house, or gone away?

We didn't wait to see. We rushed through the door, stopping in the little living room.

The house was all quiet. Then we heard a skittering rush and a black shape can hurtling out of the darkness, landing with a skidding bump, and ending up shoved against Thomas' legs. Monty's eyes gleamed white, and his teeth flashed as he gave us his characteristic grin.

Tori followed down the stairs, eyes heavy and dark with sleep. Her eyes focused on Thomas, and she froze.

"Thomas?" Her voice was rough and her hair a tangled mass.

"He's here!" I said, pushing the door closed behind us. "He's either inside, or he's gone around back."

Tori's eyes widened and she immediately started sprinting up the stairs. I knew she was heading up to her sister's room, and Thomas seemed to agree because he was just behind her. I stood at the base of the stairs, Monty next to me and leaning up against my leg. I could hear them in the hall above, opening Liz's door.

"Okay, it's just you and me," I said softly, and started back the hallway. We moved quickly from room to room, snapping on lights and throwing open doors. I was trying to be quiet, and startled Tori as I entered the kitchen. We met up there, Monty acting like he hadn't seen Thomas for hours rather than minutes. Tori still looked pale.

"All's clear upstairs," she said in a quiet voice. "Liz is still asleep. Are you sure you saw someone?"

"We saw someone outside, that's for sure. But where he ended up, I'm not sure." Thomas paused and looked around the well lit room. "Is there anywhere else we should check?"

Tori frowned, running her hands through her hair. "Just the basement," she said quickly.

"Then let's go," Thomas let Tori lead to the basement door, and she swung it open. She reached to the side of the door and flipped a switch, a light brightening the stairway. "Let me go first," Thomas said. He ducked his head, and we followed.

At the base of the stairs, the room widened. And there was something on the floor.

"Plainly, he is telling us something!" Tori said angrily. She was pacing the living room in short steps, hands on hips, hair whipped up like a tornado had flown around her head in a fury.

I was sitting on the chair, my legs unable to hold me any longer. And Thomas, well Thomas was gone.

"Is he just telling us he's back here? Like taunting us. See how easy I can get in? I can do anything I want?" I felt sick at the thought that he was out there playing with us.

Tori mutter a curse and dropped to the chair. "Times like this I wish I drank!" she exclaimed. At my expression she sighed. "No, I don't. We need to be totally ready if we're going to catch this bastard."

"Catch him?"

She looked at me squarely. "Don't you see? That's where we are now. It's either we get him, or he gets the cross, and the ability, and God knows what else!"

I shivered and put my head in my hands. I felt like screaming, like pounding my fists against something. "This stinks!"

"I'm sorry all this had to happen tonight," Tori said, arms crossed across her chest, "and that it had to happen like it did. I know that you have bilocated, but I guess seeing someone else, especially your brother disappear, is a little crazy."

I put my hands over my face; my skin felt cool and clammy. Just minutes ago, we had been standing in the basement, looking at the 'gift' all splayed out on the concrete floor. As I glanced around, Thomas' eyes had caught the light, and I could see something different in them.

"Van," he had said. "I've got to go. You call Drew and tell him to come over."

"Thomas?" I asked, but I could tell something was changing.

"Oh, my God." Tori was staring at us in the darkness. "He's not glowing!"

And when I turned back to him, he had vanished as though he had never been there at all.

"Savannah," Tori broke into my thoughts. "I'm calling Drew to get him out here. Thomas and Thea should be here in the morning. You just sit here for a minute."

She stood and went into the kitchen, and I wondered idly if she didn't want me to hear the conversation. I was shocked, that was very true, but I had a reason to be. It was one thing to appear and disappear in 'dreams', to not know what is real and unreal with your won experiences, but it's totally another thing to see someone disappear like a stage magician. I felt another tug of sympathy for Travis. My world had gone crazy, but on a chance, I had pulled his world off kilter too. Not fair, but it was true.

"Drew is on his way," Tori said softly. "I'm going to throw on some clothes and do something with my hair."

I looked up at her. "I guess I should too," I said softly.

"Are you kidding? You look like you just stepped off a modeling gig. But if you want to…"

I grimaced. I doubted I looked good at all, probably all haunted and waifish, but I needed to move. "I'm coming," I said, and climbed to my feet. The day was about to begin, and I wasn't ready at all.

"What is it?" Drew was standing at the basement stairs, looking at the heap on the floor.

"I don't really know," Tori replied softly, "his calling card? A warning?"

And it might have been a warning. The soft leather bag had been ripped open and the contents displayed, looking very much like someone had gathered up their bounty and then left it carelessly on the floor.

"How many knives are there?" I asked, feeling a little sick at the thought.

"Looks like five," Drew said, "and whatever is wrapped in that fabric."

"We have to get these out of here," Tori said urgently. "They can't still be down here when Liz gets up."

Drew nodded. "Then let's get some garbage bags. We need to get it all wrapped up. But I don't want to touch any of it with our bare hands."

"Fingerprints?" I asked.

He shrugged. "I don't know, really. Maybe I've watched too much TV, but I don't feel safe with those blades."

Tori nodded and headed upstairs at a jog.

"It all looks really old," I said, still standing back from the pile.

"I agree," Drew said, sounding distracted. "I'm wondering if we are looking at more of the pirate's belongings. It makes a weird kind of sense."

"But why leave them here?"

"To show that he's on to us? That he knows what we know, or that he knows that we know."

Tori came bounding down the stairs with several black garbage bags, a few plastic bags, and assorted other paper bags as though the very selection would help us with getting rid of the evidence. "He knows that we know what?" she asked, picking up on the last of the words.

"He may have left some of the pirate things to show us that he understands we are on the same trail that he is. I think it's a threat. Like he's saying, see, I'm further than you are, and I can get in here and show this to you. Obviously, he must have figured out who vandalized the grave years back and who had gotten most of the grave goods that were taken." Drew took the bags from Tori and headed down the last stair.

"The only thing he didn't get was the cross, and that's only because the old man got to it sooner." I agreed thoughtfully. "And maybe that's what he really wants to say. If we give him the cross, he won't come in again."

"Like I would believe that," Tori said bitterly. "He wants whatever the cross can do, but if he has any idea that we know the abilities that come along with the cross, he's not going to want to let us tell anyone."

I felt another flash of fear. I looked over at Tori, her face white and set, to Drew, as he wrapped his hands in plastic bags to gingerly pick up the knives by the handles and place them in another bag. "So what do we do?" I asked.

"We keep on," Drew said. "But I think that you might be better going back home."

I opened my mouth to protest, but quickly closed it again. I was going home. I only had one day, and I would be going back to my parents' house. From there, I would be out of danger, out of the worst of it at least. But what about my brother? And the rest. "I'll be going home," I replied, "but that doesn't mean I'm out of this."

"Well obviously," Drew said, but his tone was lighter, joking. "If you're still going for your late night walks, something has to be done about you!"

He had picked up the last knife and reached for a fabric wrapped object. "Wait," I said suddenly. "We should have documented this somehow. At least taken a picture."

"I'll get my phone," Tori responded, and hurried up the stairs again. When she returned, Drew opened the plastic to display the array of knives before wrapping them up securely again. Next he carefully unwound the fabric, still using a plastic bag to cover his skin.

"It's a phone," Drew said frowning, the shiny piece of technology looking strange against the ancient cloth.

"It looks familiar." My voice was ugly in my ears, too rough, too wounded.

Drew's eyes went up to mine, and I saw the dawning realization a second before he opened his mouth. "Ah, Christ, it was Daniel's."

Chapter 11

I threw myself into my brother's arms as soon as he arrived at Tori's house. I had had enough. I had seen miracles, I had seen threats, I had seen tragedy, and I had seen the terrifying possibility that the man who was coming into Tori's house had also been at the accident site. He had been there when my brother had been killed.

Thomas' arms were tight around me. "It's okay, Van. It's going to be okay," he said against my hair. I let him lead me in the house with Thea on my other side. Tori pulled the door closed behind us and let Monty out to greet the new guests.

With rare doggy intuition, Monty seemed to understand that I needed something more. He settled at my feet, his massive head in my lap, only moving his big brown eyes to gaze up into my face as I stroked his ears.

"How did you know that I wasn't 'myself'?" Thomas asked at last, looking at Tori as she handed out cans of soda.

"I realized that you weren't glowing, but Savannah was." Tori slid into a seat and opened her drink with a hiss and pop. "I didn't really register it before, but when Drew bilocated, and I guess when you did, neither of you glowed. I mean, your real self glowed, but your second self didn't." She took a sip and sighed. "And when you are here, like truly here, then you glow. All three of you do."

"So we can assume that our bad guy is the same. When he's really here, he glows, but when he's bilocating, he doesn't." Thomas was playing with the can, gently tapping the sides until they made a ping-ping sound.

"And if I see him on the street, I'll immediately know it's him," Tori said, rather victoriously. "I don't think he knows about me yet!

About what I can do."

Thomas was nodding, and Drew said quickly, "And we don't want him to know anything about you. It puts you in a whole lot more danger. If he thinks that you can identify him…"

Tori's smile melted. "Crap," she muttered.

"And there's one other thing that I don't understand," Drew said. "When you were walking in the graveyard, and you were with Anna, you felt that presence. And you and I ran into it again when we were in the cemetery. It wasn't someone bilocating, and it wasn't some real person pulling some kind of hoax. So what the hell was it, and how does that fit in?"

"You mean when I thought that I ran through a ghost?" Tori clenched her hand around the can. "Whatever that was, it was bad. There wasn't a single good thing about it. And if that's some kind of trick that this guy can play, well that's just," she stopped, her lips clamped tightly together before the expletive crept out.

Thea stood suddenly and went to the counter. She seemed to need the movement. She started opening cabinets before turning back to Tori. "Mind if I make some coffee?" she asked, attempting a smile. "We've got some thinking to do."

Tori sighed and seemed to get some control of her emotions. "Sure. Let's do that. I need to call Blythe anyway, and maybe we can get some bonus pastries for breakfast."

Thomas looked toward me. "We're going to talk this out, and then I'm getting you back home," he said firmly.

"I'll go," I said quickly, "but I'm not giving up. I may not live here, but I have a stake in this too!"

Thea squeezed my shoulder as she walked past to grab the sugar. "It's all for one, and one for all!" she joked, and I smiled back.

Home. As much as I enjoyed being with Tori and Liz, coming home felt familiar and real. It was easy to slip into the imaginary and fantastic while I was in Crestwood, cuddled close to the historic cemetery, surrounded by things that were just too strange to be explained. But home was different. Home was a neighborhood, a house full of familiar things, and most importantly, mom and dad and Thomas. We arrived the day before Thanksgiving, better to help our mother with the preparations.

On our last day with Tori, we had gone out and purchased a live

Christmas tree from the tree stand/nursery that sat next to the train tracks. The man there had known Tori through his visits to the diner and promised to give her the friends and family discount. Since most of the town were among friends and family, I wondered how he ever managed to make a profit. He proudly walked us around the little lot, pulling out trees at random and spinning them around, allowing us to see the full 360 view of each. With a brisk thump, he would bounce the tree's trunk off the ground and show that the needles were not shedding excessively. The smell of evergreens was intoxicating, and I had to resist the urge to buy a tree for my room at home.

The man had deftly tied the tree to the top of the car and then given us a slightly blurry type sheet of paper that detailed the exact directions for caring for the tree throughout the holiday. Pleased with our purchase, we had taken the tree back to Tori's and then spent the rest of the evening decorating it, mixing in Tori's parents' decorations with the things that we had found among Mrs. Lucy's storage.

The finished project was beautiful. Liz had cried a little as she viewed the tree where it stood by the window, the fairy lights shimmering and reflecting in the glass of the ornaments. I had teared up as well. It was close to perfect. Besides the tree, we had decked the halls, the kitchen, and added a wreath on the door with a giant red bow. We had taken copious pictures of the decorations, and then laughingly posed for some photographs ourselves. Satisfied that I hadn't completely lied to my mother, I had gone home with a slightly clearer conscience.

Thanksgiving was a family day. We went to see grandparents, aunts and uncles, and cousins who generally were scatted across five states but who all came home for the holiday. For some of them, the last time we had seen them was at Daniel's funeral. Bitter sweet. But Daniel had been gone for a year, and time, like a gentle balm, was making it slightly easier.

The day after Thanksgiving was Black Friday, a traditional day for shopping for our family. My mom and I went out to join in the adventure, meeting up with aunts and cousins to finish some shopping, pretending to pursue some of the best sales, but in reality, just enjoying the frivolous fun.

Friday night I was exhausted. We had started our shopping at five in the morning, and had stopped only when our budget ran out. We ate leftovers from Thanksgiving for an early dinner, and I was asleep by ten.

And as tired as I was, I then went walking.

I was by the road. I hadn't thought that it would ever happen again, I had foolishly thought that I would never do it again, yet here I was. It was colder, but my habit for dressing for bilocation, a ridiculous idea, was paying off. I had on heavy sweat pants and a tee shirt. It had been too warm in my room to wear a jacket, but I could have used one. And the thick socks, which had seemed such overkill when I put them on, were now a sad mistake. The ground was damp, and now the socks were chilly and wet.

Now I knew what I was doing, I also suspected that there was a reason I was doing it. It wasn't a mystery like it had been before. I wasn't crazy, but this was a problem. I stood by the roadside and looked out across the dark pavement. I was here for…what?

The rumble of the motor and tires on the road broke the silence. In the dark, headlights pierced the gloom, and with that, I knew why I was there. No, strike that. I knew who I was there for. Just as my brother had come to Thea night after night, I was coming here. And before I had firmly believed that I was here for my brother, for Daniel. Now I realized that I might have had a very different reason. A reason that I would have never dreamed until the very moment. I was here for Travis.

I waved as he slowed, and watched him step out of the truck. He was dressed for work and must have been finished because he looked tired, with fine lines fanning from around his eyes. The light from his headlights threw shadows over his face, but I knew they were hitting me square in the face. I could see the blond strands of my hair falling tangled across my shoulders like filaments of fire. My pale hands seemed to glow in the harsh light. No wonder he had thought I was a ghost.

"What are you doing here?" His voice was rough, aggravated. "I thought that you were taking care of yourself. No matter what you think, this is incredibly dangerous to hang around here at night. Especially alone!"

"But I knew I wasn't going to be alone," I said surprised at myself. "I guess I'm here to talk to you," I said helplessly.

"What?" He stood, hands on his hips. "I thought you were going back home?"

"I was," I said quickly. "I did." After a moment, I mumbled almost to myself, "I am."

"It's cold out here," he interrupted. "What are you wearing

now?"

"I'm wearing my pajamas. Just like always, I'm wearing my pajamas. I seriously didn't plan on this. I never plan this. It just happens." I hugged my arms close to my body. "I'm freezing," I said shivering, "So let's go into your truck."

He was shocked speechless at my suggestion but he followed wordlessly as I strolled to the truck and opened the door. I climbed in and stripped off the damp socks, tucking my chilly feet under me as I curled up on the seat.

"Are you going to explain?" he asked.

"This is going to take a while," I replied. This was it. This had to be it. No matter if he thought I was insane, I was going to tell him the story. Because he was here for a reason. I was now certain of that. He was here for me, for my problems, for my family, for my friends. I didn't know what he could do, or why him specifically, but I had faith. Yes, for the first time in a long time, I had faith that there was something out there that was guiding me.

"I'm listening," he said. He had closed his door and turned on one of the overhead lights. The heat from his drive still lingered, but he turned on the motor and a flood of warmth came rolling out, easing my muscles.

"I've figured out exactly what is happening to me," I said firmly. "And now my family knows," I made a face, "or some of my family knows. But the point is, this is a really long story, and I'm not sure that I'm going to have time to explain tonight."

"Fine, try," he said curtly.

"First of all, you know that I'm not a ghost. I'm just a normal person." I reached out and grabbed his arm, feeling his firm muscle through his jacket. "I don't want you to think that I'm anything else."

"Sure," he said, looking down at my hand on his arm.

"See, if I were to leave, um, suddenly," I looked him in the eyes, thinking of how Thomas had been there and then with no warning, gone. "I want you to know that it's real, and I'm real, and you're real."

He blinked at me, now more confused than irritated. "Okay."

"So I want to meet you tomorrow. Can you come and meet me? We can go to the same coffee shop."

"When?" he asked.

"When can you meet?" I felt a strange feeling of pulling, like my mind was getting distracted, but my body was following. Time was short. I could tell.

"Two o'clock," he said hurriedly, like he could sense my urgency.

"Okay, that's fine."

I could feel the heat of the air pouring into the cab, caressing my bare arms, loosening my muscles. But I could feel a strange draft, and then a wet heat against my cheek, and as I turned my head…

I woke in my bed, Daisy lying close. She had rolled over in her sleep and her muzzle was inches from my face. I couldn't say if I had sensed her movement on the bed, but something had jolted me. Something had made me come back.

"Daisy, girl, my life is definitely taking a strange turn," I said softly.

She huffed a moist breath into my face, and I gently redirected her nose so that she wasn't breathing directly on me. I tugged up my blanket. My feet were still cold and clammy. But my socks were on my feet, and they were dry.

The coffee shop smelled delicious, and I bought coffee and a cinnamon roll, disappointed that it wasn't as good as Blythe's. I was pouring in cream and sweetening my coffee when Travis came in. I stifled the urge to hug him. He didn't know it now, but he was about to become an integral part of my life, and my problems.

He came over to my table and sat down without even getting anything to drink. He looked rough up close, eyes heavy with fatigue, hair ruffled, unshaven. He sat down rather heavily and propped his elbows on the table.

"I'm glad you came," I said softly. The café was almost empty. A few serious caffeine addicts were sitting at tables with computers propped in front of them, and a mother with two dark haired children were sitting by the window, the boys drinking milk out of a prepackaged container.

"I haven't been to bed," Travis said, his voice rough. "I can't sleep. I can't get my head around all of this. I have to admit, I'm a little afraid that if I go to sleep, I'm going to not come out of this dream."

"I understand." I leaned forward. "This isn't a dream. This isn't a nightmare. This is real life, and if it makes you feel any better, it's not just you."

"So tell me? Tell me how the hell you were sitting in my truck last night in your pajamas, and a second later you were totally gone.

Because I'm just about ready to check myself into the nut farm to get this fixed. I can't do this. I can't just go crazy right now!" His voice had become strained in his vehemence.

I reached over and took his hand like I had before. He was a stranger, but I suspected that I knew just how he was feeling. "This is going to take some time to explain," I said gently. "And it's going to sound more than crazy. But you need to just listen to me for a little bit."

He sighed. "Okay. Fine. Explain."

So I did. I had spent a long time the night before trying to piece together the story in my head to figure out how I could best explain it to Travis. Did I start with my own situation? Did I tell him of all my nightly walks? I had told him some of that before. It wouldn't be exactly new for him. But that meant a lot of backtracking in the telling. Just as I had learned of the true situation, it had been a convoluted way to understand the situation.

So I started at what I thought of as the beginning of my piece of the story. I started with the first time that I had come to Crestwood with both my brothers and Drew. I described what little that I remembered from the visit, the fact that I truthfully wasn't sure of what we were looking for at the time, and Daniel's persistent pursuit of the mysterious and unusual.

When Travis looked like he might interrupt, to ask a question, I held up a hand. I needed to get through as much of the explanation as I could before answering any questions.

I told him about the accident, about the death of my brother and the long weeks of waiting, waiting for my other brother to come out of his coma. I didn't mention what was going on with Thea. That just seemed to be too much to bring up just then. But I told him about my feelings, how difficult everything had been for me, and I told him about Thomas' recovery.

As I talked about my first dream, the first time that I had bilocated and appeared in the cemetery, I realized that I had not remembered the event in detail. As I looked back at it more deliberately, more of the conversation seemed to unravel for me, lines that I had forgotten. And I had forgotten much of what I had said.

"I think I knew that something crazy had happened even before the accident," I said slowly. "I remember telling Thea that I wanted Daniel to fix us. Like I knew that something had gone wrong during that first visit, and I thought that it was somehow his fault. Or at least, I felt like he could fix us, fix me."

"What do you mean?" Travis leaned forward. "What went wrong? What is wrong?"

I looked into his eyes. "It always happens when I sleep but not every night. When I sleep, I am actually existing in two places at one time. And before you say anything, I do have proof."

He was still staring at me wordlessly when the door to the café opened, and Thomas came in. I had wanted to first talk with Travis on my own, but knew that my word might not be persuasive. On the other hand, having a second person that agreed with the story might be more believable. And especially if that person was Thomas. There was just something in Thomas' calm, his steady gaze that made it easier to accept what he might say.

"Travis, this is my brother Thomas," I said gently. Travis's eyes went from me to Thomas and back. I was well aware of the family resemblance. When heredity had rolled its dice, the characteristics that it had chosen for all three of us had been eerily similar. While the boys had been identical twins, and therefore exactly the same in all of their features, when I looked in the mirror, I could definitely see the small, more feminine from of the same lines.

Thomas took a seat at the table and nodded to Travis. "It's nice to meet you finally," he said.

"You too." Travis didn't sound very sure of himself, like there was a chance that my brother's presence might cause another ripple in his reality, but he was polite.

Thomas leaned forward, arms on the table. "I know that this is not something that you have had to deal with every day, so I understand if you think this is a bunch of garbage," he glanced around us, but there wasn't anyone close enough to hear, nor was there anyone who looked to be paying any attention to our little group. Thomas continued, "but we have been trying to figure this out for over a year now. Something has happened to us, to my sister, and my friend, and I, and we have been trying to track down what we think might be the cause." His gaze went to me and he said slowly, "It wasn't until a couple of weeks ago that we learned that Van was having some of the same experiences. She didn't exactly come to us to talk it out as soon as it was happening. But for some reason, she's been meeting with you, and that has left us with no choice. We're going to have to trust you."

"I can't see myself telling anyone else," Travis said honestly. "I don't really know what is happening, and if what you say is wrong, than the only other sensible answer is that I'm losing it."

"You're not," Thomas assured him. "Because what you've seen Savannah do is the same as what other people have seen me do."

An hour later, I went and got a refill for my coffee and Travis walked with me to the counter. He looked, well, thoughtful mostly, and a little confused. He now knew enough to know that he wasn't the crazy one. Or if he was crazy, he was in good company.

"I really do want to help," he told me softly as the barista went to get my coffee.

"I know you do. And don't get me wrong, I'm thrilled that you do. But I'm not surprised. I had a feeling that, once I realized that you were being purposefully sucked into our problem, you were going to have to help us."

His smile was wry. "I'm glad you felt so sure," he said after a moment.

I took my coffee and went back to our table. Thomas was on the phone. When he hung up, he looked back at me.

"That was Thea. She and I are going to have to head back tomorrow. We have three weeks til Christmas break." He studied my face. "Are you going to be okay?"

"I'm fine," I said firmly. "I'm better. I feel like we're getting somewhere."

"But the threat," he said quickly.

"I think it's more directed at Tori. And that does scare me. This person seems to think that she had the cross. And he wants her to know that he thinks that."

"And Daniel's phone," Thomas said, a trace of pain in his voice.

"It proves he was there. And it might be saying a whole lot more than that." I shook my head. "If this guy is trying to say what I think he is, trying to tell us that he had a hand in the accident, than he's way more scary than we thought he was."

"I agree," Thomas said. He was watching as Travis paid for his coffee. "But what can we do about it?"

"We'll stay on guard, keep researching, and try to watch out for each other," I replied. "And Travis will help."

My parents were in high spirits having Thomas home, so it was difficult for all of us to see him leave. We knew that he needed to get back to school, his grades were good but he was taking a heavy class load and couldn't risk missing any sessions. But my dread was very different from my parents. There were too many questions. Too much that we had left undone.

With more time on my hands, my thoughts went back to all of the times that I had bilocated. I pulled out my journal that I had started writing in just after my brother's death and went back to my first entry. But that entry hadn't been my first experience with bilocation. That first time had been when I had gone to the cemetery with Thea. And that experience was the one that was least clear in my mind. I didn't know if it was the stress, the grief, or perhaps the medication that I had been taking to help me sleep, but something had fogged the memory.

In my journal I made a notation to talk to Thea again. If I had said what I thought I had, that I felt guilty because I believed that I had begged Daniel to 'fix' us, than I had known long ago that we were changed. And it was reasonable to think that if we were changed, if Thomas and I and Drew were different, than maybe Daniel had been as well.

But now that seemed lost to us. In none of the documentation that we had read from the flash drive did Daniel ever imply that he had bilocated himself. Rather, the information was mostly information that he had collected, with occasional annotations, rather than his actual thoughts and beliefs.

And the one other piece of information that might have had was locked up in the dead phone that had been left on Tori's basement floor. We had tried fixing it when it didn't turn on, we had plugged it in and waited until it seemed charged, and we had plugged it into the computer to see if any of the files had been transferred. But none of our efforts could make the phone accessible, and it was still an ominous blank screen when we had left to go home.

Thomas had it now. The phone was carefully packed among his things, but he had decided that he would call on some of his college friends. He knew some people that were more skilled in technical areas, and might be able to understand the functions of the phone better than we could. They might know something about the machine that would allow them to access the files, even if the phone never functioned again.

But whatever was hidden on the cell phone was a mystery, as was the greater question. How had our scary visitor gotten it? And why had he left it in Tori's basement?

I decided that I needed to do something to help with the background of the mystery. We needed to know all there was to know about that cross. We needed the facts about Saint Francisca and the pirate, and we needed to know the story of the grave robbery. The closer to the source of the information we got, the more clear the picture should be.

The least I could do was follow up on the call that I had made to the professor. I had the number still, and I called and left a message with my own cell phone number. It was midday the following day when the professor called back. He was very polite but a little short. I was persistent anyway, and managed to get a promise that I could come and speak to him in person. We set up the time, and I sat back, satisfied that I was finally doing something to help the cause.

"You don't have to go with me," I told Travis over the phone.

His call had jolted it out of my reverie. I had been sitting on my bed, a text book in front of me, thinking that I needed to write on the paper that my mother had given me to complete.

"I'm calling to check on you," he had proclaimed bluntly.

"I'm fine, really," I replied. I had known whose number it was before I answered it, but now that I knew that Travis was part of our group, or part of our experience at the very least, I knew I had to answer it.

"You made it home?"

"Sure," I said trying to sound upbeat and positive. "I'm staying here until Thomas can come home for the holidays. He prefers for me to be here just now."

"It makes sense," he said, but I could tell that he was being cautious.

"Look, Travis, I think I'm going to try to get some information about the history of our experience. I'm going to go meet with Professor Morrison. He's the one that helped Daniel find the information in the beginning. He says that he doesn't remember Daniel, but I find that difficult to believe. I think seeing me will jolt his memory."

"Is Thomas on board with this?" Travis asked.

"I told him what I was doing. He just said that he didn't think that I should go alone." I stopped, knowing that I was forcing him into joining me. I didn't regret it, though. I needed him, and in some ways, he needed me. I was part of a mystery that he was involved in. And even though it was my fault that he was there, I knew that he was supposed to be there.

"So I'm going," he agreed.

"It won't be a long drive. The University is just a few miles away." It was a little farther than that, but he knew the distance. "And I already talked to Professor Morrison. He's expecting us the day after tomorrow," I said hurriedly.

"Okay," he said cautiously. "What time?"

"I told him two o'clock. I figured by then, you would have had time to get home from work and rest some before we left."

"Two is fine," he replied. "Do you want me to pick you up?"

I hesitated. He was part of the mystery, but since I was sucking him into my life, I felt like I needed to let him in a little. "Yes, that would be great," I said. "If we leave by one, we should have plenty of time."

"Alright, one o'clock," he said.

I found myself smiling for no good reason. "See you then."

Chapter 12

In early December, the weather could be anything. I was pleased to see that it wasn't raining, but it was cold, a bone chilling cold that bit at your fingers and nose and made it almost painful to breath.

I told my mother that I had met a new guy and watched her eyebrows creep up her forehead with shock.

"He was one of Tori's friends," I said, exaggerating the truth. "We've met a couple of times, and now we're going to the University of Ohio. He wants to tour the campus and I said I'd go along."

"He's thinking of going to college there?" my mother asked.

"Yes, he's working right now, but he wants to go back to school." I wasn't sure if that was true. I knew he worked, but I had no idea what his future plans were. And to think about it, I didn't know how old he was or if he already had a degree. On the other hand, I didn't know what my plans were either.

"So how long will you be gone?" my mom asked.

"Just until evening," I reassured her. "We'll be stopping on the way back and having dinner. We'll come home then."

"And he will be going back home?"

"I assume so. He didn't say he was going to work." I realized that I had just taken it for granted that he would clear the whole day for me. Presumptuous, I knew, but it seemed right. "Anyway, we won't be out too late."

My mother's smile was tight, her eyes doubtful. She had assured me that she had seen a big change in my demeanor. But that didn't mean that she wasn't still worried.

I was not surprised to see that Travis was punctual. I knew that he would be. He climbed out of his truck while I watched from the window, and I called to my mom that I was leaving. I could hear her quick footsteps approaching and smile wryly. As I opened the door, Travis reached the porch, and since my mother was just behind me now, I did a quick introduction. I didn't want her asking too many questions, but I wanted her to see Travis, who was looking very respectable, handsome even.

"You all be safe," my mom said from the doorway as we strolled down the sidewalk.

I smiled and waved quickly before climbing into the truck. It was funny how familiar the seat felt. I had been there twice, but never when I was actually, truly, 'there'. But it reinforced my belief in the crazy bilocation. I had sat in the truck, feeling the heat pour from the vents, and known exactly where I was.

"Are you ready?" Daniel asked me, climbing in the driver's seat and pulling the door closed.

"Yep," I said quickly. I glanced once again toward the house and saw my mother in the doorway. I smiled again and waved a small gesture.

As we pulled out onto the main highway, Travis switched on the radio and soft country music gave us a little background noise.

"Is this okay with you?" Travis asked, nodding his head toward the radio.

"Sure, I'm good," I said. "And thanks for taking me."

I was surprised at how quickly the time passed. Although it was freezing outside, the truck was cozy warm inside. I found myself asking Travis about his life, realizing that I knew very little about him. He been born in Tennessee, close to Nashville, but had moved to Kentucky when he was still very young. His mother's family was still in Tennessee. He had two siblings, an older sister who was a nurse at an emergency room in Tennessee, and a younger sister that was still in college. He had finished two years of college himself, but had stopped to work when his business had gotten exceptionally busy.

"How did you get into landscape?" I asked.

"My grandfather had the greenhouses. My dad didn't really have the passion for it, but I grew up running through the aisles, playing in the dirt. I loved everything about it, the damp smell of the earth, the feel of the steam in the summer, watching the plants grow and bloom. I started working there when I was old enough to help, probably at ten. I came to Kentucky every summer after that, and any extra time that I could, long weekends, holidays."

"So you decided that you wanted to get into the family business?"

"Not really decided to. I just fell into it. It always seemed like the place I was meant to be." He rubbed his hand over his face. "I am trying to take classes in business at the community college in the morning and work in the afternoon and evening. When it gets dark, I have to do paperwork, orders and invoices. It is wearing me out."

"Oh," I said surprised. "I thought you were just working the late shift."

"I work all shifts," he said wryly. "It's just that some seasons are a whole lot busier than others."

"Like the spring?" I guessed.

"Sure, and just before Christmas with the poinsettias. And the fall with mums. Actually, we don't have much down time at all." He grinned and I could tell that he loved his job.

"But in the meantime, just walking in the greenhouses, it must be soothing."

He glanced at me out of the corner of his eye. "It is," he agreed, "I wouldn't want to work anywhere else in the world."

The University of Ohio was sprawled over several city blocks, but the Google map led us directly in front of the building that housed the history department. We parked the car in the visitor's space and hurried up the sidewalk. We were just on time with not a minute to spare. We had the number for his office but wasted a few moments getting turned around in the confusing building. When we finally found the correct number, the door was closed. I stepped up close, feeling an odd weight on my chest. This must have been what Daniel had done. He must have come to this man for help at some point. He must have stood by this door, but for him, it would have been exciting and an avenue to a new adventure. For me, it was slightly melancholy, more like a pilgrimage.

At my knock, the familiar high rather nasal voice from the telephone bid us to come in. The room could have been any corner of a university library. It was framed by bookshelves, all tall and dark with age, stuffed with volumes of all shapes and sizes. They were all hardback, however, and there wasn't one in the collection that I could see that might have been printed after the 1950's. The spines were lined with military precision, marching across the wall in an order that perhaps only the Professor knew. And the man at the desk looked like a professor. He was small, with fine boned hands and sharp features. His eyes were dark in his pale face, but he smiled in a very friendly manner and jumped to his feet to greet us.

"Savannah," he said with enthusiasm. "I have been racking my brain to see if I could remember your brother, but now that I see you, I knew exactly to whom you were referring."

"We've been told we all look alike," I agreed, and smiled back at him, taking his proffered hand in mine. His skin was soft, the hands of a scholar.

"And you do, you really do. But I was so sorry to hear about your brother's death. Now that I can see him in my mind's eye, I can recall what a bright spirit he was, what a fine young man."

"Thank you," I said, feeling my throat tighten a little. A bright spirit was a good descriptor for my brother. A flame that burned bright.

"And you came to ask about why he visited me?"

"Um, yes, if you don't mind."

He gestured and I slid into a seat across the desk from him. He waited until I was seated before slipping into his chair. "And how rude of me!" he exclaimed. "I didn't ask about your companion!"

I glance to the chair next to me where Travis was settling in. I was embarrassed a little myself. I should have remembered to introduce them, but in my preoccupation with memories, I had forgotten the common courtesy. "This is Travis," I said quickly. "He's a friend of mine. He agreed to drive me."

"Oh, you don't drive?" Professor Morrison asked, his voice full of concern. "Of course you don't. Memories."

"No," I said quickly. "I drive, but I asked Travis to come with me."

"Very kind of you," the Professor said softly, but I detected a strange edge in his voice. Did he think that Travis was taking advantage of me? Did he have the wrong idea of our relationship? But that wasn't my greatest worry, so I just nodded my agreement.

"We had seen some of the papers that Daniel had copied," I said, changing the subject. "We wondered where they came from."

"They were mostly from my private library," the Professor explained. "He asked to review some of my books for a paper he was writing. He must have found some good information, because he also asked to make copies of some of the papers." He sat forward and steepled his fingers beneath his chin. "We have a photocopy machine down the hall, so I allowed him to copy the pages there. I didn't want the documents to go any further. They are very old and very fragile." He shook his head slowly. "But I never knew what he did with the information. He told me that he would send a copy of his paper to me when it was almost completed. I had offered to proof read it for him and give him some of my professional insight."

"That was very generous of you," I said quickly, noting that he might expect that reaction. I could tell from the way that he presented the information, that he had believed he was doing Daniel quite a service.

"Yes, well, I do live to help educate." He paused and sat back in the chair, a small sigh escaping the cushion as he repositioned his slight frame. "But I never heard anything more from your brother after that time. I did wonder if he ever completed the paper. Do you know?"

"Oh, I don't," I said, a little embarrassed and caught off guard. I seriously doubted that there was ever a paper planned. It seemed more plausible that Daniel had used the excuse to borrow the information with no intention of using it for anything scholarly.

"I had hoped to get a copy," he said, his voice wistful. "You would send me a copy if you found it, wouldn't you? I would love to see what he was able to do with the information."

I felt a prickle of guilt when I agreed, knowing that we would never see the draft of the false paper that my brother had proposed. "We'll send you any draft we find," I said nodding. "We just haven't found everything that Daniel was working on." I rubbed my chilly hands together. "But I was wondering if we could look at some of the books that Daniel had taken the copies from?"

He was already shaking his head slowly. "I'm afraid that is impossible," he replied, his tone regretful. "I had a break in here at the office shortly after your brother's visit, and most of the volumes were taken. I couldn't imagine who might have wanted them. They really weren't worth much to anyone but a scholar like myself."

I stared at him, totally shocked and dismayed by this revelation. The information was gone. Gone. All that we had left were the copies that Daniel had made, and those seemed a poor substitute for whatever else the volumes might have held. "I am so sorry," I said, meaning the words. This man had made collecting these old books for a big part of his life. And then they had been taken from him. And I had the awful feeling that I knew why.

"So someone broke in and took your books?" I had almost forgotten Travis was there until I heard his voice.

"Yes, books, some statuary, a few odds and ends that I had sitting around. Nothing of great value beyond the books."

"So the books were expensive?" I asked.

"Oh, my dear, the worth of books cannot be counted in money." He stood and went to the shelves that blanketed the walls from floor to ceiling. "Some of these books I found in Europe in the 1960's. Some were from collections being auctioned off, others I found at rare bookstores. I have a few first editions as well, but I don't keep them here," his voice had dropped as though this part was a secret.

"And how many were taken from you?" I asked. It was difficult to imagine a thief sneaking out of the university building with a bunch of heavy books under his coat.

"Seventeen," he said, sounding very certain in his count. "There are seventeen missing from my collection. Not all of them valuable, to be sure, but still…" He looked pensively out the window.

"That is a shame," I agreed. And what to do now? He didn't have the original texts that Daniel had looked at, and he didn't seem to be that aware of what Daniel had been looking for. So that left little to be done in our investigation here.

"And do you know if your brother was able to find any more information about his subject?" The professor had turned from the window and the silvery light was cast about him, throwing his thin face in shadow.

"I don't really know," I responded honestly. "We've seen some scans of papers that he had, but not everything."

"Oh," he said, but didn't expand upon his thought, whatever it might have been.

"Well, I guess we'd better head back," I said, feeling suddenly awkward under his unseen gaze.

"Of course," he replied slowly. "You must be careful on your ride home." He had walked away from the window, and I could more clearly see his face. His expression was completely benign.

"We will," I said, and stood. Travis was quick to stand, and stopped at the doorway to let me walk through first. I felt a thrill of warmth for the gentlemanly curtesy.

As we walked down the hall, the office door closed behind us. I turned and looked back down the hall. A few students were meandering slowly, deep in discussion. But there was no one else there. In spite of the emptiness, I felt watched. My skin crawled at the sensation, and I increased my steps.

We had decided to go by the library since we were already on the campus. It seemed such a shame to come all this way and then turn around empty handed. But after an hour with a librarian who had shown extreme patience with our search and checked on the computer for anything with our search words, research ideas, or names, we had to leave empty handed.

We were close to home when we stopped for dinner. We picked a place with a crooked sign out front and a handwritten menu with the specialty of handmade pasta and Mama's Sauce. As it turned out, the choice was a good one. The food wasn't fancy, but the garlic bread was fresh baked in house, and the pasta was rich.

We talked about everything, about his family, the family business, and what it was like to grow up in the green house. He was very close to his family. I could tell that by just listening to him talk, and it reassured me.

On my part, I told him about growing up with the twins, the funny ways that they had fooled teachers with their identical looks, and our little family unit. I found myself talking more about Daniel, his love of the mysterious, and the adventures that he had pulled us into on occasion.

"He seemed to always seek out things that were unusual," I said thoughtfully. "It was a family joke. We always said that he was going to end up being an archeologist, find the next King Tut." I sighed, so much lost. "But he ended up studying accounting." I laughed a little. "I don't know if he would have stuck with it."

"Not likely," Travis said. "I have felt like that. When I was in business classes, I felt like I was being tortured. I wanted to do well, but it just wasn't going to work. Although I have needed some of the lessons to help run the business, so it wasn't wasted."

"That's what I think. I think he would have stopped those classes. He should have gone into history, something like that." A wash of sadness, so deep and intense, swept through me. He had missed so much.

Travis seemed to catch my mood and covered my hand where it rested on the table. "Savannah, this is none of my business, but I think you should know." He took a deep breath. "I believe in God, in religion, and the whole heaven/hell thing. But most importantly, I believe that people don't just go away when they die. They continue to experience a life, just a different one. And I believe that your brother will continue to look for mysteries."

I ducked my head and nodded, blinking away tears. Without thinking, I turned my hand in his and wrapped my fingers around his palm, feeling the strength and the warmth. I couldn't help but admit it. I liked this man. And I knew very well that we hadn't known each other very long, but there was something so steady in him, so true.

We shared a decadent chocolate dessert, laughing a little about our strange lives. On the way back to my house we discussed the story we would give my mother. I felt guilty again for all of the deception. But at least I could share with someone. Travis had come into my life when I needed him.

Once home, I invited Travis inside, knowing that my mother would want to meet him. Dad was home too, so the introductions were completed before Travis had to head home. I walked him out to his car, and hoping my parents weren't watching out the window like I was some vulnerable 15 year old, gave him a swift but heartfelt hug. It wasn't a romantic embrace, but it said what I couldn't. Thank you. I care about you.

Once in my room, I called Tori to give her the newest information.

"You mean you went to see him by yourself?" Tori demanded, talking about the Professor.

"Not by myself, no, I took Travis. I had been the one to call him in the first place. I thought he might be more inclined to talk to me."

"Savannah, that was pretty brave!" Tori said, her voiced laced with amusement.

"Yes, well, I'm stuck here with nothing to do while you all are trying to solve this without me. I wanted to do something!"

"You have done something. You are doing something," Tori protested. "And you are going to do more. We have been making plans."

"We who?" I asked suspiciously.

"Thea, Drew, and your brother. We are trying to divide and conquer."

"So what am I doing?" I asked quickly, a little eagerly.

"You need to come here again this weekend. I know that Thomas would like for you to stay out of this, to stay safe, but there's no avoiding it now. We have to have everyone's help. We're going to make plans."

"Okay, I'll be there," I said smiling.

"And bring Travis if he'll come," Tori said. "We might as well get him involved since he is already."

"I'll call him!"

"Great," Tori said, and our plans were made.

Travis was happy to meet with us. I had called him to invite him, and then I felt like I had to backtrack and explain more of the situation. Why was it necessary to have a meeting with everyone? Why now? But that didn't seem right either. It wasn't all my story to tell.

"Look, just meet me at Blythe's diner this evening," I said on Friday morning. "We'll meet up there for dinner and then go from there."

"Go where?" he asked curious.

"I'm not really sure," I admitted. "Can you just live not knowing?"

"I can," he said, his voice warm with humor, "I've lived with bigger mysteries."

I knew that I had been one of the bigger mysteries, but I let the comment drop. "Okay then," I said, trying to sound brisk, like his tone wasn't making me feel somehow better, and a little soft inside.

"Okay," he said.

At Blythe's, Tori was just finishing her shift. She had grabbed a table for us, and Drew was already sitting there drinking a soft drink out of a frosty glass. I slid into a seat across from him. I had gone to the counter to order a milk shake, feeling a little reckless with the thought of all of those calories. But I still was too thin for my frame and a couple pounds would only do me good at that point.

When Thomas came in, I saw that Tori was watching him critically. I wondered if he was glowing more. Tori had said that the aura she could see around us differed depending on how frequently we had been bilocating. I knew that I was still doing it, not often, but it was happening. I didn't know about my brother. He hadn't bilocated since coming out of the coma except the one time that I had seen him outside of Tori's house, the night we had discovered Daniel's phone. Now I wondered if he was doing it more frequently than that, checking on us, investigating behind closed doors that only he could go through.

Thea followed him closely. Her curls had been caught in the wind, and she was busy trying to tame them into a pony-tail. She had spots of paint on her jeans, and I figured she might have come directly from an art class.

"Is that what you're having for dinner?" Thea asked as she stood next to the table.

I smiled and shrugged. "No, not really. This is just the appetizer."

"Really?" she joked. "On a health food kick?"

"Nice," my brother said from across the table. "I think I'll try one too."

Anna, Tori's friend and one of the other waitresses at the diner swung by and caught part of the conversation. "Are you all going to order now?" she asked, "or should I come back later."

"Well Savannah is eating in shifts, so I guess we can go for the first course," Tori joked.

"Okay, so what do you all want?" Anna asked.

Most ordered drinks, but Thomas was true to his word and ordered a milkshake like mine.

"I'll be back in a minute," Anna said.

"Can you take your dinner with us?" Tori asked her friend. "We'll be here for a little while, so we can wait to eat until you're ready."

"Sure," Anna replied. "I'll break around 6:30. The sidewalks roll up around here early, so the rush should have died down a little bit."

I felt a little relief. Tori had told Anna just a little about what was happening to us. Anna had been in the cemetery with Tori when she had experienced her haunting, and knew some of Tori's history, but wasn't privy to the full extent of our craziness. As long as she was around, we would have to curtail the serious conversation. And it would give me a break from having to stress about all that was happening around me, and to me.

"Is Travis coming?" Thomas asked.

"Yes, he said he would be here." I glance around as though with my words he might walk in the door, but he didn't.

"Maybe just running late," Thea said.

Anna brought by our drinks, and we sipped as we talked about normal stuff, the weather and the holidays, friends and family.

Travis came in almost thirty minutes late looking harried and stressed. He was dressed in clean jeans and a crisp shirt, but his hair was mussed. I had a brief feeling of alarm when I saw him. I had to stifle the urged to rush toward him and throw my arms around him. Now where had that come from?

"Is everything okay?" I asked as he approached.

"It's fine now. I just had a weird experience. I was looking for some of my information from my truck, I need to change out one of the headlights and thought I had a bulb in the glove compartment, when I realized that a bunch of my papers are missing. I can't figure out what I would have done with them. It's just the usual insurance and government things that I've always kept in my glove box, but now I guess I somehow lost it." He stopped next to the table.

I disregarded the break in, thinking that I was just happy to see him. It didn't occur to me that someone might have been looking into my companion, his identity. "Sit down," I said quickly. "We'll go through introductions in a minute, but why don't I grab you something to drink."

"I can get it," he said. "I've been sitting down too much already." I watched as he strolled over to the counter. I glanced around the table and saw that almost everyone else was watching him as well. He was the newcomer in the group, the wild card.

"He was really good when we went to visit Professor Morrison," I said in a soft voice, keeping it low for only our table to hear. "He just listened mostly. I think he hears and notices a whole lot more than he lets on to." I frowned a little. He had gone to the Professor's office with me, and now someone had taken papers from his truck. It would be a weird coincidence, but I couldn't see how it could be anything else.

"Well we kind of discussed the situation and decided that considering everything that he's already seen and what he already knows, we might as well take advantage of another set of eyes. Hopefully he can help us out." Thomas seemed to be speaking for the group, but that wasn't a surprise. He was gaining some leadership qualities that he had lacked before, although he had always been the calm and reasonable one of the brothers. "We're trusting you about his character," he added, one pale eyebrow quirked in a teasing way.

When Travis came back, we changed the subject and a few minutes later Anna returned to take our orders. Blythe was by as well, making sure that we had enough to eat, and truthfully just checking on us. I knew that she had two boys of her own, and was protective of most of the local kids. She had watched a lot of them grow up, including Thea, and like an honorary aunt, viewed them as part of her extended family. Her relationship with Drew and Tori was similar. When Drew had come to Crestwood after the crash, still reeling from what he had gone through, she had helped him back on his feet, giving him recommendations about where he might find some odd jobs to help support himself, besides providing him with some free or bargain meals.

When Tori had moved to Crestwood with her sister after the death of their parents, she had come to the diner with little money and little direction. Blythe had offered her a job and someone older and wiser to talk to. She had helped build the foundation for Tori's new life. Through Blythe, Tori had become part of the tight little town community.

Thea had lived there all of her life. She had carried her own peculiarities. Living next to the cemetery, having a father that was a funeral director, and making art pieces out of dead flowers, first gathered from the graves outside her door and later hand-picked and dried in her basement, she remained a town curiosity much of the time. But Blythe had known her mother before Thea had ever been born, and the bond there was long lasting and strong. When Thea had gone through some of her worst times, when she had seen my brother and thought that she was really seeing a ghost, Blythe had helped her pick up the pieces. It seemed only right that we would be in the diner, sorting through our problems.

Around Anna, the talk was of college and careers, future plans and small town gossip. Thea's best friend, Lindsey, had been away at college in New York State and would be returning for Christmas after a long time being gone. It would be one more person to help in our little group, although Lindsey, like Anna, didn't know the whole truth.

We had debated who to tell, and how much to tell. For now, they were staying with a need to know policy with Anna and Lindsey, but for Travis, they had decided that he needed to know more. I knew what they were thinking. They wanted him to be my backup not in the least because he was the one that seemed to always see me when I bilocated. For whatever reason, he had been put in that position, and my brother wanted to make sure he was up for the job.

After dinner, we went to Tori's house. Tori's sister was out for the evening with a friend, so we had the house to ourselves for a while. Drew and Thomas went upstairs to gather the things that we had taken from Mrs. Lucy's collection. When they came back down, we took some time spreading out the strange museum pieces and documents on the kitchen table.

Thomas handed over Daniel's flash drive to Tori, so she could print out some of the documents that they had only gotten to skim earlier. Much of the information that had been printed out the first time had been taken on the night of the fire at Tori's house. Now we needed another copy. While she was busy, Thea and Thomas started sketching in some of the background story of the items on the table with Travis, using their explanation to fill in some of the parts of the story that we hadn't ironed out.

For his part, Travis listened in relative silence. I sat back and listened myself, rewinding the story in my mind. It seemed we had most of it figured out. The Saint gave the cross to the pirate after his conversion; someone stole it from the pirate's body. Then the cross was lost for a time before the old man found it. From there, it traveled to the United States where the little boy had gotten his hands on it, and it had disappeared in what we supposed was a tragic accident when the boy had fallen into the well. The grandfather had searched for it, but some time just around the time of the boy's disappearance, the old man had died.

End of mystery.

Until our present situation. And that was the part that made the least sense to me. For some unknown reason, when Drew, Daniel, Thomas, and I had come to Crestwood, to Floydsburg cemetery and Duncan Memorial, we had triggered an anomaly, a miracle, which we had known nothing about. That was assuming that Daniel hadn't known about it, and considering Daniel's preoccupation with the strange, we weren't so certain. But the fact was, after that point in time, we had been changed in some fundamental way.

The result was astonishing, extraordinary, and would have been frightening in itself. But it was now so much worse because of him. Him. The intruder, the ghost, the thief, the murderer? If it hadn't been for him, we might have had time to deal with it. But he was the newest mystery. The one wild card that none of us could explain. There was one more person in our midst that had the same ability and very different intentions. If he could actually do the same thing that we could, and we were pretty sure that he could, than he too had been exposed to the cross. And we could only assume from his behavior, that he wanted the cross. For what reason, we could only speculate, but we were sure it had to do with the power, the ability.

"You know, if I hadn't seen Savannah just disappear, I would think you were all crazy. Or just really bent," Travis said, looking at the cross that Thomas had pulled from the protective pouch.

"Yeah, I agree," Tori said holding up a stack of papers. "This is like something from a movie, or worse, a made for TV movie."

"So do you think the grave robbers knew what they were doing?" Thea asked, paging through the documents and skimming the new article that covered the crime. "Do you think they were going after the things because they were valuable, or because they had a story connected with them?"

"Any religious artifact would probably bring in more money in the right circles," Thomas said. "Let's face it, anything that is rare tends to bring in a higher price. If someone knew that a saint had given it to the pirate, they would have probably been willing to shell out more for it."

"It's sacrilegious!" Thea exclaimed.

"The church has done way worse than that. And remember, the thieves didn't have to believe in anything themselves. They may just have known some of the history." Thomas looked at Travis. "So now that you've heard the story, what are your thoughts?"

"I guess my main problem with this is how are you going to make it stop? Savannah can't just keep showing up in the woods by the side of the road every time she goes to sleep."

"Now wait!" I interrupted. "I am trying to work on it! Drew has been showing me how to control it. I'm just not there yet!"

Travis frowned. "You're not saying that you want to continue this way, are you?"

"No," I replied quickly. "I feel like a science experiment gone wrong. But if I could control it, at least I wouldn't be a danger to myself. I could choose to bilocate or not."

Travis nodded but didn't look convinced.

"Our first priority is to figure out who this maniac is that is sending us messages. I want to stop him. I'm not really sure if he was involved in my brother's death, but if he was," Thomas' voice was firm with a little edge, "he needs to pay for what he did." He looked around at us all meaningfully. "My second goal is to get rid of this ability."

I felt a chill flood my bones. He was right. If the man had had Daniel's phone, than he had been at the site of the accident. Since no one could remember what had caused the accident, it did beg the question, could it have been less an accident, and more a murder?

Chapter 13

We started organizing our information in a crazy web drawing on the back of a desk sized calendar page with Sharpie markers. Starting with the first incident of bilocation, we traced the sighting of the Saint Francisca in the battle of the pirates when she saved Juan Madino, and then progressed through his life. There was the portrait of the Saint with the cross necklace, and then the same necklace among the pirate's belongings. Our next connection was his burial spot and the subsequent plunder. I picked up the photograph of the gravesite. It was in black and white but still creepily clear. His skeleton was intact, dressed in some finery including shoes on his bony feet. They hadn't moved the body itself, but you could see where the lid of his coffin had been shattered, leaving splinters of wood and clumps of dirt on the chest and legs of the body. And the article noted that any valuables had been looted, including jewelry.

"It sounds like most the things taken were never retrieved. I don't know if that means that they are spread out all over the place, or if someone ended up with the whole collection. But either way, we have one that turned up." Thomas looked at the cross and nodded his head.

Thea held up a couple of sheets that they had printed out. "It's these documents from Morrison's books that link the cross to the pirate. The grave robbing was a more modern event."

"I can't imagine thinking it would be a good idea to rob a grave," Drew said, his face looking strained. "That shows desperation."

"Or greed," Tori added.

"And no respect for the dead. Or the Church for that matter. This was done on sacred ground." Tori looked up and saw that Travis was looking at her quizzically.

"The pirate was friends with Saint Francisca and after he witnessed the miracle, he became devoted to the church himself. After he died, he was buried in a Chapel. When the grave was robbed, it was done within a church. Whoever did that had no respect for religion."

"Or the dead," Thomas said, his face grim.

"I wonder if the old man knew what the cross was when he came upon it. I wonder if he knew that it came from Saint Francisca, or from the pirate." Tori's face was thoughtful, her eyes on the picture that I had been looking at of the open grave. "Seems like I would be uncomfortable having something that had been taken from a dead man."

"Well, whoever is after it now doesn't seem to care either," Drew said, looking with open distaste at the cross.

Thomas scooped up the necklace and replaced it in the bag. "I'll keep the cross with me, but that doesn't seem like it's changing this guy's mind. He's coming back here, even if the cross isn't."

And the rest of our night seemed to spin around that idea. Whoever he was, whatever he was, he was there for the cross. Except that he wasn't. For whatever reason, he seemed to want to get to us, whether we were in the possession of the cross or not. He was proving a point. We had what he wanted, but he wasn't giving up.

We agreed that it was odd that our ability, and his, might have come with the cross but no longer seemed to rely on it. It didn't matter where the cross was located, we were still able to be in two places at once. And while that might have seemed to be a pretty useful talent, the implication that someone had the ability and an evil intent was terrifying. We would all happily give up our gift.

As it began to get dark, Travis decided to head home. He was plainly exhausted, his brain full of strange facts and stories. I walked him out onto the porch, suddenly feeling young and shy. The longer I knew him, the more attractive he appeared. His broad shoulders, thick hair with just a touch of curl, his gentle southern accent, were all becoming dear to me. I stood on the top step as he stepped to the one below me, our eyes now even.

"You need to take care of yourself," Travis said, his eyes conveying an even deeper meaning.

"I am," I said, leaning lightly against the railing on the porch.

"I'm not going to be traveling down that road tonight. So you just stay in your bed, okay?"

I nodded, my cheeks going pink.

He looked at me and flashed a smile. "See ya," he said, and stepped off the porch and out into the night.

Tori, Drew, Thea, Thomas, Liz, and I sat in the comfy living room at Tori's house to watch some movies. I nodded off at some point because when I became aware of my setting, Thomas and Thea had left. Tori walked me up to what I was now considering my room, and I dropped on the bed, still too awake after my extended nap. Monty had chosen my room again, pacing until he found the exact place that he wanted to lay, then pacing again as he tried to find the best position.

I pulled out my pajamas and put them on, fairly confident that I couldn't be going walking that night. After coming my hair and brushing my teeth, I brought a book to the little bed to read. I was getting ever so slightly sleepy when I heard a light knock on the door to my room.

"Yes?" My voice was soft.

"Savannah? Are you still awake?"

"Yeah," I responded and sat up straighter.

Tori carefully opened the door and slipped inside. She closed the door after her and tiptoed over to where I was sitting. "I saw someone outside," she whispered.

"Where?" I asked, my eyes going to the covered window.

"Out front. By the street. Savannah, I see someone glowing. And it's not Drew or Thomas. And here you are."

"So it has to be…"

"It must be him." She rubbed her hands up and down her arms as though she had a chill. "There's no one else who it could be," she said, her voice still pitched low.

"And how do you know it's not Drew?" I asked hopefully.

"I called him," Tori said. "And Thomas too as soon as I saw the light. I knew that you weren't likely to go wandering out in the dark."

"Do you still see him?" I asked, fear creeping into my voice.

"No. I mean, I kept looking, but I'm not seeing him." She looked toward the closed window as well. "But you know what this means. He's getting bold enough to travel without bilocation. That's really him out there."

"In a way that's good," I said quickly. "He can't blink in and out of places if he's here in the flesh."

"True," Tori said, "but it still makes me so nervous. Why is he here?"

"He wants to be seen, I guess."

"I'm going looking for him again," Tori said, now sounding almost angry.

"Wait!" I cried, getting to my feet.

"Wait for what?"

"I'm coming," I told her, and we slipped out of the door together.

Monty followed, and when we reached the bottom of the steps, stopped when Tori caught his collar. In the silence, the house seemed to settle comfortably around us. We hurried to the front window and peered out into the darkness.

The yard stretched out in a gentle roll of black. The road was a shiny ribbon curving off into the distance. A flutter of fall leaves caught my eye, and I watched the drift as it settled in the yard. Beyond the road was the rustic stone wall outlining the cemetery property. At the far side, I could see Thea's house, the golden stone a lighter shade than the background. The chapel itself was lit, warm, pretty in the picturesque was that older buildings have when settled.

But no glowing man. At least, that Tori reported. I wouldn't see the glowing, but I was pretty sure I might see movement. There was nothing out of place that we could see, so we rushed to the next window. But even after peering through every window on the first floor, we saw nothing amiss. Whoever had been there was either in hiding, or had left.

"Damn," Tori said frustrated.

"We should have known that he wouldn't show up again. He did what he wanted to do. He's gotten us up and alarmed. Now that we're freaked out, he doesn't need to be around."

"Unless he wants to watch," Tori replied, her voice low and troubled.

"We'll close the curtains and show him that we don't care to watch him anymore. Then we can play a card game or something, so we don't think about him either." I was trying to sound confident.

Tori stood with her hands on her hips, her hair in a wild disarray around her shoulders. She looked ready for a fight. "Okay, fine, it that's how he wants to play this," she exclaimed, and started closing the curtains.

When the sun peeked through the window, I turned over to get a few minutes of sleep. I hadn't slept at all for the night, waiting with Tori in case that person, that man, might try to break in again. When the edging around the window had gone from a deep navy blue to pearly gray, I had stood and walked up the stairs, head feeling heavy and off balance. Tori had fallen into a doze on the couch, a hand of cards still in her fist, wild tangles of hair falling against one cheek.

When I woke again, the sun was fully up, and I was starving. The house had a silence that felt empty, and I went downstairs to see a note on the kitchen table. Tori had gone to work. Drew would be checking in on me later. Thomas and Thea were going into downtown Louisville to do a little more research. Monty was on watch, and although they were sure that I would be fine, he was my security for now. That left me some time to myself. I went back upstairs and slipped into a pair of jeans and a loose sweatshirt. I ran a brush through my hair but left it down, glancing in the mirror. I was looking better. My hair was smooth and glossy. My eyes were clear despite the lack of sleep the night before. I knew that I was doing better as well. I had gained a few much needed pounds, and better yet, I was able to smile more easily. It was a strange feeling, coming out of mourning even with all of the mysteries swirling around and unsolved.

I grabbed my cell phone and the book I had been reading and jogged down the stairs. With Monty on my heels, I went rummaging through the cabinets, and found, to my delight, some of the left over pastries from the day before that Tori had brought from the diner. In one of the upper cabinets I found coffee and filters. I used the coffee pot to make plenty of the brew and pulled out the cream and sugar. After I had warmed up the sweet roll and fixed my coffee, I sat at the table in the gentle light of late morning.

I spent a contented morning reading. I found the Oldham Era, the local paper, filled with stories of the local schools, the social events, church notices, and some personal pieces about longtime residents from the area. After I had finished my breakfast and washed my dishes, I took Monty outside on his leash. It was chilly, even in the autumn sunlight. I was surprised when I saw the truck come around the curve and then pull into the driveway. I hadn't heard from anyone, but had thought I might see Drew later, not Travis. But Travis climbed out of the cab and waved at me. Monty seemed to remember him, or perhaps he habitually greeted everyone with the feel of a long lost relative because he launched himself from my side and hit Travis with two paws against his chest, his big nose right in Travis's throat. I could hear Travis grunt in surprise and then laugh at the goofy face the dog made. He gently pushed him down, but pet Monty's curly head in a sign of affection.

"Hey," Travis said to me as he approached. "I didn't know how long you were going to be in town, so I thought I would come by early."

"I'm leaving this evening. It was an unexpected trip anyway." I really didn't have any plans for once I went home, I needed to do some schoolwork, true, but it seemed rather minor compared to the other supernatural events that were happening in my life.

"I wondered." He walked with me to the porch. "So that's the cemetery?"

"Yes," I replied, looking across the road to the land enclosed by the stone wall. "Haven't you been here before?"

"I might have when I was smaller, but I don't recall. I had other places that I liked to hang around." He was smiling a little wryly.

"True," I said. "Do you want to walk over there?"

He took a moment to consider. "Sure. I'm kind of curious to see it all now," he said. In all of our research, we had reviewed the stories of the cemetery, its history and the map of the land. We had also found the articles describing the building of the Chapel and the people that were buried there. And among Tori's things, she had kept the article from the paper describing the discovery of the poor missing boy in the well that they had found last summer. It too was now a part of the lore of Duncan Memorial.

"Let me put Monty inside. I don't want him doing anything rude while we're over there." I ran inside and put Monty in the bathroom where he usually stayed during the workday. When I came back out onto the porch, Travis was standing by the road looking down the pavement. He looked good. His jeans were neat, his collared shirt fit his wide shoulders well, and his brown hair was touched with golden highlights. The wind had stirred up some curls, making him look younger.

When he heard the door close, he turned to look at me and smiled again. "Sure is a nice day," he said conversationally as we crossed the road to the sidewalk by the stone wall.

"It is," I agreed. "But I didn't get any sleep last night." I filled him in on our visitor from the night before. It was a strange tale, but stranger yet that he could listen to it and not doubt me.

"Tori was sure that it was him?"

"She said she had talked to Drew and Thomas. Neither were out. That's why she went looking for me. And as far as I know, we're the only people, besides him, that would be glowing." I shook my head. "I can't believe I'm actually talking about something like this seriously!" I walked through the open gates with Travis by my side, suddenly glad for his large presence. The grounds of the cemetery were still mounded with fallen leaves, heaps of them gathered at the foot of grand tombstones and tucked into crevices between the ground and the wall. Some flower beds had been freshly turned, waiting for winter to pass. To one side was the chapel, a peaked roof with a cross signaling to every one of its religious affiliations. Tori had told me that it was a nondenominational chapel, used by all religions for weddings, funerals, and other celebrations. A black drive looped around and within the property, cutting up the lawn in so many uneven plots with clusters of stones and monuments within. On the left hand, sheltered by the surrounding wall, was the well. It was made of the same stone as the wall, with a quaint roof and a few stone benches placed strategically around it. We walked that direction first, the leaves stirring at our footfalls. The trees above us were bare, and I could see that some of the leaves were starting their deterioration, their veins standing out like lattice.

"So this is where Tori said that she and Anna heard something."

"Not heard," I corrected. "They felt like someone was here, and then Anna's phone was moved from where she dropped it to the side of the well. Or actually, they were never sure how the phone had disappeared. They just knew that it wasn't in Anna's pocket any longer. And then it was gone. That doesn't sound like any ghost to me. That sounds like someone was trying to warn them away."

"Scare them, at least," Travis agreed.

"And Drew and Tori ran into something here as well. She really described it as a ghost, but now I wonder."

"Wonder what?"

"Well," I began, and turned toward him a little as I walked. "Say this guy is better than Drew. He can project himself easily. Who's to say that he couldn't choose how much to project himself? I mean, when Thea saw Thomas, and when you saw me, we seemed like we were totally there. Just normal people although in weird places." I paused, my brain trying to catch up. "What if he can partly project himself? What if he was sort of there when they came out by the well? He might have suspected something strange about the well, maybe he knew that the cross might be there, and decided to warn them away. So when they came out here, he took advantage of that and tried to scare them. He made himself a living ghost!"

"Do you really think that someone can do that?" Travis looked really worried.

"I don't know, but it would explain what Tori says she has seen and felt. I'd rather think that one person is behind all of it than think that we're dealing with a crazy man and a couple of ghosts."

Travis nodded. "True."

We stopped at the side of the well and looked into the top. A brand new grating had been fastened across the top of the opening, and I explained that it was a more recent addition. "After the boy was found, they debated about whether it should be filled in completely or covered over. In the end, they just made sure that the cover was virtually impenetrable." I put one hand over the grate, feeling the metal vibrate under my palm. But I felt nothing else. No strange feelings, no creepy sensation of being watched. It was just an old place with lots of history and many memories, both good and bad.

Travis had stepped up close beside me and put his hand out on the top as well. In the silence, I wondered if he was thinking or praying.

"I'm glad you came by," I said softly not looking at him but at our hands resting on the top of the well.

"I had to," he said softly. I felt his hand on my shoulder and looked up into his face, his eyes so clear and true. He leaned forward, his face just inches from mine. "Would this be the wrong place to kiss you?" he asked.

I shook my head mutely. This was a place of weddings and celebrations, of baptisms and funerals, the beginning of life and the end. And that's how the kiss felt. Like the soft beginning of something very precious, very important, and the end of my edgy loneliness. His hand tightened on my shoulder and I turned into him, falling against his chest, his arms circling me, and our kiss deepened. When we pulled apart, I rested my forehead against him, hearing the heavy beat of his heart and the sharp pulse of my blood. I knew that I had been waiting for this, and maybe waiting for my whole life for this, for him.

"We're going to cause a scandal with the neighbors," he said, humor in his voice.

"Kiss me one more time, and I'll enjoy the scandal," I replied, and he did.

We went to Tori's house, but I was reluctant to let him go, and I didn't think he wanted to leave.

"Do you have to go to work?" I asked from my place on the porch steps.

"I'm leaving it to some of my people," he said. "We have a great team."

I smiled to myself. I was going to enjoy this day, this moment. Love,

I thought to myself. So this was what it felt like to fall in love. I hadn't seen it coming, I hadn't felt the fall, but now here I was. I leaned back against him where he sat on the step above me.

"So what are you doing this afternoon?"

I thought about that. What to do? My investigations were stalled out. My lessons had stopped. I had nothing to do.

"What do you want to do?" I asked, throwing caution to the wind. I would follow my heart and gobble up what joy that I could.

"How about a date?"

"You're on," I said. "Give me a minute to get ready, and we can go out."

"Where do you want to go?"

"You know, I really don't care."

Our afternoon was blissful and silly. A comedy movie, a thick cheeseburger on a homemade bun, a little shopping at a few stores. I texted Tori periodically, letting her know who I was with so she wouldn't worry. I knew she would get in touch with Thomas. We ended our day with a second walk in the cemetery where we stole another kiss at the side of the chapel. Travis closed his arms around me and laid his cheek against my hair.

"The girl of my dreams," he said, a laugh in his voice.

"Um, literally," I agreed, and smiled.

On Sunday morning I headed home. I didn't want to leave Crestwood, not now with my heart so full and my head so empty, but my parents waited. Travis came to see me off. But, of course, so did everyone else. We had coffee at Tori's house, the whole group of us. Thomas and Thea would be returning to Lexington, and I would be going home. We would be stalled for a while longer.

Travis sat close to me, and I was amused by the lifted eyebrows on Thomas' normally blank demeanor as we sat opposite from him. No one commented. And for that I was glad. We finished our breakfast and went our separate ways. Travis helped me take my bag out to the car, even though I didn't need help. Tori and Liz told me goodbye as I headed through the living room, and Travis met me outside.

"You have gas in the car?" he asked.

"Yes," I replied, trying not to sound amused.

"And it's in good repair?"

"Yes. And now you're starting to sound like my dad. Who, by the way, had my car tuned up last week even though I'm old enough to get it done myself."

"Okay, I'm just checking," he said, the picture of patience. "Will you call me when you get home?" Now his voice had deepened and lowered, losing some of the matter of fact tone.

"I can," I replied. "I think I have your number."

"I know you do, and I would like to hear from you."

I couldn't help but grin, and he blinked. "I'll call!"

"You're beautiful," he said, still looking a little stunned.

"Well thanks," I replied, feeling the heat in my cheeks.

"No, I mean, you're really beautiful. Hasn't anyone told you that before?"

"I'm nothing but average," I said, "and I think you must be a little biased."

"I am biased," he said, coming closer to me, "but you are not average."

When he kissed me, I thought that I could hear the breath of wind in the trees, the flutter of birds, the heartbeat of the world. It was all so right, so blissful and fine. When we stepped apart, I said, "I don't really care if I'm average. Being with you is special enough, and I don't want to be different in any other way."

He gently tucked a strand of my hair behind my ear and looked at me carefully. "Being special isn't so bad. It's just the type of special that matters. And you're the best type."

I threw myself into his arms and gave him a quick hard hug. Then I stepped away and climbed in the car. I needed to leave now before I said something utterly foolish, or proclaimed my love for him on the spot. Because that was truly what I felt. I loved him, and I knew it in every breath that I took.

He bent over the open car door and looked at me. "Buckle up and be safe," he said.

"I will," I returned as I shoved the key in the ignition and started the engine. I pulled on the belt while he watched and he smiled at me. Then he closed the door and stepped back. I sketched a wave through the windshield, even though I couldn't see him clearly.

The street was clear in both directions so I pulled out, glancing once at the cemetery to my right side as I drove toward the main road. If someone had told me just two days before that I would be looking so fondly at that cemetery, I would have said they were dead wrong. Before this, it had seemed as much part of my nightmare as my brother's death. But now it was different. It was just a place. And I had found both extreme grief there and extreme happiness.

My drive was not long and I listened to the radio and sang along as I drove. I strongly suspected that when I got home my mother would detect a change in me immediately. She had always been pretty perceptive, but now that she was starting to come out from under the cloud that we had been living in, drowning in, she would probably notice my change in attitude. But that was probably good as well. That was a normal concern for a mother, to watch her child fall in love. And normal was good for us.

Chapter 14

The call came in the middle of the day. The December chill had finally set in and a dusting of snow frosted the front lawn, the trees and bushes, and made the pavement glisten like a scatter of black diamonds. Snow like that was beautiful. My mother had returned to work part time, now feeling surer that I was getting back on my feet, returning to the world of the living. The house felt empty, but not in a bad way. I had gotten a lot done in the morning. I had completed a paper for school and done some math work that I had been putting off. I had to watch demonstrations for the on-line math instruction, but had finally gotten a better understanding of the steps in the problem.

To treat myself for my good behavior, I made a cup of hot chocolate with extra marshmallows and curled up on the couch. Daisy wasn't allowed on the couch, but she didn't accept that well, so I spread out a blanket to mask her shedding and let her climb up next to me, resting her head on my knee. She would roll her eyes up to look at me in that warm worshipful way that dogs have, and I pet her silky ears.

I was growing a little sleepy when my cell phone rang, but I came immediately awake.

"Hello?" Daisy lifted her head from my lap and looked up at me as I spoke.

"Savannah? This is Professor Morrison."

My mind scrambled. I knew who it was, but the sound of his high voice was startling.

"Yes, um, hi," I said, clearing my throat and pulling myself into a more upright position. It made me feel like I had been caught sleeping in class.

"I felt like I needed to contact you," he said softly. "I have recovered one of the books that was stolen from me, and I believe I found a note in it that might have been written by your brother. He is the only other person who has had access to the book besides myself."

"Really?" I asked, feeling a tinge of excitement. "What did the note say?"

"It's an entire page of text and some drawing as well. It would be difficult for me to explain over the phone. I think it would be best if you were able to see the note and the book together."

"Oh, well okay." I was trying to get my brain on track.

"But my time is limited, I'm afraid. I plan to go on sabbatical from the university next week, so this will be my final day at my office. We are packing my belongings in preparation for the move. If you want to see the book, you would want to come immediately."

I hesitated. There was no one in town that I would trust to go with me to see the professor. And it would take anyone else at least an hour to get to me, and another hour before we were able to get to the university to see the professor. Since I would probably not be able to take the book, I would want to try to make as many copies of pages as I could. "How long do you plan to be in your office?" I asked.

"I can wait for you to come, if you are able to come today. If you are not, well, I can inform you of my arrival after my sabbatical. I should be back to the city in 18 months or so."

My heart sped up. I couldn't wait for 18 months! There were too many things that I didn't know, and I was sure that if he left, I wasn't likely to find out what notes Daniel had left for us. The thought lingered in my mind. There was that chance, a real chance, that Daniel had known something that we didn't. He had been one step ahead of us the whole way. So it would be safe to assume that he would have left something behind to help us. And we hadn't found the answer just yet. At least it didn't feel like we had. So the answer might be in that book.

"No," I said quickly. "I can just hurry out there to meet you. I can leave now. I just need to call my other brother."

"Of course. Yes, call your brother and let him know your plans."

"Great! So I should come to your office?"

"I'll be here at the university for a few more hours."

"Alright," I checked my watch. It was just a few minutes past 2. From our last trip, I knew that it would take me forty five minutes to an hour and a half to two hours to get there, depending on the traffic and construction. "I'll be there by 4. Is that all right with you?"

"Certainly," he said cordially. "I will be here."

As soon as I disconnected the call, I texted my brother and Travis. Strange that those were the first two names that I thought of. I rushed around, throwing a sweater over my tee shirt, and switching my ratty jeans for a pair that looked more presentable. I was thinking of pulling on the tennis shoes left by the door, but decided on a pair of boots instead. I stopped for a moment, checking in the mirror to make sure I wasn't looking too slovenly. The professor struck me as something of a stickler for tradition. I suspected he would notice if I was a mess and might read into it too much of the truth.

I stopped at the kitchen table, searching for a pad of paper that I knew my mother usually had sitting out. I growled in frustration until I found the paper, and then had to search around again for a pen. Finally I was able to scribble out a note for my mother. But what to say? What reason did I have for going to the university again?

"I hate this," I mumbled as I quickly wrote out the lie. "Going shopping." It was vague. It would have to do. I had my phone, and I could always check in with my mother later. "Sorry, mom," I said softly and dropped the note on the table, anchoring it with a salt shaker.

I was on the road five minutes later, my purse on the seat next to me, the directions to the university programmed into my phone in case I got mixed up. I had plenty of gas, the cold had brought frost but no snow, and the sky was now blazing blue.

I arrived just on time. Traffic had gotten thicker as I drew closer to the campus, but I was able to find a parking space for visitors after only ten minutes of searching. I switched off the car and checked my phone. I had seen no responses from her texts. Nothing from Travis, nothing from Thomas. I frowned and gave up and called Tori.

"Hello," Tori said, her voice hurried.

"Hey, it's Savannah," I said. "Sorry for bothering you during work, but I can't get an answers from Thomas or Travis and I wanted to let you all know that I was going back to University of Ohio to visit Professor Morrison."

"What?" Tori seemed distracted, "Where are you going?"

"Professor Morrison called. He said that he found one of the books that Daniel had been looking at. He said that there was a paper in it with notes. And I need to go out there so I can look at it."

"Savannah, I think you should wait for someone to go with you." Tori sounded alert now.

"I can't," I argued. "He said he's going out of town on sabbatical. He won't be back for over a year. I need to go now if I want to see any of it. And we need to see what Daniel had been researching."

"Surely he could wait one more day," Tori said. "Hang on, let me pull over so I can talk."

I waited in silence for a few minutes before I heard Tori come back on line. "Look, I'm already here. I'm at the University and parked. I'm going to run in and look at the book. I'm going to see if I can get a few copies, and then I'll bring it home and call you all."

"Savannah, I don't like this. We know that there is someone out there who doesn't want us involved. Do you think going in by yourself is a good idea?"

"He said now, or we have to wait for over a year. This is something that I have to do right now." I glanced up for a second. "Besides, this guy seems really harmless. I think he felt bad about what happened to Daniel. This is his way of showing that."

"Okay, but I'm calling Drew."

"Sure, call Drew. Call anyone. They won't be able to make it here, but maybe we can make plans to meet."

"And you'll call as soon as you're done there."

"Absolutely," I said quickly. "I'll call. And thanks."

"Thanks for what? I didn't do anything to help."

"Thanks for listening. And being my friend," I said quickly.

"Oh," Tori's voice was a little faint.

"I'll call you in a little bit." I disconnected the phone and looked at the handset. It was very true. I did feel like I had some new friends now. It was a nice feeling.

I sighed and tucked the phone in my pocket. I slipped out of the car and shut the door behind me. I held the keys in my hand for a moment and then slipped them in my purse. The building looked a little abandoned this late in the afternoon. I wondered if they had classes this late, or if there were only a few teachers and staff wandering the halls. The front door to the classroom building was unlocked, however, and I strolled in as though I belonged there.

His office was lit from within; I could see that through the frosted pane of glass on the door. I knocked once, but since I knew he was expecting me, went ahead and opened the door.

The room was shockingly bare. The full bookshelves that had dominated the room were empty but for a few loose papers shoved in a stack on one of the shelves. The old desk, rather beaten and shabby, no doubt a University provided piece, was completely cleared off, the only remaining piece a cheap curved lamp that illuminated the bare surface of the desk top. Neither of the two chairs that Travis and I had occupied still sat on the opposite side of the desk. There was only an office chair pushed up behind the desk, but no other furniture or bit of decoration.

Professor Morrison was standing at the window looking out on the cold landscape. He looked like a professor. His jacket was a tweed in a mustard color and his pants were an unfortunate shade of brown. I doubted he was married. He didn't have the air of a man who had someone at home doing his laundry and commenting on his wardrobe.

"Savannah," he greeted me, and came toward the doorway. "Come in! You just made it in time."

"Oh," I stepped inside, and he slipped around behind me to close the door, "good. I was afraid that I might not. But the traffic wasn't too bad." My eyes scanned the room looking for the book and the papers. I had come here for one thing, and I was anxious to be done with it. I didn't like traveling alone. I glanced around, looking for evidence of the books or papers that he wanted to show me. "Your office looks so different. Are you all packed up then?" I was asking the obvious, but the silence felt heavy.

"Yes, as I said on the phone, I plan to leave and not be back for quite a while."

I was standing at the opposite side of the desk, and he had retreated to the office chair but hadn't sat down.

"Then it's a good thing that I was able to come by." I tried to keep my voice light, but I was feeling a twinge of discomfort.

"It was," he agreed, and stepped around the desk, skirting the wall of book cases. I wondered if the papers were in the desk.

"Have a seat. Just here," to my surprise, he took my elbow and guided me around to the other side of the desk, seating me in the office chair facing the blank surface. "I'm sorry I haven't got any other places to sit. I'll just be a moment." I sat with my purse in my lap, feeling strange and awkward, very out of place.

He was behind me, closer to the book cases, and I glanced back. I suspected he was getting the book for me to see, but from where, I couldn't say. I realized then that the bulk of the desk had blocked my view of a box on one of the lower shelves. Now the Professor's body blocked my view of what was in the box.

"We unfortunately have a change of plans," he said, his voice still smooth, a little high and now a little strange.

"What do you mean?" I turned more fully as I asked.

He was just behind me, and in his hand was a gun. It had a very surreal feel to it, staring at the metal like that. I had only seen a real gun a few times in my life. And I had certainly never handled one. I couldn't speak. My mouth was dry and a strange prickling of terror spread over my scalp making me feel both sick and hyper aware of my situation.

"We are going on a little trip. Just the two of us. And you will make no comments. You will not speak. You will walk with me to your car. You will unlock your car and get in. Then you will drive wherever I say." He bent until his face was closer to mine, and I could see the dark emptiness in his eyes. "Or I will shoot you in the abdomen. It is a survivable wound, very painful, and would eventually kill you if not tended to." He stood, his back straight, morphing into the professor again. "To relieve you from the irrepressible curiosity that you and your little group of friends seem to have, I will tell you this. We are going to my house. You will be my guest, albeit unwilling, until your brother brings me the cross. Then I will let you return to your family, and I will leave the country with the cross. You and the rest will never, and I must repeat, never, speak of this again. Is all of that clear?"

"But," the pain was like a slice to my face before I realized the he had struck me. The gun was not large, but it was heavy, and I supposed I was fortunate that he hadn't hit me any harder. It no doubt would be easy to break a bone with the weapon and never fire it. As it was, my eyes were filled with painful tears and my jaw throbbed where he had struck me.

"You seem to have already forgotten one of my rules. I said, no talking until I allow you to talk. Is that clear?"

I nodded slightly, fearing the pain again, feeling the impact still as it raced up the side of my face and flooded hot and sharp in my temple.

"Now we stand." He stepped back from the chair and pulled it away from the desk on its wheels. I carefully stood, using my hand to keep my balance. My other hand was still clenched on my purse, holding it by the loose fabric. I wasn't sure that I could have ever outrun him in the unfamiliar building, but with the injury, my reflexes felt dull. I wondered what my face looked like. If someone were to see me in the hall, would they see the mark? Would they be alarmed by my appearance? I wasn't bleeding, but I could feel a steady swelling and heat.

"After you," he said, and swung the door open.

I want out the door and heard him close it behind him, painfully aware of his hand clasped tightly on my arm, holding me close to his side. Just as before, the corridors were empty. No sounds could be heard from the upper floors as well, and I felt another surge of fear. No one here. No one to see me taken.

Outside, the sunlight that had greeted me in the morning was starting to wane. There were mounds of clouds on the horizon, and I knew it would be a beautiful sunset. That was when it occurred to me that I was just assuming it would be one of many beautiful sunsets. It would not be my last sunset, or my most beautiful. It would be a sunset to remember, however.

I walked woodenly down the steps and headed for my car. My eyes were constantly roving over the landscape of buildings and parking lots, alleys and sidewalks. Where were the people? There were a few, walking away, too many yards of pavement between us for them to be of any help. And their backs were to us, their heads bent. I knew I couldn't call. The barrel of the gun was planted firmly in my side, so tightly that I had the image of an imprint left in my flesh.

"Now, here are your keys," he said, pulling them out of his jacket pocket.

I was just staring at him in surprise. I hadn't seen him take them out of my purse, or even touch my purse. But now they were in his hand and there was no denying which car was mine or that I hadn't driven. The key was plainly marked with the make of the car, and I had conveniently parked just in front of the door.

He handed the key to me and said gently, "Just unlock the car. Here on the passenger side. Then you can slide over to the driver's side." I could see his logic. He wouldn't want to let me out of his sight while he had to go to the other side of the car to get in. He would rather have the gun trained on me at all time.

My hand was shaking so severely that I couldn't get the key in the lock. My trembling grip sent the tip of the key skidding onto the paint, scarring the door with scratches that would be hard to buff out. I was surprised at the track that my brain was taking. That I would be concerned about scratches in the paint was strange, but my brain still felt foggy. The pain in my jaw was keeping up a steady beat, in rhythm with my heart, which had gone from racing to just a speedy pounding. At last, the key slid home and I turned it, feeling the lock give. I pulled the key free and slowly opened the door. The interior was still warm from the prolonged drive there. I sat on the leather like seats and slowly slid over toward the driver's seat, well aware of the gun trained on my side. My mind was furiously reviewing the items in my car. I had papers and pens and pencils, tissues and gum, a forgotten plastic bag from the card shop and an empty cup from the gas station.

"A little faster, if you please," the professor said, voice low.

I finished shifting across the seat and stayed very still as he slid in next to me, his gun trained on me. It occurred to me that he seemed pretty comfortable with the firearm. He knew how to shoot.

"And lets start the engine," he said.

I obeyed, feeling the car leap to life. I followed his directions then, backing away from the building, turning out of the lot, and heading onto the city streets that I had left so recently. I almost jumped when I felt my phone buzz in my pocket. The cheerful chime let me know that someone had texted me.

Thomas? Travis? My mind went to Thomas and in a sudden flood of thought, I wondered if the end of all the mysteries was sitting just beside me. Could this man be him? The man that had terrorized Tori had broken into her house, had lingered in the cemetery looking for the cross, searching for the answer? It seemed to be an obvious conclusion.

"What was that noise?" His voice was curious, unconcerned.

I looked at him mutely.

"You can speak this time."

"It was a text." My voice sounded odd, strained. It hurt tremendously to move my mouth, my jaw, and I winced.

"Your brother?" he asked hopefully.

"I don't know," I said slowly. "It could be. Or it might be Travis. I told them both that I was coming."

"Fine, fine. I planned on that," he said contentedly. "You will turn at the next right."

I had been driving slowly, trying to consciously make note of street signs and landmarks. I didn't know the area, and my sense of direction was not the best on a good day. But I tried to keep a running list in my head. The traffic was sparse but there were a few pedestrians and random cars and trucks passing in a blur. I wished that I could feel safe enough to draw attention to us, but I didn't. I knew that this man was in his own way crazy, and I didn't know how far that I could push him. If he suspected that I was trying something, he would shoot. I felt sure of that. And I knew that we weren't going fast enough that he would feel that the danger outweighed the action.

I turned where he pointed, Mayfair Avenue, I recited to myself, and had only gone half a block when he told me to pull into a driveway. The house was a little ranch with blank dark windows. There were no numbers on the door or mailbox, and I didn't have the concentration to figure out where on the block we were. I felt sick to my stomach. My brother and Travis knew where I was meeting the Professor. They knew where we had started, but they would have no idea where we were now. And even if they did, he had a gun. This wasn't an action movie where the characters had miraculously gained the ability to wield weapons. Thomas had never touched a gun to my knowledge. And Travis? He might have at some point, but I honestly didn't know and would never ask him to risk his life to come to find me.

So I would just have to trust the professor at his word. Would he really set me free if he had the cross? And if he took the relic, what would he do with it? My mind was full of questions as I put the car in park and looked over to my captor.

"Turn off the engine and give me the keys. No fast moves, no words."

I pulled the key from the ignition and looked at him. He was watching me closely, and it was starting to make me ill. His expression was still the same, so cool, so little feeling. He took the keys, and they disappeared back in his jacket pocket.

"Time for us to get out." He looked at me. "We're going to do just as we did earlier. You will follow me out. Bring your purse. And trust me, at this close range, if I shot, I wouldn't miss some part of you." I shivered as he slid out and then I followed him obediently. As soon as I was out of the car, he pulled me close again, and we went up the little sidewalk to the house. The air felt heavy and damp. When the clouds finally caught up with us, there would be rain. A cold rain, a chilling rain, a cruel rain.

We paused just a moment in the doorway of the house. It seemed that being a university professor did not pay particularly well. Either that, or Professor Morrison was wasting his money on something other than his home. The front room was sparsely furnished with a couch in a very similar upholstery as the fabric of his jacket, and two very stiff chairs. The carpet was a matted shag, the walls painted stark white. The air smelled of old man, stale and smoky.

"Go on," he said sharply, and pushed me inside. He pulled the door closed behind us and immediately started moving down a front hall. I had the briefest glance of a kitchen with tired linoleum floors and pea green cabinets before he opened another door and flipped on the switch to the right of the door.

It was a basement. The wooden steps led down into the dark, but the bare bulb above me lit the stairs well enough for me to navigate. My legs felt weak. The movement was making my face throb again. I held tightly to the railing with one hand, but I had my purse in my other hand. At the bottom, I could see that the room spread out on both sides, but my eyes weren't used to the darkness, so I couldn't see far. He was close at my back, and nudged me forward a little. I felt a deep dread. All the horrifying movies with dead bodies hung from meat hooks, all the dissected bodies with agonized expressions on the television series that I used to watch, all the horror of entertainment made my flesh crawl and I almost cried out. His hand went out again, and he flipped a switch. The rest of the basement lit up. And it was open and empty. The room stretched in one big expanse under the house, poles stretching from well swept concrete floor to rafters punctuating the space. A cluster of utilities were set against the far wall. Furnace, water heater, and assorted pipes, but even these looked clean.

"Now, I'll take your purse for you. I don't think you'll need it down here." I silently handed over the large bag, unsurprised that he would think to take it. "And your cell phone," he said.

My heart plummeted. I had hoped that he would have forgotten the phone in my pocket. With the device, I could have sent out word to the police as well as my family. Slowly I pulled out the phone and held it out. He took it without his fingers touching mine and quickly tucked it in his jacket pocket. He looked at me assessing.

"One last thing," he said, and moved lightning quick. The blow caught me completely off guard, and this time I did fall down, my hip and hands hitting the concrete floor hard. I must have blacked out because I didn't see him leave the room.

When I woke, I didn't know if it had been an hour or a few minutes. The pain in my face was extreme, and I suspected that he had broken something this time. My teeth felt loose to my probing tongue, and my mouth tasted of blood.

I sat up slowly. The room seemed to shift beneath me, and I laid back for a moment until it seemed to steady. When I sat up again, I cautiously looked around.

He had turned off the light. But there was still illumination, enough for me to see my immediate surroundings. There was a window. It was one of those small single paned basement windows high up on the wall, large enough to fit my body through. But when I studied it more closely, I realized that it was painted closed. Had I a weapon, I would have been able to break the glass and crawl through. But the room was empty. I could hear the footsteps creaking above, so I knew that he was still home. Was he planning his next move? Was he calling my brother? Setting up a time for the exchange?

When the door squealed, I flinched away from the stairs. I tried to hold myself up, trying to look like my face didn't hurt so much.

"Good," the professor's voice was very calm. "You're awake. I'm sorry that I had to do that, but I can't have you getting any ideas. For now, I am in charge. I am not a cruel man. I don't like hurting you, but I have to protect my interests. I need that cross, and for that, I need you."

"And after you have the cross?" My voice was hoarse, my speech slurred from the swelling. "You said that you would let me go."

His smile was pitying as he shook his head slowly. is smile was pitying as he shook his head slowly. "An unfortunate accident," he continued. "You have been mourning the death of your brother. You can't stand it any longer. So you will do something drastic to end your misery."

Bile slid up my throat and I swallowed hard. "But they know. My brother will know."

"They will know only that I was here, and now I am gone. There will be no proof that I have done anything. You see, the cross doesn't belong to you, and you have never actually shown it to anyone outside of your little group. I've been keeping a close eye on you. You're secrecy has been very helpful." He moved closer to me, and I saw that he held a water bottle. "Have a drink and a rest," he said. "I'll contact your brother soon enough."

When he placed it on the floor by the foot of the stairs, I shrank away from him. I wouldn't be drinking anything that he gave me. I was relieved when he went back up the stairs and closed the door. He had left the light on, but it only helped me see how impossible my situation was. There was no way out of the basement, at least not on my own. My head ached in a fearful way, and I wondered if I had a concussion. All I knew is that I had to get out of there before he was able to get his hands on the cross. If not, I was sure he would go through with his plan, and I would never make it through alive.

I honestly was surprised at how calm I was. It was as though I was standing outside myself, logically analyzing the situation. The unreality of the situation was like a cushion to my fragile nerves. I tried to shift my weight so that I would be more comfortable.

I needed to figure out a way to communicate. When I tiptoed, I could see the brick of the house next door. The glass was surprisingly thick and strong for its age, and I wondered if he had had it replaced. Perhaps it wasn't as old as I thought. And outside, the color of the sunset had drained to the gray of evening, and a light splatter of rain had begun to decorate the glass.

But there was no one to hear me cry, no one to see me wave, no one to come to my rescue. I spent valuable minutes following the walls, looking for any weakness, anywhere that I might be able to escape. But the windows, three of them, had been painted shut and a nail driven into the base for good measure. The door was locked; I tried that as well, twisting the knob but knowing that he wouldn't have left something so obvious for a means of egress.

I sat on the cold concrete, laying down once to let the cold press against my swelling face. I didn't know how hurt I was, but I knew that the steady pain was fogging my brain, slowing me down. After a few minutes I sat up. No phone, no way to escape, no way to tell anyone where I was. If only I could let them know. I feared not only for my life but for theirs. If Thomas did come to trade me for the cross, how did I know that Professor Morrison would let him leave? It seemed more likely that he would be willing to take out any witnesses.

I needed to talk to someone. Travis's face swam in my mind. If I could just talk to him. Just once more. I pictured our meetings in his truck, feeling the warmth flowing from the vents, the relief of not being alone.

Then it struck me. I hadn't actually been there on most of our meetings. With bilocation, I had been able to see him while still remaining in my room at home, existing in two places at once, my gift and my curse. But could I do it deliberately? I had tried with Drew. I had tried the training, settling my mind so that I could force myself into that state. And I had failed tremendously each time. What were the chances that at this point, when it was a matter of my life at stake, that I could actually control the power? But I had to try. For myself and my brother, and Daniel too, I had to get out of here and stop this man.

I laid down on the concrete again. I couldn't concentrate. I couldn't empty my mind, and when I tried to concentrate on my breathing, I found myself panting. This wasn't going to work. I closed my mind and prayed. I found myself seeing my brother's face, Daniel, concentrating on the depth of his eyes, the knowledge and the spirit. What was left of my brother.

And I felt a fat cold drop of water strike my face. When I opened my eyes I was in the woods at the side of the road.

Chapter 15

I stood, my head still heavy, pain still tripping up and down the side of my face like tiny shockwaves. I was dressed in the clothes that I had worn in the basement, proof that I wasn't always in my pajamas when I went wondering. I took a deep breath and put my hand on the side of the tree next to me, getting my balance. It was seriously raining, hard chilled droplets that traced a wet path down the back of my shirt and snaking through my hair. I realized that it had finally turned completely dark, but I had no idea what time it was. It had been evening when I had gotten to the house, but I had been hit twice and wasn't sure how long I had been out on the second occasion.

I realized that there had to be a reason I had shown up here. With that thought, I forced myself away from the tree and closer to the road side. As if called on by magic, head lights began to swell in the distance, high off the ground, and the subtle roar of a truck broke through the pelting of the rain. I stepped out on the dark pavement, waving my arms and crying out, even though I was sure he couldn't hear me.

Travis seemed to see me at a distance because he had significantly slowed by the time he had gotten to me. He quickly steered off the road and popped his door open as he put the truck in park.

"Savannah?"

I limped toward him and then threw myself in his arms as soon as he was close enough. The press of his coat against my swollen face made it sing with pain, but I still held him tightly.

"What the hell are you doing out here?!" He pulled away, and then became speechless as he looked at my face.

"I can't explain," I said, holding his arm for balance. "I don't know how much time I have, so you have to listen!" My words sounded garbled, and I realized the swelling was getting more severe. Not fair. Why was it that even my injuries had carried over?

"Get in the truck," he said quickly, guiding me toward the vehicle.

I let him hoist me up into the seat, and he climbed in next to me, the engine still running.

"We're going to the hospital," he said, his voice close to frantic.

"No!" I leaned over and grabbed his shoulder. "Look at me!" When his face turned my way, I put my hand on his cheek. "I'm not here. I'm not really here. Professor Morrison has taken me from the university and locked me in the basement of his house."

"What?"

"This isn't me. Not all of me!" I felt a surge of desperation. "I have to tell you where I really am so that you can get help. So listen."

He went very still showing extreme control and concentration. His eyes focused on mine. I told him of the car ride, reaching the main road, the turn off. I tried to think of landmarks that I had seen. I told him about the house, the blank windows carved into the brick façade.

"I'm there now. But I think I'm sleeping. As soon as he comes back, I'll wake up, and I won't be with you anymore." I took a deep breath, "do you understand?"

"Yes, but…"

"There are no buts, there are no questions. I don't have time for that. You just have to find me!"

"Okay," he said his voice choked, and leaned over to kiss my cheek gently. "We're going now."

He quickly put the truck in gear and with a sharp turn, reversed back the way he had come.

Once on the wider road, the truck was moving so fast that I could barely get a breath past my tightened throat. The road slipped by like an oiled slit in the earth. I looked at Travis's taut jaw and tried not to see the desperation there.

"Get my phone," he said nodding to the center console between the truck seats. "We'll call Thomas to get more help. I don't know where he is, but he'll be able to meet us."

I pulled the phone from the pocket where he kept it and switched the device on. I dialed quickly.

"Put it on speaker phone and let me talk," Travis instructed. "He's going to get too confused if you speak."

I nodded even though he couldn't see me and listened to the phone ring on the other end of the line. When the message picked up, I moaned in frustration but held the phone up so that Travis could speak.

"Thomas, this is Travis. You have to call me back immediately. Savannah is with the Professor, he's taken her to his house, and she is in serious trouble!"

When he was silent for a moment, I hung up the phone and cradled it in my hand for a moment, praying that it was a mistake; that my brother was actually there and would see the message and call right then. But the phone was silent.

"Do you know anyone else's number? Travis asked. "Drew's or Thea's or Tori's?"

"No," I said frowning. "They're all programmed into my phone, and he's got that."

"Okay, then we call the cops," Travis said, his voice edgy.

"And tell them what?"

"I'll tell them that you called me. I'll say that some maniac has kidnapped you."

"Do you think they'll believe you?"

He glanced my way. "If we can get them to knock on the door, it would be enough to make him run."

"Or do something rash," I said fearfully.

He seemed to take this in, a dark frown on his face, the oncoming headlights flashing through the wet windshield against his features. I felt a bloom of panic in my chest. Was I going to find a way out of this? What would happen if Travis didn't make it in time? What were the Professor's plans for me?

"I'm going to call my mom," I said, turning the device back on.

"Why?" he asked.

"I want to talk to her, ok?"

He was silent for a moment as though digesting my words. "Savannah, look, we're going to get you."

I felt my heart break just a little. If they didn't? If the Professor was able to go through with his plan, to kill me, to get the cross, to leave my family thinking that I had chosen death! That I had taken my own life! That was inconceivable, unforgivable. No, I wanted that chance to talk to my mother, to hear her voice, and let her hear me.

"I need to call, Travis." I said, and dialed the number the tones sounding into the silence.

"Hello?" my mom didn't recognize the number.

"Mom? It's me, Savannah," I said.

"Where are you?" she asked curious. "When I got home, you had just left."

"I had to run an errand," I said. "I won't be long." I waited a second, trying to catch my breath. My speech still didn't sound normal; my tongue felt swollen in my mouth. "Do you know where Thomas is?"

"No," she said, still sounding curious but not alarmed. "Why do you ask?"

"I was just trying to call him, and he didn't answer," I said truthfully. "If you hear from him, can you have him call this number?"

"Okay," she replied. "When are you going to be home? I was going to make brownies tonight. I thought we could catch up on some of the shows we've missed."

I felt an ache deep in my heart and my hands shook slightly. I wanted to be there with her, curled on the couch, feeling the familiar warmth of home. "I'll be home in a while," I said. I caught my breath and rushed on, "And mom, you're the best! I love you and dad so much."

I heard her make a breathless chuckle. "All for brownies?" she asked.

"Sure," I said, talking through the lump in my throat. "You're brownies are really great."

"Well I love you too, sweetie," she said.

I felt a strange sensations somewhere in my stomach, a stretching, pulling sensation, singular and disturbing, and I knew that my time was limited. "Ok mom," I cleared my throat with difficulty, "well, I'll see you later," I said quickly and disconnected the call. I looked toward Travis, and his eyes looked suspiciously glassy. "I don't have long, I think," I said.

"Hold on," he said with urgency, glancing toward me and back to the road. "Just hang in there, Savannah."

"I will," I said. "Just drive, Travis!" I unbuckled by seatbelt, feeling the odd pull still. I leaned over and pressed my lips to his cheek. I inhaled deeply of his spicy scent and closed my eyes for just a second.

And when I awoke, I was on the concrete floor. The door had snapped open, and I watched as the Professor minced his way down the steps. In one hand he held the gun, trained in my direction, and in the other was another water bottle.

"I brought you a drink," he said, stopping at the foot of the staircase. He tossed the bottle in my direction, and I watched as it rolled and then settled next to me. The pain in my face had returned with a vengeance. And I honestly wasn't sure if he expected me to speak or not. I wasn't risking further beating if I could avoid it by keeping my mouth shut. "I have tried to contact your brother, but he isn't answering his cell phone. Ironic, isn't it? He can't be bothered to answer such an important call? But he will." He seemed to hesitate, but then he sank down on the second step, the gun still trained in my direction. "You know, I do remember your other brother. I remember Daniel very well. You see, I knew him very well."

"How?" my voice was choked.

"Didn't you know? He came to me. I had been scraping together the story of the Francesca cross for years. I had bought every book recorded, followed the leads to Spain, to the island where Juan Madino was buried. I visited his gravesite, you know. It was after the robbery." He stopped and looked thoughtfully at me. "It amazes me that your brother, with no work at all, stumbled upon the one link that had eluded me. He found the old traveler and knew about his trips, his studies, and his settlement in Kentucky." He glanced up at the ceiling as though seeing through the wood into the rooms upstairs. "I never found out how the thieves managed to get the cross into the market in Spain, but there is no doubt that is where the old man found it." His laugh was low and mean. "He didn't know! He bought it only knowing that it was old, a valuable piece for the gold and jewels. It wasn't until he started his own research that he realized what he had found." He stopped. "But you know what it did, don't you."

"Did Daniel?" I asked, avoiding his question. "Did Daniel know what it could do?"

"Your brother never admitted the truth," he said, a mocking tone lacing his voice. "I have to assume that he knew, because surely he was doing it as well. Bilocation? As good a term as any. I feel sure that your brother used his talent to get into my space, to make those copies, to take my possessions!"

"He didn't steal anything from you!" I protested.

"He took my chance. I had to follow him to Kentucky, to the graveyard. I followed the whole little group of you. No one saw me; no one suspected. And even then, he didn't know where the cross really was. But then it happened! We were all given a gift!" His voice had risen with excitement, his eyes gleaming with something not quite sane. "A little quake in the earth's core and a miracle was released! And we were all enabled! There we were, the five of us, blessed." He grew quiet and put his head back. The gun had gone slack in his hand, held to his side.

"So you went to ask him about the cross?"

He laughed, low with no humor. "I didn't need to. I had what I needed. It was just tying up loose ends by then. That's what the car accident was for. A finale to get the witnesses out of my hair."

"You were there," my voice went high and weak, and I had to stifle the impulse to stand.

"Of course. He saw me there in the middle of the road. I knew exactly where he would be. He had told everyone his plans to return to the cemetery. So all I had to do was wait."

"You caused the accident."

He nodded. Then he lifted the gun again so that it was trained on me. "I got rid of one big problem, but created several others. Your other brother, for example. But I needed to keep searching for the cross, not sitting at his bedside waiting for him to die. Because that's what should have happened. He should have died."

He shook his head regretfully. "I'm pretty sure that you would have given up without them," his voice was low, evil. "I need that cross. I needed to find it. That's when it occurred to me that it might never have left the old man's house."

"So you broke in Tori's house and tried to find it."

"Tried," he said, his voice tight. "But I was restricted in my movements. I had hopes that I could pursued them to move by other means."

"So the fire." I looked at him both afraid and too curious not to ask. "And the night that Tori's friend lost her cell phone and they found it later?"

"Was my experiment in trying my ability." He finished the thought for me. "But doing that partial bilocation is incredibly exhausting." He sat back. "As soon as I have the cross, I will be able to study the effects. I will have a powerful knowledge."

"What are you going to do with it?" I half expected him to say that he would hide it away like the old man.

"It will be my key to changing the world!" He looked at me and I suddenly saw the fanatic's gleam in his eye. This wasn't for money, or for the ability. He was, and always had been, an academic. This was knowledge, and for him, knowledge was power. The thought seemed to motivate him, to energize him, and he stood up quickly. "Now to finish our business, I will try to contact your brother once more." He turned back toward the stairs. "In the meantime, please make yourself comfortable. Your wait won't be much longer."

A thousand hours snuck by in forever, and I felt like my body was going to sleep. The basement wasn't heated, so the space was cold and getting colder with the night settling in. I had been praying, thinking, wallowing in memories. I had examined every crack in the wall, every seam of the window. I had stripped off my sweatshirt and wrapped my hand in the material, slamming it against the glass in the vain hope of breaking the glass. When that hadn't worked, I had pulled off my shoes and tried again until I heard footsteps above. I had gone back to my place on the floor then.

I was sitting very still when I heard a rustle and what sounded like the sole of a shoe hitting the floor. The room was dim and the rain outside had blocked what little light there was. I shifted and looked up to see my brother. "Daniel?" My voice was weak, my brain still soft.

"Oh, Van!" I realized that Thomas was standing over me, and I had thought for a split second that my other brother had come to me to take me away. Now Thomas bent and caught my chin in his hand. "What did he do to you?"

"Thomas?"

"It's me, Van. And we're getting you out of here." He straightened. I could hear a strange noise by the window. "That's Drew. He's going to pry this thing open, and we're going to get out. Then we'll call the cops." His voice had gotten low and rough.

I stood slowly feeling every pain and twinge. But Thomas' arm was around me. "How did you find me?"

"Daniel's phone. My friend finally got the data off of it, so we were able to see who called. It was the Professor that he called the most. We were on our way up here to confront him when Travis called in. He had the directions to lead us here."

The window trembled and then crashed open, panes of glass shattering inward and littering the floor like spilled jewels. "Got her?" Drew's face was at the window and it suddenly occurred to me what I was seeing. How could Thomas be here beside me when the basement door was still locked, and the window hadn't been opened? How could he have gotten in my prison? The thought was like a shot of ice water. This wasn't Thomas. Not completely. He had done as I had earlier with Travis, and he was lying somewhere unconscious while he projected himself in here.

"I've got her. Let's go." Thomas took my arm and guided me to the window. Drew was clearing the glass around the frame. I felt Thomas grab my waist and hoist me higher. Drew caught me under the arms and started hauling me through the open window. The cold air was shocking, and I felt my head bump the frame as I was lifted through, throwing lines of pain through my head and jaw.

"Oh," I muttered and grunted in pain, but a minute later, I was on my hands and knees on the brittle grass, sprinkles of rain still pattering against my back. I tumbled over onto my butt and looked as Drew bent through the window again.

"Okay, big man. Your turn." He was bent double and had Thomas' arms when I heard the sound. For a frozen second, I didn't know what the sound was. And then I knew. A gunshot.

Thomas' hands fell open against Drew's sleeve, his skin pale in the moonlight.

"Thomas?" My voice was a sigh, a cry. "Drew?"

Without a sound, I watched Thomas disappear, not fall back, but just blink from there and then gone.

Drew wheeled back in surprise, hands empty and face pale with shock. A second shot sounded and Drew turned, grabbing my hand and dragging me away.

"But Thomas!"

"He's not there!" He shouted back at me. "He never was!"

We made it to Drew's car. I heard a slam and suspected that the Professor had run to the front door and was coming for us. I didn't know what he was doing until I heard the shot ping off the car. He was still shooting! He had lost his mind, and was randomly firing toward the car. I prayed that no one would be in his line of sight because I was sure that he would hit them with accidental bullets.

"Get down!" Drew commanded, and he yanked the door open. I slid into the seat and curled up, keeping my head low while Drew fired up the engine. Another ping greeted us as we accelerated into the street.

I had seen car chases on television; I never thought I would be in one. But there was no chase. As soon as we had turned onto the busier road, a siren screamed in the distance and a police car with lights flashing came from the opposite direction. He turned just next to us, and Drew slowed to a crawl. I turned around, watching the figures of the police as they approached the house. The Professor was framed in his doorway.

"Thomas?" I asked breathlessly. He had been shot, but yet he hadn't. He had been there, but he hadn't, and now?

We stopped at a Wal-Mart parking lot. There was something so reassuring about it, the harsh lighting, the gaudy ads, the parking lot still busy with late night customers. I saw Thea's car parked in the side lot. Drew pulled in next to her car. The rain had slowed to a drizzle. I swung open the door and hurried to the station wagon. Through the glass, Thea peered up at me, her face a pale damp oval. I grabbed the handle and pulled the door open.

"Thea?"

Her gaze went to my face, gasping a little when she saw me. But then she looked back in at my brother, lying still, too still.

"What's going on?"

"He stopped breathing!" She was panting, her hands shaking. Her face in profile was a portrait in terror. "He just stopped, and then I tried to do mouth to mouth. After a few times he started breathing again on his own, but he won't wake up! I don't know what happened!"

I edged closer in, bending down and looking into my brother's pale face. It was such a flashback, a painful replay of those horrible days when Thomas had lain in the hospital bed, not stirring. "Thomas?" I bent closer. Thea shifted so I could slide in, and I leaned over the seat back to where he lay. I put one hand on his cheek. He felt so cold. Too cold. What had we done? "He came to me in the basement. He lifted me out the window when Drew got it open. And as he was handing me through, I think Professor Morrison shot him." My voice was flat and odd.

"Shot him?" Thea stared at me, and then back to his face. "But that can't be. He was really here with me."

"He disappeared as soon as I felt the impact of the bullet hitting him," Drew said. Drew's expression was equally tense, and he was leaning in the other side of the car.

"Now what do we do?" Thea sounded like she was crying, and I felt the same. Too much shock, too much pain.

I heard the insistent chime of a cell phone, and Drew leaned over and picked one off the driver's seat. "Hello?" I heard him say into the receiver. He was silent for a moment. "Travis. Yes, we're here. We got her, and the cops showed up just as we were getting out of there. But Thomas," his voice failed and he stopped. "No, he's with us here, but there's something wrong with him." He listened for a moment more. "You're right. We'll meet you at the hospital."

He clicked off the phone and turned to us. "We need to get you both to the hospital. You need treatment. And maybe they can do something about Thomas. I don't know."

"If we go to the hospital, what are we going to say happened to me? I can't imagine explaining this to anyone."

"We'll think of a story." He suddenly seemed to pull himself together. "We're heading out. We'll talk on the way."

As he drove, Thea and I huddled over Thomas in the back. I looked at his face, so still and expressionless. This wasn't right! We had come so far. All because of the cross. It all centered on that. And I had heard it from the Professor himself. He had killed Daniel, and had tried to kill my other brother and Drew as well. If he had had his way, none of us would have been around to tell the story.

"Where's the cross?" I asked Thea. I had no plan. It was just an impulse.

"In his pocket. He always keeps in on him."

I reached around him, patting him down until I figured out where he had tucked the cross. I dug into his jacket pocket until I could get a firm hold on the pouch, and I yanked it out. I had to stifle the urge to throw it.

"Give it to me," Thea said softly, her voice even.

I looked at her. In the dim light, her eyes were still damp, but her face was determined. I dumped the cross from the protective pouch and handed it to her, feeling the warm links of the chain trickle through my fingers.

She took it, looked at it for a moment, and then slipped it over her head. She tucked it under her shirt against her skin. Her hands made a quick gesture, lightly touching her forehead, her chest, and her shoulders, a Catholic sign of the cross. Then she took my brother's hand in hers and held it. I forced a long breath and imitated the movement. I took his cool hand in mine and closed my eyes, trying to ignore the swaying of the car. I prayed.

And I felt his fingers move.

I wasn't feeling well at all, but I made them take me home. I was so afraid that if we visited a hospital anywhere close to the University, that the professor would magically appear. We knew, more than anyone, what he could do, even if he were put in jail. We got as far as the east side of town when I decided that I could handle the pain no longer. Thomas was awake. He looked terrible, not as bad as I did, but close. He called our mother, who by then was frantic. She knew something was going on since she hadn't been able to get in touch with either of us for a few hours. She had also gotten a call from the police explaining that they had my phone. It had been in the Professor's possession when he had been taken in, I supposed. The glittery pink case had probably given away the fact that it wasn't his. But now my mother knew something was going on. How to explain that?

We went into the Urgent Care center and sat in an uncomfortable group. Travis had met up with us while still close to the campus, and followed us to the center. He kept his arm around me as I went into the harshly lit medical center. We sat on an uncomfortable plastic couch, my head on Travis's shoulder, while Thomas checked me in for treatment. The woman behind the counter kept looking at him curiously, no doubt noticing his sickly pallor.

We had gotten some of our story together. I had gone to the University, and while going down a set of stairs, I had fallen. It didn't exactly explain my appearance, but I was out of other ideas.

I was taken back immediately as soon as they got a closer look at my face, and they took me into a room for examination. Thomas was staying out in the waiting room with Thea, wanting to catch our parents before they saw me. He looked so odd himself; he said he was going to have to claim a migraine. I agreed. His story was so much more fantastic than mine.

Drew and Travis both wanted to accompany me back to the room, but I refused. Drew needed to wait for Tori. She was on her way as well. The whole gang would be together shortly. We would be busy trying to figure out how to explain that to my parents as well. But I knew my mother well enough. She would invite them to come to our house, feed them, and give them somewhere to sleep, just grateful that we were all okay. That was before the interrogation would begin, and then heaven help us all.

The doctor poked and probed until I had tears in my eyes again, and then ordered a set of x-rays just to make sure that the damage was only tissue deep. I sat, my eyes closed and leaning against Travis again. When the nurse took me back, I heard a commotion and knew that my parents had arrived. I sat obediently still as they manipulated my body in all positions so that they could finish taking the pictures.

The same nurse guided me out. This time it was my parents that were waiting for me. My mother looked appalled, and I knew how tempted that she was to try and smother me, to scold me. But she held it together and we waited there, my parents each on one side of me, holding me upright, until the doctor came in.

"You're little girl is very lucky," the doctor explained. "She has had a head injury, so we're going to have to watch for any signs of concussions. That means neuro checks throughout the night. But she doesn't have any bone breaks."

I checked out then, leaning against my father's side as the doctor spoke with my mother, handing over stacks of papers with instructions and summaries of treatment. I was in a daze as we left, trailing a line of people, Tori and Drew, Thea and Thomas, and Travis. It was a velvety night with stars piecing the darkness, the cold making our breath bloom like smoke flowers. I was too tired to think, to worry, to do anything. I knew that my night would be a long one. My parents would have to wake me up periodically to see how I was doing, how my brain was functioning, but I was pretty sure I knew. I would be fine.

In the morning, I woke early. Daisy was tucked next to me in bed, snoring softly. On the floor of my room, two pallets of padded blankets held the sleeping forms of Thea and Tori. Thea was sound asleep, but I could tell that Tori was awake. The subtle flair of light from her phone screen reflected off the wall next to her in a blueish haze.

"Hey!" I whispered.

She rolled over, her phone in her hand, and waved. "I'm checking the news. I wanted to see if there were any new stories about maniac professors having a shootout in the middle of a neighborhood street."

"And?"

"Nothing yet." She propped her head on her hand. "How are you feeling now?"

"Ugh." I responded. "But I'm alive, so I can't complain."

"Travis was telling me about it last night." She sobered. "What all did he tell you? Professor Morrison?"

"He told me a whole lot, like he was bragging about it. He's a sick man." I paused. "He killed Daniel." As I said it aloud, the words felt so sour in my mouth. "He said that he purposefully came out on the road to cause the accident. He knew that Daniel was going to find the cross before he was. He knew that Daniel had some information that he didn't. And he was just getting rid of the competition. But he had been doing it for so much longer than we have, the bilocation. He had much better control than any of us have ever had."

"That is sick," Tori said bitterly. "So he caused the accident?"

"He caused it all," I responded slowly.

"We've got to make him pay." Thea's eyes were open, but her usual sweet face had a vengeful edge.

"How are we going to do that?" I asked.

"We'll have to wait and see what happens with last night," Tori said thoughtfully. "Going nuts like that in the street is bound to have some serious charges."

"I hope he didn't shoot anyone else by accident," I said worriedly. I felt a subtle guilt for the way things had ended.

I heard a soft knock at the door, and slowly pulled myself up in bed. My head throbbed a little. Daisy shifted and moaned a little in her sleep. Thomas stuck his head in first.

"All decent?" he asked giving us a half smile. Then his smile disappeared and he said, "God, Savannah, you look like hell."

"Thanks," I muttered, pushing a strand of hair out of my face.

Thomas stepped in, opening the door wider so that the other two guys could enter with him. Thomas looked remarkably better. For all of his near death experience, he was recovering nicely.

"We heard you all whispering," Drew said, folding his long legs until he was sitting on the blankets next to Tori.

"They woke me up," Thea pretended to complain.

"We were being quiet," Tori said. "You just can't handle a little distraction."

Travis came in and sat gingerly on the side of my bed, on the opposite side where Daisy was still laying, her eyes open as she watched the people settling in her room. It was a little strange having Travis here with my brother in the room, sitting with all my childhood remnants surrounding me. "How are you?" Travis asked.

"Fine. Okay. Terrible." I sat back against the headboard. "Glad that it's over."

"I heard what you said," Thomas said, standing very still, face set. "He caused the accident. Why?"

"He said he knew about the cross a long time ago. He must have come across the stories in some of his collecting. That was his whole world, collecting those rare books and documents. He was looking for the cross and had been to the sight of Juan Madino's grave. But it had already been plundered years ago and the cross was gone. He said he was missing the one link. And it was the link that Daniel had." I studied my brother's face, watching pain and anger flash by in even waves. "He said that Daniel came to him because he knew that the professor had collected some of the history books about the story. And something that Daniel said led him to believe that Daniel had something that he hadn't been able to find. So he didn't let Daniel get the material. We had always thought that he had, and he led us on, acting like he had given the books to Daniel so that he could make the copies. But he said that he told Daniel no."

"Do you think Daniel broke in?" Thea sounded curious and a little incredulous.

"No, I think he bilocated in like Thomas did last night in the basement. He got the things that he needed and put everything back." I looked at Thomas' face again. "The professor said as much. But then he had figured out where Daniel was going, to Crestwood, where the cross probably was. That's how he found the connection to us, through Daniel. He was there when we first searched the graveyard, and even though there was an earth tremor, we never even noticed. But it caused something, and the professor knew it. So after he had that information, he decided that the cross had to close, it had to be in the house where the old man lived."

"And he broke in," Tori said angrily.

"He bilocated in and searched the place, over and over again. He even tried to drive you away with the fire and the stunt that he pulled in the cemetery."

"What do you mean?" Travis finally spoke up, and I realized that he was missing some of the pieces of the puzzle as well.

"When I first moved here, and my friend and I went out into the cemetery, I felt something out there. I was sure that there had been a ghost. And it happened again with Drew and me. You felt it to," Tori said, looking at Drew next to her.

"The professor admitted it was him," I replied.

"So no ghost out there," Tori said wonderingly.

"He said he had better control of his ability. Apparently he could partly bilocate. Not always the same form. But it wore him out to do something like that. So no, it wasn't any kind of ghost."

Thomas was shaking his head, "and when we found the cross, he knew it."

"Your finding the boy was in the paper," I said, referring to the summer tragedy when Drew had climbed down into the well and found the bones of the lost boy. "No one ever said what the boy had with him, but I guess he figured out that on his own. He knew the cross was there. He knew what it could do. And he knew that we were acting differently than before."

"So why now? Why did he wait?" Travis was looking frustrated too, but I knew much of that had to do with looking at me, seeing my injuries.

"I contacted him. I let him know that we knew he was part of the story. He realized that we might know more than we were letting on, and we might be making plans to do something with the cross. I mean, what would happen to him if the cross were returned to its rightful place? That's the question we've all been asking. If it were to go back where it belonged, would we go back to normal?"

"I would hope so," Drew muttered.

"And so would I," I agreed. "But he didn't feel that way. So he decided that he had to get the cross from us. That was his ultimate plan. He truly only wanted the cross. He wanted the control, the power."

"Travis said he just took you," Thomas said.

"I went up to meet him. He said that he had one of the books that Daniel had looked at, and it had some of his notes still in it. He knew that I wouldn't be able to resist. And we weren't suspecting him of anything. I went right to him," I said ruefully.

"Why did he do that to you?" Travis said, gesturing to my jaw, the swollen and purple marks.

"I don't know. I think he wanted to keep me under control. He didn't want to shoot me, really. He wanted to get Thomas to come to him with the cross. But he told me he wasn't planning on letting me live," I shivered at the memory. "He needed to cover his tracks, and I wasn't a loose end he was willing to tolerate."

Travis leaned over and put his arm around me, and Thea reached up and took one of my hands. I blinked back tears.

"Well we've got you now, Van," Thomas said in a firm voice. I could hear some movement outside my door, and knew that my parents were stirring. "Okay, well now we have to face the day. Let's go get breakfast," Thomas said abruptly. "Leave the talking to me," he told me sternly.

In a group we rose, all in differing states of dress, a tattered looking little group. Tori and Thea looped their arms through mine as we entered the kitchen, the guys close behind, and I was smiling a little when my Mom looked up from making her coffee.

Christmas break was a huge relief for me. I had agreed to return to school in January to complete my senior year, and although I was excited, I was stressed. I had tried to contact some of my friends that I had neglected from school, gone out for lunch and Christmas shopping with a couple of my closest friends, and was feeling a little more in the mood.

The bruises on my face had taken a few weeks to heal, first going into an ugly plum color, then black, then a sickly green, before settling into yellow as they were now. My parents had insisted that I go for a checkup as well, and the prognosis was affirmed. I would heal.

As soon as finals were over, Thomas came home. He knew that after our latest adventure, he would need to give my parents a little more of his time. They had been suspicious of our story, but they hadn't asked for too many details yet, and we hadn't volunteered them.

The Christmas holiday was odd. We were still trying to get used to the feeling that something was missing, and it certainly was. It wasn't as terrible as the year before, so we treasured just being together. But we knew that we would always miss Daniel. On Christmas day, we went over to our grandparent's house and followed our Christmas traditions. When we went home, we sat together in our living room and watched old movies, talking and laughing, occasionally touching on the missing member of our family, but fondly.

Thomas and I agreed to go to Tori's house for a small Christmas celebration on New Year's Day. We had a few errands to run as well, and it seemed like a good time to do them. There was something of a fresh start to our meeting.

Tori greeted us as we came in the door with a mug of hot chocolate topped with a festive peppermint stick. "Merry Christmas!" she exclaimed grinning. "Drew and Thea are in the living room. Liz is with them, but she's planning on going out with Mike soon." Mike was Liz's new love, a fellow banker who was average in every way except for his smile, which was brilliant and just perfect. He had an awesome sense of humor, and really liked Monty, which made us sure that he was a good guy.

"Have you seen Travis yet?" I asked. I knew that he was due to arrive around the same time that we were.

"Not yet, but I'm sure he'll be along." She led us into the living room. "Grab a seat. I've got home made lasagna in the oven. It took me all day, so you are going to like it!"

"I'm sure it will be great!" I agreed grinning.

"After we eat, we have an appointment to go to," she said cryptically.

"Where?" I had stopped in the doorway and turned to look at her face.

"We have some of our own loose ends."

Fifteen minutes later, Travis arrived and was greeted with a mug of hot chocolate. Liz excused herself, heading out for her date, and we settled in the living room, watching the sun wash warm colors over the cold landscape.

"So Thomas said that you all had news about the Professor," Tori said, dropping into her seat after checking on our meal.

"It's taken some work," I said, casting a glance toward Thomas. "But we finally got the complete story."

"I have an old buddy that's a cop. He's a newbie on the force, but he still gets the inside talk. He filled me in on the arrest." Thomas leaned forward. "You heard how Morrison's crazy shooting was witnessed by pretty much the whole neighborhood. And he also hit the poor guy across the street." We had seen the story in the paper about how Professor Morrison had fired several shots, reloaded, and fired three more. The fact that he had consciously reloaded had given the police the evidence they needed. No accidental shooting. He had meant to hit someone, and when they had arrested him, he had started raving about the miracle. It sounded like his mental state had deteriorated after that until he was taken, sobbing, into the police car. A few minutes later, it was found that a neighbor had been hit by a stray shot. It wasn't fatal, but the man had been hospitalized for a week after undergoing surgery to remove the bullet from his upper leg. "But the Professor never really came out of his hysteria," Thomas said. "He kept telling people that they couldn't hold him. That he would get out, that all he needed was the cross. My friend said that by the time they had him in a room at the station, he wasn't making any sense at all. They had to call in the medics to get him calmed down."

"And now?" Travis prompted.

"When he wouldn't answer any of the questions, they took him to the hospital. He hasn't been moved sense. He hasn't recovered enough to even be formally charged."

"They called back about my phone," I added. "The police did. I said that I had lost it when I fell at the University. I figured that someone had picked it up."

"So what will happen?" Tori looked a little fearful. "Will he be set free when he gets better?"

"We don't really know what will happen to him at this point. His psychotic break looks pretty severe. And if he gets better and keeps insisting that he can bilocate, that's not going to look great for his case." Thomas shrugged.

"At least we know that we're safe for now," I said and forced a smile. I had put my life on hold for long enough. I wasn't going to do it anymore.

Dinner was fabulous. Working with Blythe had given Tori some great pointers for cooking, and along with the homemade bread, the lasagna was very good. After we had finished eating and cleaned up, we piled into Thea's station wagon for the short ride to St. Benedict's, the Catholic Church.

I had only met the priest on one other occasion, at the funeral for the little lost boy where he had, with the pastor of the Baptist Church, conducted the funeral. He plainly had been waiting for us and opened the door as soon as we had gotten to the porch.

The house was a unique landmark in the little town of Pewee Valley, tucked close to Crestwood. Its property had once been just part of a home, but now the Church owned the house and land, and the home was residence for the local priests that came to work at the church. The furnishings were mostly antiques, things collected by the different owners as well as gifts from friends and family.

The library was especially impressive. It held as many books as the Professor's little office had, and more, with slick covered paperbacks, westerns mostly, to gilt edged tomes. Father had anticipated our arrival and had set out some extra chairs for us to sit in. There was an air of confession about it, and Thea had reassured us that none of our information would go beyond the walls of the room.

Once seated, Thomas pulled the heavy cross with its gold chain out of his pocket and laid it on the desk.

Father looked at it thoughtfully. "I've heard your story, and I've reassured Thea that I would keep your council," he began. "I am a man of God, but I know well that our world is full of mysteries and miracles. But I think that you are right in your plans. This belongs to the Saint, and she wanted it to remain with Juan Madino. I have called my superiors in the church, and they have agreed to place it back with him."

"And you've told them that there is a possibility that someone might eventually try to take it again? That it has some fantastic stories that go with it?" Thomas looked concerned.

"I have," Father replied. "In circumstances like this one, the Church is well able to provide adequate security. And this will not be a well-documented event. We will keep it quiet. Better to let something like this rest for a while."

Thomas nodded, and I knew how he felt. In the short time since the kidnapping, none of us had bilocated. But we hadn't tried. We didn't know what would happen to our ability once the cross had been returned to its rightful place. We were just hoping, and praying, that we would go back to our normal, non-miraculous lives.

"Within the week, the cross will again rest with Juan Madino," the priest assured us. "And then, if any of you continue to experience anything out of the ordinary, I want you to come to me. I will not break your confidence, but I would like to help you." He looked meaningfully to each of us. I smiled back at him. There was something special, reassuring, in his gaze.

"Thank you, Father," Thea said.

The priest took the cross and tucked it back into its pouch. "I will let you know when it is placed with Madino. I hope that it will give you some peace."

Two weeks later we each received a short note from the priest. Inside was a small silver holy metal with the image of Saint Francisca. Along with it was a short note informing us that the item had been returned to its proper resting place.

Drew was the first to test our theory. He had the best control of our ability, and had done it on demand the most. He called us immediately after to tell us the news. It seemed that our ability was gone.

Epilogue:

I smoothed the long skirt of my dress, enjoying the way the folds of the gown rippled around my ankles. I had gotten to help choose the dress, and the color, a soft teal, was my favorite. All the dresses were a similar color, with different shapes and cuts to suit our differing fashion and figure. Thea was considerate like that. Once the wedding was over, I could have the gown shortened and still wear it to other dressy events.

Tori came in and shut the door behind her. "You need to talk to your brother," she said, closing the door behind her. "Thea is almost ready, but Thomas and Drew are still out in the car listening to the game."

I sighed. "Ever since he graduated, he can't seem to stand not listening to the basketball games live," I said frowning. "And this one is just an exhibition game. It doesn't even count toward the season."

Tori shrugged. "I don't understand men," she said, but she was smiling. She could smile. Her wedding day wouldn't be for another six months, and in the spring, there wouldn't be any sports to distract her groom.

I checked the mirror one last time. I was ready, my hair up in an intricate braid, my silver earrings catching the light. The necklace that Thea had given each of us was beautiful, an ornate cross with a ruby in the center, a little reminiscent of the cross that had been returned to the tropical island off the Spanish coast.

As I was heading out the door, I saw my brother rushing into the chapel through the back entrance. He looked very handsome in his tuxedo, his hair slightly windblown; his eyes alight with the anticipation. I turned back and entered the Chapel itself. Thea had spent hours weaving gorgeous flower arrangements to set at the front of the church. She had chosen some dried and some fresh flowers, and the mix was beautiful. Another flower arrangement, full of bright colors, and weighted down with shiny blue marbles, would be placed at the grave of the little lost boy after the ceremony. It seemed right that he would be remembered today too. All of the flowers had some significance for us, and I knew Thea's gift would be well appreciated. Her talent had led to a very satisfying job at the local art museum where she was able to work on other artist's displays while still pursuing her own pieces. Some of these would be prepared after the wedding and placed on exhibit in the museum once the wedding was over.

The familiar priest was standing at the altar, helping some young servers in long white gowns light candles to prepare for the service. He saw me at the end of the aisle and waved as he walked toward me.

"All going well?" he asked.

"We're fine," I said. "Almost time."

"It is," he said, and I saw a subtle movement at the front of the Chapel. "This marriage is going to have some very special angels attending, I'm thinking," Father said smiling.

"Savannah! Come on," Tori hissed from behind me. "The guys are coming in."

I grinned at the priest and turned back to the door. As I slipped out and around to the side of the building, my shiny shoes cushioned by a carpet of multihued leaves of gold, red, and orange, I saw Travis come around.

He stopped when he saw me. “You look amazing,” he said, his eyes warm.

“So do you,” I said, admiring the way the jacket hung on his broad shoulders.

“Can I kiss you, or will it mess up your makeup?” he asked, already leaning in.

“Kiss me, and I’ll fix my makeup,” I responded. His lips were warm and flavored with mint. I sighed as he kissed me, feeling the wonderful flood of warmth and belonging. The ring on my finger, a lovely antique engagement ring passed down from his grandmother, was still new feeling. After two weeks, I was still examining it, giddy with the future. I kissed him again, hard, and released him. “I’ve got to go. I’ll see you at the alter.”

He grinned. “I like the sound of that,” he said.

I rushed to the small side room and met up with Thea and Tori, Thea’s mom and my mom standing close by. Thea’s dress was simple, a fit and flair that had been completely covered with antique lace topped with a few seed pearls. Her hair was up off her face, a few curls escaping to soften the look. Her veil was lace as well, attached to a small wreath of flowers that she had made. Her bouquet was made of fresh flowers that had been grown in Travis’s greenhouse for the occasion. Old fashioned roses with fat blooms in white, pale gold, and pale pink.

She saw me and held out her hand. “Is it time, sister?”

“Sister,” I said, and nodded as the music swelled.

Acknowledgment:

I'd again like to thank my publisher, Tony Acree (award winning publisher!), my wonderful editor, Lynn Tincher (and awesome writer), and my beta readers including my mother, Kathleen Lanham and Jeannine Konesko.

I would also like to give my thanks for my wonderful community in Oldham County Kentucky where I as born, raised, and still remain.

And to my readers, thanks for finishing the story with me!

About the author:

Rachael Rawlings is a full time mother, wife, writer, pet owner, and Speech Language Pathologist. Her main goal is to tell a good story, dream a little bit, and share her joy about the world we live in. She lives with her husband, James, a professional architect; her three children, Faith, Nicholas, and Chase; and two dogs. She grew up and lives in the small town of Crestwood, Kentucky and is proud to call it home.

She thrives on good coffee, chocolate, and great friends and family. To learn more about Rachael's work and her upcoming releases, visit her on her website:
http://rachaelrawlings.wix.com/rachael-rawlings

CPSIA information can be obtained
at www.ICGtesting.com
Printed in the USA
FFOW02n2310280816
27107FF

9 781942 212287